SHORT ENDS

SHORT ENDS

A VINCE MCNULTY THRILLER

COLIN CAMPBELL

First published by Level Best Books 2025

This novel is entirely a work of fiction. The names, characters and incidents portrayed in it are the work of the author's imagination. Any resemblance to actual persons, living or dead, events or localities is entirely coincidental.

Author Photo Credit: Colin Campbell

First edition

ISBN: 979-8-89820-067-1

Cover art by Level Best Designs

This book was professionally typeset on Reedsy.
Find out more at reedsy.com

For Reed
For your support and friendship

Praise for the Books by Colin Campbell

"Very real. And very good."—Lee Child

"There's nothing soft about Campbell's writing. If you enjoy your crime fiction hard-boiled, the Jim Grant series is a must read."—Bruce Robert Coffin, author of the Detective Byron series

"A cop with a sharp eye, keen mind, and a lion's heart."—Reed Farrel Coleman

"Campbell writes smart, rollercoaster tales with unstoppable forward momentum and thrilling authenticity."—Nick Petrie

"Grim and gritty and packed with action."—*Kirkus Review*

"The pages fly like the bullets, fistfights and one-liners that make this one of my favourite books of the year. Top stuff!"—Matt Hilton

"An excellent story well told. A mixture of *The Choirboys* meets Harry Bosch."—Michael Jecks

"Sets up immediately and maintains a breakneck pace throughout. Its smart structure and unrelenting suspense will please Lee Child fans."—*Library Journal Review*

"This is police procedural close-up and personal. A strong debut with enough gritty realism to make your eyes water, and a few savage laughs along the way."—Reginald Hill

"Fantastic story, fantastic characters—fantastic everything."—Chris Mooney, international bestselling author of the Darby McCormick series

Prologue

Vince McNulty sat in the extra legroom window seat and felt the turbulence shake the passenger jet as it made its final approach to Manchester Airport. He looked out of the window but could only see brief snatches of ground through breaks in the clouds. The clouds looked dark and angry, and a strong gust of wind tried to knock the Boeing 737 off course, but the pilot held firm. Even though McNulty was almost back on English soil, the ground seemed to be a long way down. He popped another mint in his mouth and sucked to ease the pressure in his ears. The plane was buffeted again. His ears refused to pop.

The overnight flight from Boston had been long and uneventful, the brief layover in New York being the only chance for McNulty to stretch his legs before being strapped into the long metal tube that had no right to defy gravity. The upgrade to extra legroom was a thank you from Larry Unger, the movie producer, proving surprisingly understanding about losing his technical advisor right in the middle of Titanic Productions' latest shoot. McNulty had argued that he should only be away for a few days, but even he didn't believe that.

The plane shook again. McNulty gripped the armrests, his knuckles showing white in the dull grey light. Northern England was still Northern England. Dull, wet, and windy.

The whine of the undercarriage being lowered was barely audible above the roar of the engines, the plane slowing some more as the giant wheels caught the air.

Final approach. Seven minutes, according to the flight tracker on the seatback monitor in front of him. He distracted himself by playing a little police game even though he wasn't a policeman anymore. That had never stopped him before. Once a cop, always a cop. His favourite mantra. In his mind, he set up an imaginary crime, say theft from somebody's cabin luggage, then scanned the passengers nearest his seat. He ticked off the three main elements that would make somebody a suspect. Means, motive, and opportunity.

Means. Being physically able to reach into the bag and steal the item.

Motive. To sell the item, desire it, or simply want to deprive the owner of it.

Opportunity. Being in the right place when the bag was left unattended.

If years of being a cop in Yorkshire, and for a shorter time in Savage, Maryland, had proved anything, it was that cops didn't put much weight on motive. McNulty had lost count of how many crimes happened because some lowlife piece of shit thought it was a good idea to steal, assault, or kill in a fit of passion, anger, or boredom. Lowlife pieces of shit didn't need a reason. They didn't have a motive apart from being lowlife pieces of shit.

The plane hit an air pocket and suddenly dropped twenty feet like an elevator with its cables cut. There was a collective cry of panic from the passengers as the cabin lights briefly went out before the engines found air again and the Boeing settled on its final approach. The ground was rushing past beneath the window.

McNulty put another mint in his mouth. His ears popped, and the cabin noise stopped being muted and became a roar. What if the crime was crashing a passenger jet? How would means, motive, and opportunity work with that? Terrorism would probably be the motive. Or maybe hiding the death of one passenger amid the deaths of everyone else. McNulty shook his head. He'd been working for Larry Unger too long because that sounded like an overused movie plot.

He looked out of the window. Roads and hedgerows rushed by, then there was a long expanse of grass verge, and finally the oil-streaked tarmac of the runway. A gust of wind sideswiped the airplane, and it was suddenly flying at a crazy angle. The cabin shook with the impact as the undercarriage hit hard, then skidded sideways. A child was screaming. Some adults, too.

McNulty touched the tattoo that ran up one side of his neck, the black branches of a dead tree that was a permanent reminder of Crag View Orphanage, where he grew up. He wasn't thinking about growing up; he was wondering about his motives for being here. After surviving the Northern X massage chain, the snuff video gang in Quincy, and that shit with Jim Grant in Colorado, was he really going to end his life splattered on the runway at Manchester Airport? He wasn't even back in Yorkshire yet. And why? What the fuck was he doing coming back to England after all these years?

I

PART ONE

MEANS
The ability of the defendant to commit the crime.
—Blackstone's

Chapter One

"You know? This whole walking like a duck thing? It extends to when he was in the Air Force."

"You want him to *fly* like a duck?"

Larry Unger chose to ignore the facetious remark and gave McNulty a dirty look. "He's not quite walking like a cop yet, back then. Not that John Wayne roll."

"Because John Wayne walked *exactly* like a cop?"

Larry threw McNulty another dirty look. "It's a flashback scene. Rewind the cop walk back a few years."

* * *

Two days before McNulty got the news that sent him flying back to England, Titanic Productions was filming at Lawrence G Hanscom Field, a small regional airfield ten miles northwest of Boston. Larry Unger still harboured ambitions of going full Hollywood, but the expense of filming in Los Angeles had forced him back to his old stomping ground in Massachusetts. For authenticity, the producer claimed. For budgetary measures, McNulty reckoned. Larry was a cheapskate, that's why he still hired McNulty to do the job of three men, technical advisor, stunt coordinator, and on-set security. Today was a technical advisor day.

Larry scanned the hangars at the side of the parking apron. "I thought Hanscom Air Force Base would have looked more, well, Air Forcey."

McNulty followed Larry's gaze. "The buildings are an easy fix. Dress 'em up, and you could make 'em look like World War Two."

"It's not that much of a flashback."

McNulty shrugged. "Whenever you like. But this hasn't been a flying base since the seventies."

Larry sighed. "I know. I was just expecting combat paint and camouflage nets."

"Green paint and netting come cheap. Making Alfonse look younger. That's a work of art."

The other big change since Titanic Productions moved to Hollywood had been replacing Alfonse Bayard with ex-firefighter Chuck Buchinsky, mainly because Bayard had priced himself out of the market and Buchinsky was cheaper. It had worked out fine, Buchinsky proving a solid upgrade on the walk-like-a-cop front, but now Bayard was back to reprise his role as a tough-as-nails detective. And that meant stopping the actor walking like a duck all over again.

Larry turned his gaze on the makeup trailer that was parked with the rest of the Location Services vehicles behind the hangars. "Works of art is what Amy does. Why don't you go check if Alfonse is looking young again yet?"

McNulty thought Larry was trying to hide a smirk, but he set off for the makeup trailer before the producer could say anything else. It seemed that nothing was secret in the close-knit community of Titanic Productions. It was like working in a travelling circus; your business was everybody's business. McNulty having a relationship with the makeup lady was everybody's business. Amy Moore keeping it quiet and McNulty being discreet didn't make any difference. The secret was out.

"You could always use digital de-ageing, like De Niro."

Larry's smirk vanished. "Amy is cheaper. Go make sure she isn't using too much foundation."

* * *

"Ouch, it stings."

"Oh, stop being a baby. I haven't even started yet."

Alfonse Bayard was a long way from being the tough-as-nails detective as he sat in the makeup chair with his head back. A wall of light from the bulbs surrounding the mirror lit the actor's face, but no amount of light was going to hide the creases and wrinkles of the years since his debut feature with Titanic Productions. He looked more like a weathered cowboy than the pampered actor he had become. Amy Moore looked as beautiful as ever.

McNulty watched her from the door. "Larry says not to use too much foundation."

Amy smiled at McNulty. "That's okay then. Alfonse doesn't want me to use any at all."

Alfonse held his hands up. "Not arguing. Just saying."

Amy remembered the angry support player who had got rough with her during Alfonse Bayard's debut feature. "You going to spray him in the eyes and make him scream?"

McNulty smiled back. "It was water. The scream was his fault."

"The scream was him being scared what you'd do next."

McNulty shrugged. "Fear of violence can be as effective as violence itself."

"In stopping the bully getting rough with the makeup lady?"

"He stopped, didn't he?"

"He couldn't talk for two hours after you fed him Chanel Ultra Velvet."

"It was a non-speaking part."

Alfonse held a hand up like a schoolboy in class. "Sorry to interrupt, but are you sure this will hide the wrinkles? I'm supposed to be twenty years younger."

Amy moved close behind him and pulled the skin back from the temples and cheeks. The wrinkles smoothed out. "I'll use invisible tape and hide it with makeup. You'll look like a teenager so long as Larry films from a distance."

McNulty chuckled. "He looks like a kid I used to know. Put a condom over his head that smoothed him like a penis."

Alfonse looked at McNulty through the mirror. "You calling me a dickhead?"

McNulty noticed the Sellotape holding the cracked mirror together after a different incident in Los Angeles. "I'm saying don't act too hard, or your face will explode."

He made an explosion shape with his hands. "Poof. Smoke and mirrors."

Amy corrected him. "Foundation and sticky tape."

Alfonse gave a little smile. "I never act hard."

McNulty nodded. "Oh, and Larry wants us to work on the cop walk thing."

Alfonse looked offended. "I thought we'd sorted that."

"He wants more of an Air Force walk."

"What's the difference?"

"More duck, less John Wayne."

McNulty noticed the ID pass hanging from the back of the chair. "And don't forget your security badge. This *is* an Air Force Base. Don't want you getting shot your first day on location."

Chapter Two

Hanscom Air Force Base might not have been a flying base since the mid-seventies, despite being adjacent to Hanscom Field, but it was still an Air Force Base. Most of the command buildings had been upgraded, but there were plenty that harked back to the fighting days of World War Two. There were barrack blocks, an officer's and a sergeant's mess, as well as two pre-war aircraft hangars and a motor pool that had been repairing unit vehicles since D-Day.

It all looked very military. Until it wasn't.

The Massachusetts Port Authority ran Hanscom Field, which was a civil airport that served as a corporate reliever to Boston's Logan International. McNulty didn't know what a corporate reliever was, but assumed it provided overspill for the main international airport. The two runways ran north to south and east to west with a parking apron that seemed to be permanently underused.

Even the Air Force Base had an air of calm that disguised what went on beneath the surface. 66th Air Base Group was proud of its mission statement, to acquire war-fighting systems for the Air Force and its sister services. Those systems provided connectivity between its warfighters with radar, communication, and intelligence systems. It also provided command centres, network infrastructure, and cyber defence. It said so on the base's website. McNulty had checked it out when Titanic Productions had done a deal with the base for its flashback scenes.

The other thing McNulty had checked out was the 66th Security Forces Squadron that provided security for the base. Everything might appear to be calm and low-key on the surface, but men with guns and body armour protected it. Women, too, as the website proudly proclaimed, the issue of female-specific body armour. It all added weight to McNulty's comment, "Don't want you getting shot your first day on location."

It was also why every member of the film crew had to wear a visitor's badge. Being an invited guest would only get you so far. Not wearing your badge could get you shot. The two men crossing Vandenberg Drive toward Building 1624 didn't want to get shot.

* * *

"Why they got to call it Building 1624? Ain't more than a dozen buildings on the whole base."

"Makes 'em feel big and important, I guess. Like Area 51. You really think they've got another fifty Areas?"

"I really think they've got alien autopsy shit."

Jaime Koch stopped and looked at his partner. "They've been spinning that tale since nineteen-forty-seven. Don't you think they'd have found a bit more evidence by now?"

Sal Mineo gave Jaime a conspiratorial wink. "They found plenty. Just keeping it under wraps. Like Area 51."

Jaime let out an exasperated sigh. "Well, there's no aliens in Building 1624. And whatever we get, it'll set us up for life."

Sal got serious. "After the fire?"

Jaime got serious, too. "If you've got to shoot, aim low. Body armour rides high on the waist."

* * *

McNulty found the armourer at the Wild Blue Yonder diner on the corner of Vandenberg Drive and Marrett Street. The production office had taken over the Hanscom Fitness and Sports Centre next door, but the tables in the diner were more practical for Bob Atkins to lay out his wares.

"They let you bring that stuff through security, Ace?"

Titanic Productions had been calling him Ace ever since he'd put three rounds through the ace of spades at a hundred yards. One hole. Blasted the ace right out the middle of the playing card. Ace looked up from cleaning the collection of handguns and assault rifles.

"Had to jump through a lot of hoops. Prove that they've all been plugged."

"Won't that show on camera?"

"Not the way Larry shoots a movie."

McNulty let out a gentle chuckle. "I'm surprised he didn't just buy a handful of black-market guns and stick chewing gum in the barrels."

Ace laughed back. "You're not far off. These aren't so much decommissioned as blocked with black rubber earplugs."

McNulty nodded. "Speaking of earplugs. Larry's not listening when he wants the hero gun to be a nickel-plated Colt .45."

Ace finished reassembling a snub-nose .38 Police Special. "With pearl handles like Patton used? Yeah, I heard. Is Alfonse playing General Patton?"

"Not even close."

"Then tell Larry there's only one George S Patton and nobody but a pimp in a two-nickel whorehouse would use a pearl-handled firearm."

"Carry more weight coming from you. Maybe you could shoot the ace out of his contract."

Ace smiled. "There is no ace in a Titanic Productions contract. I thought you'd have learned that by now."

"I've learned that Larry sees the world different to the rest of us."

Ace nodded. "Then I'll shoot the ace out of his argument. Air Force flashback? More realistic if he's packing standard issue. He can go all pearl-handled once he's a cop. That's your field of expertise."

McNulty snorted a laugh. "I worked in Yorkshire. Had a penny whistle and a truncheon. Used to shout, 'Stop or I'll shout stop again.'"

"Works for me. I'd stop."

"You wouldn't be running."

The waitress came over, drawn by the table of guns but mainly by the English accent. She waved an order pad in front of McNulty. "Can I get you something?"

McNulty turned to look at the waitress. "You still open?"

The waitress waved a hand toward the kitchen. "Can't you smell the home cooking?"

"Chef doesn't cook it here?"

"Figure of speech. Point being, yes, we're open."

McNulty indicated the window booth. "Even with guns on

the table?"

The waitress shrugged. "It's an Air Force Base. There's guns everywhere."

McNulty glanced out the window. Members of the crew were busy moving set decorations and lighting equipment to the primary location at the athletics track. They had been here since dawn, but the first setup wasn't due to be shot for at least another hour. Flip Livingston, the DoP, was lining up the camera for a shot with a vintage Air Force jet in the background. The WWII jet fighter was angled so it looked like it was flying, the six-foot stand tastefully decorated to blend with the bushes and flower border. Alfonse was still de-ageing. Larry was busy being Larry. Nobody needed the technical advisor just yet.

"Do you do an all-day breakfast?"

The waitress nodded. "All day."

"Full English?"

"You mean you don't want pancakes and syrup?"

McNulty shook his head. "Pancakes are for Shrove Tuesday and fat folk. Sausage, eggs, and bacon is the English way."

"And that's not fattening?"

McNulty patted his waist. "Not if you work it off."

The waitress got the wrong idea and gave McNulty the hint of a smile. "And how do you plan to work it off?

McNulty didn't have a wedding ring to point to, so he indicated the swing gang and carpenters moving dolly track and backdrops outside. "Lot of heavy lifting today. I need to save my energy."

The smile faded, but she was still friendly. "Full English for the Englishman."

"Yorkshireman."

"There's a difference?"

"Would you say that to a Texan?"

"They're not English."

"Don't consider themselves American either."

The waitress scribbled on the order pad, then tore the page off. "Texas holds itself to a higher power. And they carry guns."

This time, McNulty smiled. "It's an Air Force Base. There's guns everywhere."

The waitress turned her smile back on. "Touché."

"Tea with milk and sugar would be nice as well. Thanks."

The waitress took the order to the kitchen, and McNulty sat in the next window booth so as not to disturb the armourer. Ace wore a troubled expression. McNulty looked out the window. Crew activity was intensifying, everybody moving with purpose as they headed toward the vintage jet fighter. Everybody except for two.

McNulty watched two men heading in the opposite direction, away from the primary location. One was carrying an olive green jerry can, and the other was wheeling a lighting reflector stand. Both had official crew passes around their necks. And both were checking over their shoulders as if they expected somebody to stop them. McNulty had seen enough suspicious characters in his life to wonder what these two were up to.

Chapter Three

What Jaime Koch and Sal Mineo were up to was making a grab for their slice of the pie. The pair had been brothers in all but name ever since Jaime had rescued Sal from an abusive father when the younger man was thirteen. Jaime had only been nineteen but had already learned at the school of hard knocks. Being almost twenty had made him the old man of the pair, and he had knocked out two of Sal's father's teeth and broken his nose. If there was one thing Jaime detested, it was pervy bastards that wanted to fuck young boys. Now at twenty-three and twenty-nine respectively, they were still looking for the American dream. The trouble was, that seemed to be all it was. A dream.

"Stop looking over your shoulder. You look like your dad."

Sal bristled at the implication. "My dad never looked over his shoulder. He was too busy looking over mine."

Sal had a point, so Jaime clarified. "You make us look suspicious."

"You're looking over your shoulder as well."

"To see what you're looking at. Stop it. You'll draw attention."

Sal gave a sly little sideways smile. "If there's alien autopsy shit in there, we'll get plenty of attention."

Jaime stopped wheeling the reflector and turned to face Sal. "It's a research and development building, not Area 51. We ain't gonna find no alien autopsy shit. We're gonna find fortune and glory."

Jaime sometimes worried how much damage Sal's father had done, knocking Sal about from the age of five and trying to get into his pants since he was ten. That kind of stuff could send anybody a little off-kilter. Sal was so off-kilter it was a wonder he could walk straight. "Forget the weapons development, we're going for radar and communications. The future of warfare is cyber attacks. They said so in American Warrior."

Jaime was an avid reader, figuring if you cribbed off intelligent people, you didn't have to know much yourself. The article in American Warrior magazine had gone into great detail about Hanscom Air Force Base and speculated about even more. Jaime's mistake was in believing that the people who wrote for American Warrior were intelligent people; the magazine hardly being a step up from Famous Monsters Of Filmland or Redneck Roadkill. You might as well believe in alien autopsies based on the National Enquirer.

Sal nodded and faced forward. "Which one you reckon is 1624?"

Jaime proved he had a bit of intelligence of his own. "The one with the biggest aerial on the roof. To transmit all that cyber shit."

* * *

McNulty watched the two men stop to argue in the middle

of the street before disappearing behind a stand of trees that provided shade on the hot summer days. Today was a long way past summer, so the tactfully planted trees simply added greenery to an otherwise grey day. That and the smell of freshly cut grass would give the impression that summer wasn't long gone if McNulty could have smelled it over the sausage eggs and bacon smells coming from the kitchen.

He craned his neck to see if any other crewmembers were going in that direction, but they were the only two. So, if the primary location was the jet fighter, why were they wheeling a lighting reflector toward the building with the transmitter mast on the roof?

* * *

Building 1624 was one of the original concrete buildings in a secluded corner of the base. The building next door had been demolished and was being replaced by a more modern office block that was still under construction. Most of the other buildings along Barksdale Street were corporate offices of one description or another, all steel and glass and ugly-ass signage. It was sad to see the once-famous Air Force Base being turned into corporate America. Jaime would have preferred Hanscom to still be combat paint and camouflage netting. In that regard, he wasn't that different to Larry Unger. Except he had a gun tucked down the back of his trousers.

"This way."

The construction site had spread beyond the footprint of the new office block. The service alley between it and Building 1624 was a glut of industrial dumpsters and piles of building materials. Tarpaulins protected some of the unused stacks while the stacks of scaffolding and planks were half depleted. The bulk of the work was on the building itself. The storage alley was quiet. Jaime glanced up at the back wall of Building 1624. Construction supplies blocked two of the four CCTV cameras. Of the other two, one was pointing toward the parking lot, and the other covered the mouth of the service alley. Two men carrying equipment among the building supplies wouldn't look suspicious.

"Put that down and give me a hand."

Sal put the jerry can on the ground and helped Jaime position the reflector to obscure the mouth of the alley. They were now beyond the view of the remaining CCTV camera and could go to work unseen. Jaime opened the lid of the jerry can and smelled the gasoline.

"American dreamers."

Sal's expression grew serious for a moment. "You think this'll really stick it to the man?"

Jaime put the jerry can down and gently placed both hands on Sal's shoulders. He spoke softly and with genuine feeling. "Government's been putting us down all our lives. Small towns, drying up and blowing away. Rust Belt spreading right across America unless you're some kind of entrepreneur or Facebook guru. We're just taking back a bit of what's ours."

Sal let out a sigh. "Trial by fire?"

Jaime nodded. "And shoot anybody who tries to stop us."

* * *

The waitress brought McNulty's Full English on a tray the size of an aircraft carrier. McNulty was in awe at the girl's strength and balance. She put the tray on the table and began to unload the plates that included the main course, toast, jam, and a side order of hash browns. A teapot, milk, and breakfast mug completed the ensemble. McNulty let out a whistle.

"I know I said Full English, but I didn't mean for all of England."

"How about all of Yorkshire?"

"Not that either. But thanks."

"You're welcome."

McNulty reckoned the welcome extended to more than the breakfast, but he turned his attention to the building with the transmitter mast. The last time he'd seen one that big had been in Drake, Colorado, and that had ended with a megalomaniac engaging in cyber warfare and a shootout that had left Jim Grant for dead. He wondered what two men pretending to work for Titanic Productions might want with a transmitter that powerful. He pushed the breakfast away and glanced at the armourer for moral support. The look on Ace Atkins' face brought him up short.

"What's up?"

Ace was silently counting on his fingers. When he'd finished, he clenched his fists and rested them on the table. "I'm two short."

McNulty knew how serious a movie armourer took his job. "You've lost two guns?"

"Yep."

"Shit."

"That too."

McNulty shook his head and jerked a thumb at the window. "No, I mean shit. I've just seen two fellas skulking around over by the research building."

Ace followed McNulty's gaze. "Two men with guns?"

Before McNulty could formulate a response, Larry Unger came bursting into the diner. "Ah, there you are." He slid into the booth opposite McNulty. "We've got a problem with the short ends."

Chapter Four

In the end, the producer's problem with the short ends had to take a back seat to the two men with guns. Firearms always elevated a situation; that's why McNulty was glad he'd never been armed as a Yorkshire cop. He might well have been exaggerating when he'd said he only had a penny whistle and a truncheon, but, in truth, he hadn't had much more. Uniform patrol officers in England carried CS spray, a side-handled baton, and handcuffs. Worst came to the worst, they also had the panic button on their radio. If there was a firearms incident, they would fall back, secure the area, and call in a mobile firearms unit. McNulty didn't have a mobile firearms unit at Hanscom Air Force Base. Larry didn't either.

"And they're pretending to work for me?"

"Got visitors' passes and a lighting stand."

"And two guns from Titanic Productions?"

McNulty let out a sigh. "Yes."

Ace tapped the table for emphasis. "Blank firing."

Larry wasn't impressed. "Unless they've got live rounds and a pair of pliers."

McNulty looked at the producer. "They're not really plugged with earplugs?"

"As close as. But however they use them, we're shut down and kicked out. Forget the Air Force flashback."

* * *

Jaime Koch scanned the rear of building 1624 and located the fire exit door on the corner furthest from the construction supplies. It was on the ground level with a metal fire escape to the second floor. There would no doubt be another fire exit on the other side of the building, but this one suited his purposes just fine. He waved a hand for Sal to help pull some of the scaffolding planks across the alley.

"Bring some of that tarp as well. It'll burn like a mother-fucker."

Sal pulled a length of tarpaulin off the building supplies, almost getting crushed by a cascade of tumbling planks in the process. "You do know that a motherfucker is basically a father. You know, the one who makes the babies."

Jaime couldn't believe the stuff that came out of Sal's mouth. "Right now? While we're getting ready to rob the Air Force? That's what's on your mind?"

Sal layered the tarpaulin with half a dozen splintered planks. "Just saying."

"Well, say this. If a motherfucker is a father, what went wrong with yours?"

Sal dropped a plank on his foot, but the pained expression on his face was from a much darker place. "Oh my dad's a motherfucker. Just not in the baby sense."

Jaime held up a hand. "Sorry. But let's stay focussed."

Jaime took out his gun and checked the load. "If there's any shooting, we want it to be us shooting at them."

Sal tapped the jerry can with his foot. "It's the fire part I'm looking forward to. Like Old Man Petrie's barn. You remember that? Went up like a Roman candle."

"It looked nothing like a Roman candle. It just burned."

"All that livestock. Smelled like a Sunday roast."

Jaime gave Sal a sad little shake of the head. "You're gonna have to stop doing that. Them cows ain't hurt nobody."

Sal looked deflated. "No more fires?"

Jaime indicated the jerry can. "After today."

Sal cheered up. "Hell yeah. Roman candle time."

* * *

"What you mean we can't call security? That's what the 66th is here for."

McNulty was right, 66th Security Forces Squadron was here to protect the 66th Air Base Group, and 66th Air Base Group would definitely want to protect the building with a transmitter mast big enough to start Cyber World War Three. Larry Unger had a different perspective.

"We don't need to trouble the 66th if you go have a chat with them."

McNulty puffed out his cheeks. "Them being the two men with guns."

Larry waved a hand at the armourer. "Blank firing."

McNulty wagged a finger. "Unless they've got live rounds and a pair of pliers."

"They won't."

"What makes you so sure?"

Larry patted McNulty on the back. "Because I have faith in you."

"Well, I don't have faith in them."

Larry held up a placating hand. "Think of it logically." He turned to Ace. "When did you last have all the guns?"

Ace scratched his chin. "About an hour ago. Before I went to the restroom."

Larry turned back to McNulty. "So, until an hour ago, these two guys didn't know what guns we had. Therefore, they didn't know what ammunition they'd need. Or that the guns were plugged. They're opportunists. Snatch and grab. This was a spur-of-the-moment thing. No live rounds and no pliers. Probably didn't even know we were using guns today."

* * *

Jaime made sure the gun was secure down the back of his trousers while Sal sloshed gasoline over the tarpaulin and planks. Jaime was amazed what you could learn online. He wasn't a super hacker, but his friend at the VA was, taking less than half an hour to hack the Titanic Productions business site and pull up today's call sheet. The call sheet listed all the cast and crew that were needed, including times of arrival. It also listed the locations and set dressing and what props were required. Costumes and makeup had a separate sheet. The crewmember that had interested Jaime was the armourer. The list of props included a selection of handguns and assault rifles. Walking around Hanscom Air Force Base with a rifle would definitely look suspicious. Knowing the calibre of the handguns was the key factor. That and where the armourer was going to set up.

"Splash some more over there. Up the wall."

Sal checked how much was left in the jerry can, then

splashed the last of the gasoline up the back wall of Building 1624. If this was going to be his last foray into arson, he wanted it to be a good one. He dropped the empty can on the ground. "Which door you think they'll come out of?"

Jaime took out the Zippo with its Marine Corps badge. The badge was scratched and faded after two tours in country, and he had a moment's pause as he wondered what the rest of the VA would think about a soldier who had fallen so far from his ideals. He let out a sigh. They probably wouldn't think anything at all. He knew lots of veterans who had stumbled on their return to civilian life. Hell, he'd read in American Warrior that more soldiers had died by their own hand than all the casualties in World War Two and Vietnam put together. Jaime wasn't suicidal; he was angry.

He flicked open the lid and rasped the strike wheel. The flame was hot and yellow. Watching it flicker in the gentle breeze, he thought he could understand Sal's fascination with fire. This time, the fire had more purpose than being angry at Old Man Petrie. It would also be his goodbye to The Corps. He was about to toss the Zippo onto the gasoline-soaked tarpaulin when a voice with an English accent spoke from the other side of the lighting reflector.

"I hear the Air Force have one of the best Fire Departments in the military. Probably because of all those crash landings on the runway."

Chapter Five

McNulty stepped over the rubble at the mouth of the alley and moved close to the reflector stand. He pulled the fluorescent vest he was wearing tight, but didn't zip it closed. He didn't want to be restricted if he had to move fast. The bright yellow vest wasn't a nod to his friend Jim Grant's orange windcheater, but it served the same purpose: to be bright and open and non-threatening. It also meant he looked nothing like a member of the 66th Security Forces Squadron. He didn't want anybody shooting at him because they thought he was armed.

He heard voices on the other side of the reflector, then the rasp of a lighter sparking to life. Keeping his hands in plain sight, he came around the side of the reflector and put on his best English accent. "I hear the Air Force have one of the best Fire Departments in the military. Probably because of all those crash landings on the runway."

The two men he'd seen squabbling outside the diner turned to look at him. The younger one struggled to pull a gun out of his belt. The older one looked more relaxed, almost as if he was resigned to this being his final act. McNulty had seen that look before, and it frightened him. It was the look of somebody at the end of his tether.

"Not that I'm saying the Marines can't fight fires. Just that they aren't usually put in that position."

He indicated the badge on the Zippo. "But you'd know better than me. British Army has different priorities."

The older one closed the lighter. "You were in the army?"

McNulty took two steps past the reflector and found a piece of level ground with solid footing. "Friend of mine was. It affected him as well. Readjusting to Civvy Street."

"I'm readjusting just fine."

"By taking on the Air Force? I don't think so."

The younger one pointed his gun at McNulty. "Want me to shoot him, Jaime?"

Jaime glanced at his partner. "I don't want you using my name. *Sal.*"

Sal noticed the pointed use of his name, appearing to come to terms with both their names being out in the open. "I guess I'd better shoot him them."

McNulty tried to stare down the barrel to see if it was still plugged, but Ace had done a good job of blacking the earplugs. If there was still an earplug in there. He held his hands up in surrender. "You ever hear of an Englishman causing trouble in America?" McNulty wasn't sure if these two had heard of Yorkshire. "We generally just go with the flow. You know, mind our own business."

Sal stabbed the gun at McNulty. "You ain't minding your own business now."

McNulty waved his hands to get them used to the movement. "Well, I kind of am. Because you're kind of interfering with my business. The movie business? You know, the business of making a movie over there by the athletic track?"

Jaime opened the Zippo again and sparked it alight. "You'd

better be in the firefighting business if you take a step closer."

* * *

Larry saw the uniforms through the diner window before he realised who they were. The two women looked strong and capable and didn't look like they gave a shit if they were wearing female-specific body armour or the male equivalent. 66th Security Forces Squadron was an equal opportunities employer. Larry didn't want them to be equal opportunity ass-kickers.

The pair walked past the front of the diner, away from the primary film location. Larry remembered them circling the vintage jet fighter, but not looking enthusiastic about a Hollywood movie being shot on the base. Larry still thought of himself as a Hollywood producer even though he'd relocated back to Boston. Now they were patrolling Barksdale Street, scanning the corporate office buildings along the tree-lined avenue while appearing to make small talk. Each held an automatic weapon casually across their stomachs. And they were walking toward the building with the transmitter mast on the roof.

Larry moved faster than Ace had ever seen him move. Out of the booth and through the front door in a flash.

"Excuse me. Officers. Is that what I should call you? Not sure of the protocol for women with guns."

Both women turned to face the short man who had come out of the diner. One of them gave him a hard smile. "Same protocol as for men with guns. Keep your hands in sight and don't move too fast."

Larry gave them a nervous laugh. "I never move fast. That's

what I pay others to do."

The spokeswoman took a step toward Larry. "To do what exactly?"

Larry read the nametags across the front of their body armour. The talker was Bushmann, and the backup was Evans. Larry waved an apology to Bushmann. "I'm sorry. How rude of me. My name is Larry Unger. I'm the producer of our little movie over there. Titanic Productions."

Bushmann kept her finger on the outside of the trigger guard. "Watch out for icebergs then."

Larry had been hearing that joke from McNulty for years. He smiled and waved a hand toward the diner. "Could you spare a couple of minutes? Come in and give me your opinion about the guns we're using."

Evans and Bushmann exchanged looks, their fingers snaking inside the trigger guards. Bushmann stared at Larry. "You brought guns onto an Air Force Base?"

Larry held his hands up in surrender. "Blank firing."

* * *

A cargo plane circled Hanscom Field to line up with the north-south runway. The roar of its engines echoed off the back wall of Building 1624 and forced McNulty to raise his voice.

"Actor in our last film used to be a firefighter. Chuck Buchinsky."

Jaime tilted his head but didn't drop the lighter. "You made that up. Charles Bronson?"

McNulty had to make the laugh loud even though he was going for casual. "We had that discussion with Chuck. Told him if Charles Bronson couldn't make Buchinsky work, then maybe we should change the name."

"No, Buchinsky works. But Chuck? I'd go with Butch."

This time, McNulty's laugh *was* loud. "Ha. That's what *he* said."

"You should have listened." Jaime held the lighter in front of him.

McNulty held his hands up in a calming gesture. "What I should listen to is what's got you so desperate that you're willing to get shot by the Air Force."

Sal spoke up, still pointing the gun at McNulty. "We're the ones doing the shooting."

"But you won't be the ones ending the shooting. Think about it. You set this alight, and you'll get the Fire Department. Fire Department won't deploy without 66th Security backup. And they'll outnumber you four to one."

The transport plane grew louder as it made its final approach.

Sal shouted. "They won't send eight security to a house fire."

McNulty indicated the transmitter mast. "This isn't just a house."

The plane was right overhead now.

Sal was agitated by the noise. "Let me shoot him now."

Jaime raised his voice, but the plane was too loud. "No."

McNulty took two steps forward. Sal tightened his finger on the trigger. Jaime dropped the lighter and made a lunge for the gun. Flames sprang up all around him, and Sal's eyes widened with panic and muscle reflex squeezed the trigger as he shot McNulty in the chest.

∗ ∗ ∗

Earplugs and pliers. That's what went through McNulty's mind as the gun went off at point-blank range. Even a blind man could have hit him at that distance. A blind panic man might miss, but not if he fired twice. Before McNulty could lunge for the gun, the man who was engulfed in flames did the job for him. Not by lunging for the gun, but by Sal dropping the gun to help his friend.

Sal dived at Jaime and knocked him away from the burning tarpaulin. McNulty whipped off his coat and used it to smother the flames. Jaime's legs and waist were still smoking, but the flames hadn't reached his hands and face. The heat had singed his hair and eyebrows, but the skin was intact.

The transport plane screeched as it landed, and the engine noise ramped up as reverse thrust helped the brakes slow it down at the far end of the runway. It was only when the noise abated that McNulty could hear the fire alarm and the warning siren. He patted his chest, checking for an entry wound, then let out a sigh.

"Blank firing."

Jaime sat up. "You don't think I'd give Sal a real gun, do you?"

Sal was too happy to see Jaime alive to be offended. McNulty pointed out the obvious. "Maybe not. But we do have a real fire."

Chapter Six

"What? You gave him a job?"

"Actually, *you* gave him a job."

Larry stood at the table where the missing guns had been returned. "Him and his idiot friend? What use is he going to be?"

McNulty's face was still blackened from helping battle the flames. "Well, he's good at starting fires."

* * *

The fire at Hanscom Air Force Base had spread to the half-built office block by the time the two green fire tenders and a water bowser had arrived, so protecting the rear of Building 1624 had initially been down to the three heroes who had also helped evacuate the building. One of them had sustained burns to his legs and waist, but everything else was superficial, if no less painful. Construction workers had been working on the other side of the site and didn't even know there was a fire until the warning siren alerted the entire base.

McNulty and Sal Mineo had used lengths of scaffolding to lever the burning planks away from the back of the transmitter building with varying levels of success; they had managed to save the building, but had spread the fire to the rest of the construction supplies. In the meantime, Jaime Koch had helped the office workers and technicians through the nearest fire exit, directing them away from the flames and telling one of them to take names in case anyone was missing.

When the base firefighters had taken over, McNulty had guided Jaime and Sal to one side and got their story straight. He had a lot of experience at knowing what the police wanted to hear. Firstly, the pair had been working for Titanic Productions when they'd lost their sense of direction, so instead of wheeling the lighting reflector to the primary film location, they'd ended up in the parking lot of Building 1624. That's when they'd noticed flames licking at the tarpaulin-covered supplies and tried to put them out.

At the same time, McNulty had seen the men going the wrong way and gone to redirect them when he too had seen the spreading flames and joined in to help. After that, it had been a race against time. The fire alarm had sounded, followed by the base warning siren. Jaime had got caught in the fire, and Sal and McNulty had smothered the flames. Since Jaime was injured, he had taken the job of helping evacuate the building while Sal and McNulty had continued to battle the flames until the fire department arrived.

That was the story they all told.

Before that was the story McNulty had prised out of Jaime and Sal.

* * *

"How long were you a Marine?"

"You're always a Marine."

McNulty indicated the fire across the parking lot. "Until you're not."

Jaime's shoulders slumped. There was no getting away from what he had become but he was still proud of what he had once been, a US Marine. "Two tours. And the times in between."

"Two tours where?"

Jaime turned sad eyes on McNulty. "Does it matter?"

"I guess not." He changed tack. "Is that where you two met?"

Jaime snorted a laugh. "Sal? No, that was before."

Sal spoke up. "I could have been a Marine. Just circumstances, that's all."

McNulty noticed the downturned eyes and the shivering hug. Sal seemed to shrink while he hugged himself. The look in his eyes was something else McNulty had seen before. He thought about Daniel Roach's little sister, Chantelle, who was seven years old to his thirteen. She had only been four when her brother had started sticking his curly-wurly in her tuppence. He nearly didn't make it past thirteen when Vice Squad Detective McNulty had pinned the child molester against the wall of the custody suite.

McNulty softened his tone. "And he helped you, right?"

Sal nodded but didn't speak.

McNulty knew what happened next. "But then he left."

McNulty knew all about being abandoned, even if it was under different circumstances. Being dumped in Crag View Orphanage when he was too young to understand was bad enough, but not knowing that the girl who was being abused by the headmaster was his sister was even worse. He hadn't even known he had a sister. Breaking Mr Cruikshank's nose with a Bible was his coming-of-age moment. Finding his sister again in America over thirty years later was his rebirth. Family. He couldn't remember his mother and had never known his father, so his sister was all the family he had. It looked as if Jaime Koch was the nearest thing to family that Sal Mineo had.

"If you ever went into movies, you do know there's already a Sal Mineo? He was in that western with the other guy who changed his name."

Sal's expression brightened. "Charles Bronson?"

Jaime smiled. "*Magnificent Seven.*"

McNulty pointed at the two men in front of him. "Magnificent Two."

Then he laughed. "Not the film with Morecambe and Wise."

Jaime raised his eyebrows. "Who the hell are Morecambe and Wise?"

"Couple of comedians. A bit like you two. Let's see if we can't get you a straight job."

It was Jaime's turn to indicate the fire that was now under control across the parking lot. "After this?"

McNulty looked at the evacuees taking names at the rendezvous point. "After what? You just saved a hundred people."

* * *

"You gave him a job?"

"Actually, *you* gave him a job."

Larry didn't look happy about hiring the men who had almost got Titanic Productions kicked off the base. McNulty waved the producer's misgivings aside and put on his cop-explaining-to-a-victim voice.

"The story I concocted was that they were crewmembers who got lost and saw the fire. Look on the bright side. Titanic Productions stopped the fire and rescued a hundred Air Force personnel. I wouldn't be surprised if they let you have the location for free."

That got Larry's attention. "Hero discount, you mean?"

McNulty pressed his advantage. "If they work for you."

"Meaning I gave them a job?"

McNulty nodded. "You gave them a job."

Larry let out a sigh. "Consider it done."

McNulty gave a thumbs-up sign to the shadowy figures in the far corner of the diner. Jaime patted Sal on the back, and Sal puffed out his chest. He'd never been in the movie business before. McNulty turned back to Larry.

"You remember telling me that Titanic Productions was one big happy family?"

"I don't remember saying happy."

"Like running off to join the circus."

"I didn't say that either."

McNulty shrugged. "Well, whoever said it, it's true. Consider yourself the saver of lost souls."

Larry looked McNulty in the eye. "Is that what you are?"

McNulty thought about Crag View Orphanage again. "It's what I was."

Larry glanced at the two men he had just hired. "Family." Then he turned back to McNulty. "Send them to Phil at the Production Office. Tell him to start them as runners. We'll see what they fall into later."

Phil Eszterhaus had been the Production Manager for as long as McNulty had worked for Titanic Productions.

The Hungarian immigrant had started as Location Manager before progressing to the production office and finally being responsible for all aspects of the movie, from catering to carpenters. McNulty had seen how Jaime and Sal handled wood and tarpaulins. Production runner seemed like a safer place for them to start.

"Thanks."

"Now let's talk about my other problem."

McNulty slipped back into business mode. "Short ends?"

Larry nodded. "Short ends."

Chapter Seven

McNulty had plenty to ponder as he climbed the stairs to his room at the Vine Brook Motel. Some of it was good, and some of it was bad, but there was one thing you could say about working for Titanic Productions: it wasn't boring.

Titanic Productions had taken over the family-run motel between the Burlington Mall and the Lahey Hospital & Medical Center, two miles east of Hanscom Air Force Base, not only taking all the rooms but also cordoning off a sizeable chunk of the shopping mall parking lot for the location vehicles. A temporary fence had been erected to form a secure compound for the makeup trailer, the craft services mobile kitchen, and half a dozen shipping containers that housed the various departments needed when you weren't filming in a studio. Larry Unger couldn't afford a studio of his own, and renting studio space was more expensive than a mom and pop motel and half a parking lot.

Part of his pondering was about Larry's problem with the short ends.

The rest was about his conversation with Amy Moore over dinner.

* * *

The Tavern in the Square looked no more like a tavern than the parking lot looked like a square. The restaurant nestled up against a three-storey office building that housed Lockheed Martin Corporation and COMSOL Inc. It was a ground-floor extension whose only resemblance to a tavern was the wood panelling inside and the red awnings that protected outside diners. In fact McNulty couldn't remember any Yorkshire taverns having outside diners; they were always inside seating and distressed stone.

"This make you feel like you're back in Yorkshire?"

Amy was smirking, so McNulty put on a fake grumpy face. "It does not."

"No authentic Yorkshire puddings and pickled eggs?"

"About as authentic as the Chipotle Mexican Grill across the road."

"I bet the road isn't authentic Yorkshire either, is it?"

McNulty snorted a laugh. "Six-lane highway just for a shopping mall? Parts of the M1 are only three lanes each way."

"M1?"

"Main north-south motorway linking London to Yorkshire."

Amy waved a hand around the warm, dark interior. "At least it's cosy. You've got to give us Americans that."

McNulty took her hand and squeezed it in both of his. "It's cosy because of the company, not the steel and concrete covered with dark wood."

"Aw. Larry always said you were a romantic."

McNulty slapped Amy's hand. "He said nothing of the sort."

"Okay. But he did say the English were romantics. That's why they all came over here. To tame the wilderness."

"Fat chance. I can't even tame you."

Amy fluttered her eyelids at him. "Maybe you're not trying hard enough."

McNulty gulped and made a show of reading the menu. He had been flirting with the makeup artist ever since he'd joined Titanic Productions, but they hadn't started dating until Amy had helped with the runaway girl they'd found hiding during the Hollywood Collision Center night shoot. Tilly Nutton had turned out to be more than a runaway; she was the daughter of a drug cartel boss who was being sex-trafficked by her own father. Looking after the ten-year-old had got Amy kidnapped, and her fingers broken. Saving Amy Moore had been the beginning of a beautiful relationship. McNulty just wasn't very good at relationships.

The menu wasn't that interesting, and Amy knew McNulty was shutting her out again. Her voice became a whisper. "Maybe you're not trying at all."

McNulty wasn't shutting Amy out; he was shutting himself in. He really liked her, maybe even loved her, but the lack of love in his childhood had hardened him, so expecting anyone to love him now was tough to accept. If even your mother didn't love you, how could you expect a beautiful American to love you? His eyes scanned the menu, but didn't see it. When he finally looked up Amy had stopped flirting. McNulty's voice became a whisper, too.

"Maybe Larry was wrong."

"Is that what he dragged you into his office for? To tell you he was wrong?"

* * *

That was the other thing for McNulty to ponder: what Larry had told him in the Production Office after the delayed location shoot had finished for the day. The fire at Building 1624 had closed Hanscom Air Force Base for three hours while the Fire Department made sure there were no hot spots beneath the debris, soaking the planks and tarpaulins with gallons of water and spreading them across the parking lot. That meant that filming hadn't got started until mid-afternoon and they hadn't wrapped until early evening.

"McNulty. A word."

McNulty stepped into the makeshift office, expecting to be told off again about hiring a PTSD Marine and an arsonist. "Only one?"

Larry closed the door and waved for McNulty to sit. "Enough of the dry wit. This is serious."

McNulty sat in a hard chair in front of a battered desk. "What is?"

Larry leaned against the desk, giving him the height advantage. "We're being screwed out of the short ends."

McNulty crossed one leg casually over the other. "They're not stealing it to make snuff movies again, are they?"

A couple of years ago, a torture porn gang had been using the short ends—unused film left in the cans—to make snuff movies in Quincy. Several missing girls had been tortured and filmed with borrowed Titanic Productions' equipment. It had taken a monumental effort for McNulty to keep Titanic Productions out of the firing line over that, Larry basking in the glory of having his technical advisor proclaimed as a hero.

"I've been selling the short ends to this actor who wants to direct his first movie. Something about three brothers in New York. Romantic comedy."

"Why not use the short ends yourself? Are you too Hollywood for that now?"

"I'm too business savvy. The budget includes full canisters, whether we use them all or not. I can make more money selling the short ends and still have enough film for our movie."

"Money on the side? Unreported, I'm betting."

"It's extra money. How do you think I can afford to pay the arsonist and the Marine? Who cares if it's unreported?"

"The IRS?"

"They've got bigger fish to fry."

McNulty uncrossed his legs and leaned forward. "Maybe the actor will become famous, like that fella who made *The Brothers McMullen*."

"Ed Burns was famous already. This guy, he isn't even paying."

"Ah. You want to add debt collector to my job description."

"You haven't got a job description. You're an Englishman abroad." Larry waved a hand to indicate everything around him. "And this travelling circus saved your sorry ass."

"I thought you never called it a circus."

Larry ignored the truth of that remark. "I gave you a job when nobody else would. And sometimes that job includes a couple of sidelines that help keep Titanic Productions on the rails."

"You're not going off the rails. You're just grabbing some extra cash."

"But I did give you a job."

McNulty stood up and let out a sigh. Larry was right; he had given McNulty a job after he'd been fired from the Savage PD for beating up another child molester. It seemed that the shadow of Daniel Roach followed McNulty everywhere. McNulty might have come to America to look for his sister, but he'd needed a job to finance that search. In the end, she had found him after Titanic Productions and the Quincy torture porn gang had made national news. It was hard to argue that Larry Unger hadn't been instrumental in that reunion.

"Yes, you did."

"And this is part of the job. What I need is for you to put the frighteners on the Brother McMullen. Get him to pay the going rate."

McNulty puffed out his cheeks. "I've never been very good at frighteners. But I'll go talk to him. Explain how it is."

Larry touched his lips with one finger, then pointed at McNulty. "Use the English accent. That always adds weight."

"And if it doesn't, I'll use the Yorkshire accent and short sentences. That should add a bit more."

* * *

That's what Larry had told McNulty in the makeshift office. What Amy was building up to felt a whole lot heavier.

"Where do you see this going?"

"This?"

"You and me."

"The future, you mean?"

"Yes."

McNulty took a deep breath and let it out slowly. He

considered reading the menu again, but didn't think he could put this off much longer. He rubbed some non-existent fluff out of the corner of his eye, then looked down at the table. His hands were very still. His heart was racing. He felt short of breath. Once he'd gathered his thoughts, he looked at Amy.

"I'm still trying to process the past. Haven't given much thought to the future."

"Well, give it some thought now."

"About you and me?"

"Yes."

McNulty wanted to touch her again, but kept his hands flat on the table. "You know how I feel about you."

Amy's stare was hard. "I can guess. But you've never told me."

McNulty held his hands out, palms up, and shrugged. "I'm a Yorkshireman. We don't talk about our feelings."

"You do have feelings, though."

"Of course I do."

"What are they?"

McNulty's head was spinning. Why did talking to women always end up coming full circle? There was no defending against it, so he did the man thing and went on the attack. "Well, if you don't know by now, I'm not going to tell you."

"But I want you to tell me. That's how this works. Boy meets girl. Boy talks to girl. Girl knows what's on the boy's mind."

"What's on my mind is food and short ends."

Amy gave an exasperated sigh. "The boy's future. About that."

Now, McNulty was angry. There were some things he just didn't want to talk about. Ever. Why couldn't Amy understand that? What gave her the right to start prying into his most private thoughts? It was good between them, wasn't it? Why couldn't she settle for that?

"The boy's past. Is that what you want to talk about? Well, this boy's past is dead and buried, so he lives for today. Not tomorrow or the next day. Now. In the moment. And you talking about wedding rings and family and the future. That's not…" His voice trailed off when he realised what he'd said.

Amy looked crestfallen. "Is that what I'm talking about?"

McNulty couldn't meet her eyes. He couldn't tell her that being abandoned by his own family left scars he wasn't sure would heal. What if he turned out to be as bad as his mother, somebody who had not only abandoned her son but five years later had done the same to her daughter as well.

Amy saw the hurt in his downturned eyes and wished she hadn't started this conversation. She pushed back from the table and stood up. "You're right. You need to eat and sort out Larry's short ends. Short end of the stick seems to be what we both got."

* * *

And that's what was on McNulty's mind as he climbed the stairs to his room at the Vine Brook Motel. He paused at the half-landing to catch his breath. He had managed to eat half a steak and a quarter of his fries, but the weight in his chest wasn't indigestion. Why did he always manage to shoot himself in the foot? Had Crag View screwed him up so much?

He continued to the top of the stairs and turned left along the external walkway. Vine Brook was a traditional motel with downstairs rooms opening straight onto the parking lot and upstairs doors lining the balcony. McNulty's room was at the far end. It was dark now, and he glanced at the fenced compound as he walked past the other rooms. Security lights highlighted the production trailers, but the rest of the parking lot was in darkness. Burlington Mall had closed hours ago.

McNulty kicked an empty Coca-Cola can that he hadn't seen. He hadn't seen much ever since Amy left him sitting at the table. Abandoned again. He bent to pick up the can, intending to crush it like Robert Shaw had in *Jaws*. Somebody had beaten him to it. He felt more like Richard Dreyfuss anyway, with just enough strength to crush a Styrofoam cup.

He noticed the light in the end room as he straightened up. His room. The door was partly open, and *The Great Escape* theme drifted out of the room. McNulty remembered that he'd tuned the radio to a classic movies station. He reckoned it should be *The Good, the Bad and the Ugly*, McNulty standing in for the Bad and the Ugly. Amy was all Goodness, and it pained him to hurt her so much.

When he reached his room, he nudged the door open with his foot. The man sitting on the bedside chair stood up. "Are you Vincent McNulty?"

Chapter Eight

Twenty minutes later, McNulty was still holding the crushed Coca-Cola can, his knuckles white as he tried to crush it some more. The man was tall and thin and had the sombre air of an undertaker. He wore a black suit that enhanced the image, but a garish orange and yellow tie that completely blew it away. That and the smile he used like a cut-price Jim Grant to reduce the tension as he broke the news that turned McNulty's life upside down.

* * *

"It's funny, but I would have thought that somebody working in the movie industry would listen to anything but movie soundtracks."

The smile might have been friendly, but the deep voice was exactly how you'd expect a funeral director to sound. It was deep and slow and enunciated every syllable apart from the contraction of, it is. McNulty back-healed the door closed and tightened his grip on the crushed can.

"What's funny is somebody breaking into my room and listening to *The Great Escape.* Because unless you've got a good explanation, you're not escaping to anywhere."

The man appeared to consider what to say next, then gave a curt little nod. "You are right, of course. I do apologise. But if you are indeed Vincent McNulty, formerly of Crag View Orphanage, I thought this was news best delivered in private."

"News?"

"Not good news, I'm afraid."

McNulty's heart sank. His first and only thought went to Susan Carter, formerly McNulty. "My sister? What's happened?"

The man shook his head. "Not your sister."

"Her daughter."

"It's not her either."

McNulty was growing tired of the circular questions with no answers. It was coming to the end of a very bad day, what with the fire at Hanscom Air Force Base, Larry wanting McNulty to put the frighteners on some poor actor, and Amy storming out because he couldn't commit. Now here was the man in black warning of bad news but not delivering it.

"Unless you want to check how good your health insurance is, you'd better stop giving me the circle jerk."

The man held up a calming hand. "I am not doing this very well."

He waved toward the bedside chair. "Please sit down."

McNulty knew all about giving bad news. He had delivered dozens of death warnings and fatal accident reports back in his uniform days in Yorkshire. The first thing you always did was get the recipient to sit down. The next thing was to ask if they had any relatives who could come and stay with them.

"You going to ask if I've got a relative who can stay with me?"

"You have no relatives. Apart from your sister, who was

also a resident of Crag View Orphanage."

McNulty moved to the chair but didn't sit. "You keep mentioning Crag View. It burned down. Doesn't exist anymore."

The man tapped his forehead. "It will always exist for those who lived there."

McNulty had a sudden thought. "You worked there?"

The man smiled. It wasn't a very convincing smile. "No, I did not. I hardly think they would send me all the way from a derelict orphanage in Yorkshire."

"They sent you from somewhere."

"As a courtesy. Because of your heroic deeds at Northern X and your brief service with the Savage Police Department. Another child molester, wasn't it?"

"Another?"

"After the unfortunate Daniel Roach got you fired in Yorkshire."

"I wasn't fired."

"Forced to resign then."

McNulty sat in the chair but kept his back straight and his chin up. "Do I get a courtesy call for that as well?"

Despite the dour expression, the man seemed to be enjoying this. "They do say that abusers were often abused themselves. Or abandoned."

"I'll remember to ask. Next time I beat up a child molester."

The man waved a hand again. "Oh, I'm not suggesting that you are a serial abuser. Merely that being given up to an orphanage might explain your inclination to, how should I say it? Fly off the handle."

"You want to see me fly off the handle? Keep going."

The man let out a sigh, then sat on the edge of the bed with his feet together. He straightened the crease in his trousers. "I am sorry, but I do find it best to gauge how someone will react to bad news before giving them the bad news."

"You keep talking about bad news. How about you get on with it?"

The man examined McNulty's face and appeared to be satisfied with what he saw. He gave that brief little nod again. "Very well. It's about your mother."

This time, McNulty's heart beat faster. He felt tightness clamp his chest, and his mouth went dry. He swallowed and licked his lips. "I don't have a mother."

"Everybody has a mother."

"Not me. Not ever."

"I understand. Maybe this isn't such bad news after all, then."

"Spit it out."

The man straightened the garish tie, then looked McNulty in the eye. "Your mother is in a dementia care home in Yorkshire. She is very sick."

Chapter Nine

The spindly dead branches tapped the window as the storm grew louder. Rain lashed across the enclosed courtyard where children were encouraged to commune with nature while seeking inner peace. There was very little inner peace at Crag View Orphanage tonight. The winter storm had put paid to any peace in the upstairs dormitories.

Vincent McNulty saw the flash of lightning and began to count while he waited for the thunder. He had only counted to eight when the earth shook, and the glass rattled in the frame. The rain changed direction and began to attack the window above Vincent's bed. He tried to remember if the count was more or less than the last time. Was the storm coming closer or moving away?

Another flash almost blinded him.

He began to count.

One. The rain was getting harder.

Two. It felt like it would break the window.

Three. The tree danced and waved.

Four. The branches looked like sharp black witch's fingers.

Five. Somebody was sobbing further along the dormitory.

Six. Bang.

The clap of thunder was so loud that it shook Vincent's bed. It felt like the storm was going to uproot the entire building and send it into oblivion. Six seconds. The storm was coming closer. The thunder was getting louder. Soon it would be right overhead, and the wind would tear Crag View Orphanage from the earth. Young Vincent closed his eyes and waited for the end. It couldn't come soon enough.

* * *

McNulty snapped awake as the Fasten Seatbelt sign came on and the Captain announced that there was turbulence ahead. He had already told the passengers that Delta 7580 was beginning its descent into Manchester and ordered the cabin crew to prepare the cabin for landing. The overnight flight from Boston had been long and uneventful, the brief layover in New York being the only chance for McNulty to stretch his legs. There had been plenty of time for him to question the wisdom of making this trip and to bemoan the shortcomings that had meant he'd left Boston without clearing the air with Amy.

After the man in black had dropped his bombshell, he had tactfully withdrawn, staying just long enough to give McNulty his mother's name and the address of Halcyon Court Care Home. McNulty hadn't known what to do with that information and had wished he could have talked it over with Amy. The main thing to talk over was why should McNulty care about the woman who had abandoned him while at the same time wanting answers to the reason why. His first thoughts had been anger and hatred. His next had been curiosity. Somewhere in the back of his mind, hadn't he always wondered about the woman he had never known?

Doreen Wills. She wasn't even a McNulty anymore.

The next morning, after a long and sleepless night, McNulty had told Larry. The money-grabbing producer had surprised McNulty by telling him there was only one thing to do, and that was fly back to England.

"It's your mother. What else can you do?"

"I can let her rot, that's what."

Larry had become almost paternal. "No, you can't. That's not you."

"It's what she deserves."

"Deserves has got nothing to do with it. She's your mother."

Larry had brushed aside McNulty's objections, arguing that they didn't know the whole story. There was always a story. A reason. No matter how bad things had been for McNulty growing up, imagine what it must have felt like for a mother to give up her son. Or have her son taken away from her. Before that son could seek closure, he'd need to find the answers to those questions.

"You're a shrink now?"

Larry had shaken his head. "We might all be family here at Titanic Productions, but you only have one mother."

McNulty hadn't given up that easily. "Losing one child might be careless. Giving up a second. That's unforgivable."

"I'm not saying you should forgive her. Go and ask. Then put it to bed."

The plane shook again. McNulty gripped the armrests. Northern England was dull, wet, and windy. The undercarriage was lowered, the plane slowing some more as the giant wheels caught the air. Final approach.

The plane hit an air pocket and suddenly dropped twenty

feet. There was a collective cry from the passengers as the cabin lights briefly went out before the engines found air again and the Boeing settled on its final approach. Roads and hedgerows rushed past beneath the window, then there was a long expanse of grass, and finally the oil-streaked tarmac of the runway. A gust of wind sideswiped the airplane, and it was suddenly flying at a crazy angle. The cabin shook as the undercarriage hit hard, then skidded sideways. A child was screaming. Some adults, too.

McNulty touched the tattoo that ran up one side of his neck, the black branches of a dead tree that was a permanent reminder of Crag View Orphanage. There was a groan of twisting metal, then the undercarriage collapsed as the long metal tube sent a shower of sparks in the air and slid across the runway. The last thing he heard was a child screaming that he wanted to go home. McNulty had the opposite thought; he wished he hadn't come home at all.

Chapter Ten

The grubby-looking man with dirty fingernails sat at the end of the bar and nursed his third pint of Tetley's as if his life depended on it. In a way, it did, since his life had been on a downward spiral over the last few years. Sitting in a dark north of England pub an hour before lunchtime wasn't even the bottom of the spiral; he knew he had a long way to go before touching bottom. The ornate carvings and heavy wood of the bar sucked all the light out of the day. The grimy windows kept what little light there was on the outside. Three pints and a pickled egg kept his personal darkness on the inside. He hadn't sunk to pork scratchings yet, but it was early.

The front door opened and closed, giving a brief glimpse of the grey northern sky as two more Yorkshire lowlifes came in for a liquid pick-me-up. Pat Tubah didn't even look up to see if he knew them. Sitting in this pub at this time of day, he would definitely know them. He just didn't care. That's how low he'd sunk.

Tubah had come a long way since being head bouncer for the Northern X massage chain, and the journey had been all downward. He used to have influential friends and had the ear of the boss, Telfon Speed, but now he was just another

Yorkshire bottom feeder eking out a living on the fringes of crime and eating pickled eggs before eleven.

The landlord stopped polishing glasses with a towel and poured two pints after taking payment in advance. He knew all about Yorkshire lowlifes as well. There was hardly any small talk and no cheer whatsoever. Tubah took a swig of his beer and glanced up at the TV above the bar. A Breaking News banner scrolled across the bottom of the screen. A plane crash at Manchester Airport.

Tubah paused with the glass halfway to his mouth as shock bristled the hairs at the back of his neck. Not shock at the Boeing 737 that had skidded across the runway or the close-ups of a child's shoe and a teddy bear that news cameramen always managed to find at the scene of a disaster. It was the huddle of figures being escorted onto the airport bus and the face that briefly glanced at the camera. A face he never thought he'd see again.

* * *

The Evacuation of Delta 7580 had gone smoothly, the crew putting years of training into practice despite none of them having dealt with a real, live incident before. Simulations and training exercises could only get you so far; the rest was strength of character and professionalism. The Delta crew were very professional. At least the airplane hadn't burst into flames, although the cargo hold had split open, spilling luggage onto the runway.

Paramedics and fire engines had been on the scene immediately, but it was the press that surprised McNulty, camera crews filming the evacuation slides and subsequent huddle of passengers as if it were a Hollywood blockbuster. Larry Unger would have loved to have a film crew at the scene; he could have used the footage to add production value to whatever movie he could rewrite to include a plane crash. As it was, McNulty had to fend off the BBC and Channel 4, ITV having been caught on the hop covering the latest high-profile footballer signing for Manchester United.

McNulty noticed a cameraman sifting through the scattered luggage, arranging a child's shoe and a teddy bear for a close-up of the debris. A stewardess took McNulty's arm and guided him toward the mobile triage tent that had been set up at the edge of the airfield. The air was filled with shouting and crying, but the emergency services remained stoic and calm. It's what the emergency services did. It was why McNulty would forever think of himself as a cop first and a technical advisor second. A long way second.

A blanket was thrown across his shoulders, and the stewardess moved on to the next passenger. A handheld camera broke ranks from the media scrum and pushed in towards McNulty's face. He looked briefly into the lens, then told the cameraman to fuck off. He didn't think that would make the Six O'clock News.

* * *

What did make the Six O'clock News was the signing of a high-profile Spanish footballer to Manchester United and the latest transgressions of a government minister who should have known better than to kiss his female assistant in the apparently secure environment of Whitehall. There was nothing secure about Whitehall.

The third headline was the plane crash at Manchester Airport. There was some stock footage of airplanes trying to land in strong winds, followed by a shaky mobile phone video that had been recorded from the terminal window. The Delta Airlines flight was flying at an angle but appeared to straighten just before the wheels touched down. A sudden gust of wind sideswiped the plane, which took a sharp left turn before the undercarriage collapsed and the Boeing belly-flopped across the runway, skidding off the tarmac.

The rest of the news bulletin showed fire engines and ambulances racing to the scene and passengers being helped down the emergency slides, which couldn't fully deploy because the undercarriage was gone. There were close-ups of shocked faces and frightened passengers, as well as the ever-present shots of children's shoes and cuddly toys. The only things missing were balls of flame and smoking wreckage, but you couldn't win them all.

The newsreader confirmed that there had been no fatalities and only a handful of minor injuries, mainly bumps and bruises, and the inevitable shock. Questions were already being raised about whether the pilot should have aborted and diverted to a different airport. Hindsight was the prerogative of newsreaders and opposition politicians. Nobody ever questioned it when disaster was averted.

The camera mingled with the passengers, showing some relieved faces among the more common shock and pain. The coverage highlighted the shock and the pain, as well as repeating the cuddly toy and the child's shoe. One passenger looked straight at the camera and appeared to say something, but there was no audio. It didn't take a lip reader to guess what he'd said, though. McNulty had been wrong; his "Fuck off" had made the Six O'clock News.

* * *

The voice down the other end of the line didn't sound pleased to hear from him. "What do you want?"

The dirty fingernails didn't feel as dirty as Pat Tubah gripped the mobile phone he'd borrowed from one of the other lowlifes for the price of a pint. "It's not what I want. It's what I can give you."

"You haven't given me anything but indigestion in five years."

Tubah bristled at the putdown but kept his tone friendly. "Time was I gave you anything Mr Speed wanted."

The voice growled down the line. "Time was I could give a shit."

"Mr Speed would give a shit about this."

"Telfon Speed has been pushing up daisies ever since Northern X got shut down. Terminated with extreme prejudice. And the organisation put out of business. So I'll say it again. What do you want?"

Tubah considered how much he could ask for and decided to err on the side of caution. There was no point stalling negotiations before he even got his foot in the door. "I want to help settle the score."

"What score?"

"With the copper that shut down Northern X."

The voice down the line didn't sound impressed. "The copper that shut us down was an ex-copper then, and he's an even more ex-copper now. Somewhere in America. He's not worth the price of the flight."

"Might not cost as much as you think."

"Will you get to the point?"

Tubah took a deep breath and puffed out his cheeks. It was shit or bust time. He leaned against the wall and melted into the shadows at the end of the bar. "The point is I've just seen him on the telly, and he's a lot closer than America."

The voice sounded interested now. "What's he doing on the telly?"

"Telling some news reporter to fuck off at Manchester Airport."

Chapter Eleven

The main thing McNulty noticed when he finally made it across the Pennines to Bradford was just how small everything was. After spending the last few years in America, he had grown used to wide roads and tall buildings and had forgotten just how narrow a two-lane B road could be. Add illegal parking and badly planned sightlines, and driving through Yorkshire became a game of dodgems. At least sitting in the airport transfer taxi meant he wasn't driving. When he'd first moved to America, it had taken a while to get used to Americans driving on the wrong side of the road. Now that he was back in England, he was having the same trouble in reverse. If he hired a car, he'd probably spend the first two days reaching for the gear stick with his right hand.

Another thing he noticed was the weather. Yorkshire weather was notoriously fickle, sometimes giving three seasons in a single day, but mainly what it gave was cold, grey, and damp. Today wasn't cold, but it was definitely grey. "Pull up here for a minute."

McNulty had purposely asked the driver to drive through Bradford on his way to Leeds and had directed him to Five Lane Ends. The road where McNulty asked the driver to stop was Bradford Road. The building he wanted to look at was Ecclesfield Police Station.

* * *

Once a cop, always a cop. Vince McNulty had been living by that mantra ever since he'd worked at the walled-in police station that had replaced the old nick on Kings Road.

"You need to call the police?" The taxi driver glanced at the fortress McNulty was staring at.

"I am the police." McNulty had always wanted to use the old Hollywood cliché, but realised it wasn't appropriate anymore. "Used to be."

The driver saw the look on McNulty's face through the mirror. "Memory lane?"

McNulty nodded. "Memory lane."

McNulty had too many memories of growing up in Yorkshire, so he narrowed them down to his time in the police and the mistakes he had made. He glanced at the first-floor windows of the CID office that were directly above the report-writing room downstairs. The CID office was where Jimmy Tynan, the DC coordinating the missing girls investigation, had put ex-DC Vince McNulty back into the Northern X massage chain undercover. Looking at Ecclesfield Police Station now, McNulty couldn't hide the sadness inside him. He had loved being a police officer. He had loved feeling like he made a difference in the world, no doubt a throwback to the fact that he made no difference at all growing up at Crag View Orphanage.

McNulty nodded to the driver. "That's enough. Lead on Macduff."

The driver didn't know that McNulty was misquoting Shakespeare, but knew what he meant. "Hotel?"

"Yeah. Hotel."

"He's staying at the Station Hotel."

"In Manchester?"

"No."

"You're not much for getting to the point, are you?"

The voice down the phone sounded just as unhappy as the last time Tubah had called him, but at least Tubah had cleaned his fingernails and stolen a phone of his own. He wasn't up to date with the latest technology, so he'd shoplifted a Nokia that still had a keypad instead of a touchscreen and programmed in the number from memory.

"Leeds."

"There's a lot of stations in Leeds."

Tubah told himself to calm down and be more concise in future. "Neville Street. Round the back of Leeds Railway Station. Middle of town."

The voice sounded like it was smiling. "Get yourself over there and keep an eye on him. I'll have some of the fellas come and join you. Welcome back."

Tubah ended the call and couldn't help smiling himself. He paraphrased McNulty's feelings. Tubah felt like a crook again.

Chapter Twelve

McNulty tossed his overnight bag on the bed and surveyed the hotel room. It was cheap and cheerless and as faded as his jeans. He couldn't afford Queen's Hotel on City Square or the Hilton Leeds City and had settled for the Station Hotel overlooking the railway arches behind Neville Street. It didn't even overlook Neville Street, which wasn't much of a view in itself, but the railway arches, that was slumming it. There was a single tree on a triangular patch of grass that was in urgent need of cutting. The tree had already shed its leaves. It was the leaves that depressed him. Not the end-of-season feeling that the dying foliage normally engendered but the spindly black fingers of the branches they left behind. He touched the tattoo on the side of his neck. You can take the boy out of Crag View, but you can't take the orphanage out of the boy.

* * *

A stolen Subaru Impreza rumbled as it drove past the front of the hotel, the twin exhausts sounding like the throaty roar of a lion about to let rip. Tubah was more adept at stealing cars than shoplifting mobile phones and had already switched the number plates with a similar car in the twenty-four-hour Tesco car park on Canal Road in Bradford. Tubah had driven as fast as he dared without attracting attention from the police and reckoned he wasn't that far behind the man who had told the reporter to fuck off on national television. He couldn't tell by looking at the main entrance, so he phoned the front desk and said he was a reporter looking for Vince McNulty. Tubah hung up when the receptionist offered to put him through. McNulty had arrived.

Tubah reversed into a side street with a view of the front door and waited for the heavy mob to arrive. Wherever McNulty was planning on going, he would be leaving through the main entrance. If the heavy mob arrived before he set off, McNulty wouldn't be going anywhere.

* * *

After a shower and a change of clothes, McNulty felt refreshed but no less tired. He hadn't managed to sleep much on the overnight flight and was struggling to keep his eyes open. His legs felt heavy. His mouth was dry. He took a deep, refreshing swig of bottled water from the fridge and sat on the bed. He didn't remember the Victoria Hotel in Halifax offering free bottled water back when he'd been frequenting the Northern X massage parlours.

Victoria Hotel had been the last stop on his journey across the north of England. He had sat on a bed not dissimilar to this one and plotted his route on a battered Ordnance Survey map that had red dots ranging from south of Leeds to the east coast and then along the coastline north. Moving back to Leeds had been the catalyst for his further fall from grace and him becoming a person of interest when underage girls had begun to go missing from the massage parlours he had visited. Missing presumed dead, until the body of one of the girls had been discovered in a rusty oil drum behind Kwik Save, elevating McNulty to prime suspect in her murder.

All that because McNulty had come back to the place he had worked, returning home where he didn't have a home. All he'd had was a bed in an orphanage that had taken everything from him. Crag View had not only crushed his life but stolen the sister he hadn't known.

And here he was, doing the same again. Circle of life. Minus the massage parlours that he had shut down with the help of DC Tynan and Donkey Flowers. Donk was another blast from the past, a teenager McNulty had arrested so many times that Donk had finally gone straight. He had been thirty-five to McNulty's forty when they had broken the Northern X massage chain. He was the only friend that McNulty had.

"I once told you, Von Ryan. If only one gets out, it's a victory." Trevor Howard talking to Frank Sinatra in the classic war movie, *Von Ryan's Express*, the movie that had reunited McNulty and Donk at the Hyde Park Picture House on Retro Night. McNulty glanced at his watch as if that would tell him what day it was. He didn't need to look; it was Friday, and Friday was Retro Night at the Hyde Park. McNulty thought about Halcyon Court and the mother who had disowned him, then thought about the man who had stood by him when he'd needed it. Where to go first? That was a no-brainer. But first, he needed some sleep. Despite it only being mid-afternoon, McNulty stripped off his fresh clothes and got into bed. After all, a nap never hurt anybody.

Chapter Thirteen

The stairs creaked as four pairs of feet reached the third-floor landing. The three heavyset men with permanent five o'clock shadow had decided not to use the lift because the lift shaft was right next door to Room 302, and they didn't want to alert McNulty that they were coming. Tubah brought up the rear, keeping three paces behind the men who were going to break McNulty's knees.

They paused at the top of the stairs, then the leader took a cautious step along the corridor. The floorboards creaked, too; that was the kind of fleapit the Station Hotel was. The floors were uneven, and none of the walls were straight. The heavily embossed wallpaper couldn't hide its age despite having been repainted dozens of times. The lampshade dangling from the ceiling was even more stained than the window at the far end of the hallway.

The leader stopped in mid-step.

Three more pairs of feet stopped as well.

Tubah listened, trying to gauge if the leader had heard McNulty moving in his room, but all he could hear was the 8.10 from Harrogate pulling into Leeds City Railway Station. The brakes squeaked, and the wheels echoed around the railway arches that supported the tracks. A station announcement was muffled and indistinct, but was still clearly an automated announcer.

Tubah had been out of the game for a couple of years. Considering what had happened to the desk clerk, he thought maybe he should have waited in the car.

* * *

"What room is he in?"

"I'm afraid I'm not at liberty to disclose that information."

The clenched fist snapped forward, and the short jab spread the desk clerk's nose across his face and jerked his head back so fast that Tubah thought his neck was broken. The leader didn't even rub his fist. There was no inflammation, no scarring, and no reddening of the knuckles. The only evidence was the smear of blood across the broad, flat plain of a fist as wide as a bulldozer.

"If you want to stay at liberty, consider your next answer carefully."

The desk clerk was old and tired, but looked like he could handle himself. He might have been a boxer in his youth, but he was long past his sell-by date. "We've got CCTV."

The second punch crushed all resistance. "This is the Station Hotel. It barely has ordinary TV. Console yourself that the sting of your pride leaving the building is nothing compared to the sting when they stitch your face back together."

Tubah had waited over three hours before the heavy mob had turned up, the three men in a car that was too small for them pulling up beside the Subaru, driver's door to driver's door. Anybody watching could have been forgiven for thinking it was two detectives discussing an ongoing police operation. In that part of town, nobody would have been surprised. Things had moved on since Tubah's days with Northern X, but even Tubah hadn't been so brutal so fast. He had preferred to talk unruly customers down before breaking their noses. If they didn't calm down, then the gloves were off, but this fella, he launched straight in. Brutality for brutality's sake.

The desk clerk held a hand to his face but couldn't stop the bleeding. He jerked a thumb across the lobby. "Third floor. Three-oh-two. Next to the lift."

"Right next to the lift?"

"Next door. Yes."

"We'll take the stairs." A glare and a fist emphasised his next words. "Don't let him know we're coming."

* * *

Nobody let McNulty know they were coming. Room 302 was dark and quiet, if any room just across the arches from six lanes of railway tracks could be called quiet. Glass in the single-glazed window rattled as the 8.10 from Harrogate pulled into the station, flashes of light dancing across the ceiling through a gap in the curtains. Apart from that, there was no movement and no sound. Not even snoring. McNulty didn't snore.

Once the train had stopped at the platform, the room fell silent again. After a few moments, the drip of the bathroom tap began to intrude; silence had a way of magnifying every sound. McNulty had tried to tighten the faucet, but to no avail. The drip had come back every time, even through the closed bathroom door. It was a regular, monotonous drip, drip, drip.

The other noise that sounded loud in the quiet hotel room wasn't as regular or monotonous but was infinitely more dangerous. There was a creak on the stairs, then a long pause before the floorboards creaked in the hallway, halfway between the stairs and Room 302. There was another pause. The only sound was the dripping tap. Then a creaking floorboard. Right outside the door.

* * *

Tubah hung back and let the heavy mob do what the heavy mob was paid to do, cause pain and carnage and put the ever-loving shits up people. The person they were going to put the ever-loving shits up tonight deserved every bit of pain and carnage.

The leader's two subordinates flanked the leader as he approached Room 302. They had managed to make it all the way to the door without any further creaks or groans, but just as the leader reached for the door handle, a floorboard creaked right outside the room.

The giant fist paused halfway to the door handle. The man to the left held his breath. The man to the right hunched his shoulders. Tubah almost felt sorry for McNulty, but considering what had happened to Telfon Speed, his former boss, he reckoned the ex-cop had it coming. Speed had been blown up in a fireball caused by a gas leak and a microwave in the staff kitchen of the torture chamber. Northern X had gone up in flames as well, shutting down the massage chain. All because of Vince McNulty.

The leader waited. There was no sound from inside the hotel room. There was no sudden rush for the fire escape or slamming of windows. The creaking floorboard hadn't woken the guest in Room 302. Good. Shock and awe always worked best when you caught them by surprise. A giant hand tested the handle. The door was locked. Even better. Kicking in doors always added to the surprise.

The leader stepped back and raised one foot. The floorboard creaked, but it didn't matter anymore. He put his full weight behind a kick that smashed the lock and sent the handle flying across the darkened bedroom. The frame held firm, but the door disintegrated. The two men darted through the opening, one to either side, then the leader pounced on the shape under the covers and began to punch until it was unconscious.

The shape wasn't unconscious. It wasn't a shape at all, just a ridge in the unmade blankets and the partly hidden pillow. The leader ripped the covers off the empty bed, then checked the bathroom. Apart from the dripping tap, there was no sign of life. Toiletries were neatly arranged on the glass shelf above the sink. He checked the bedroom window. It was still closed and latched on the inside. The telephone was unplugged from the wall. There had been no sudden evacuation or emergency call. McNulty had simply gone out some time between Tubah pretending to be a reporter and the heavy mob turning up.

"Tubah." His tone warned Tubah to keep his distance. The clenched fist told him even more. The leader turned to face Telfon Speed's former right-hand man. "I thought you said he was still in his room."

"I said he hadn't gone out."

"Well, he didn't stay in either. Where the fuck did he go?"

Tubah swallowed to clear his throat. "Not out the front door."

"That wasn't the question."

Tubah scanned the room and found salvation on the bedside table. A copy of the Yorkshire Evening Post was folded open at the entertainments page. A ragged circle had been drawn around a late-night showing of *Where Eagles Dare* at the Hyde Park Picture House. The performance wasn't due to start until half past ten.

"Taking a cable car to the Schloss Adler?"

Chapter Fourteen

Taking the bus from City Square to Hyde Park Corner took McNulty longer than he remembered. Public transport wasn't what it used to be. He supposed nostalgia was always seen through rose-tinted glasses. If he were to really analyse that, he'd have to concede that the last time he'd bumped into Donkey Flowers at the Hyde Park Picture House, McNulty had been driving a Vauxhall Astra and hadn't needed to take the bus.

McNulty got off the bus on Brudenell Road and checked his watch. It was only quarter past nine, so he crossed the road to the King's Arms and ordered a Pepsi. The snug bar was as dark and dingy, as he remembered. The barman didn't even blink at a big strapping Yorkshireman ordering a soft drink. Attitudes seemed to have changed as much as the public transport.

He scanned the room for Donkey Flowers and wasn't surprised when he didn't find him. Donk was more of a drink after the film kind of fella. *Where Eagles Dare* was a long film, even if it wasn't the roadshow presentation with an intermission. At least there weren't any members of the press trying to interview him about the plane crash at Manchester Airport. It was the reporter calling his room that had prompted McNulty to go out the back door to avoid a media scrum. The last thing he wanted was to have a bunch of microphones shoved in his face.

It felt strange sitting in an English pub opposite a vintage cinema. He hadn't realised just how much he'd assimilated into the American culture. He'd even started calling taxis cabs and lorries trucks. At least the Pepsi came in a half pint instead of the huge glass of ice with unlimited refills. McNulty checked his watch and considered trying to catch Donk before he entered the cinema, but decided to go watch the film himself. It had been five years since he'd nursed Donk in hospital, Donk having been beaten up because of McNulty's run-in with Northern X. Donk might have stopped going to the Friday night screenings of classic films.

McNulty finished his Pepsi then crossed the road and bought a ticket at the box office. Even the ticket office was vintage, a little old lady tearing tickets off a roll behind a narrow window. McNulty let out a sigh. It was good to distract himself from the real reason he was back in Yorkshire. Clint Eastwood was as good a way as any.

* * *

The auditorium went dark, and velvet curtains opened on a cinemascope screen. The MGM lion roared, then the screen was filled by a panoramic view of a snow-covered valley at night. The surround speakers blew wind effects from all sides. McNulty felt the short hairs bristle up the back of his neck and goose pimples rise on his forearms. A subtle rhythm was played on snare drums, growing louder as the repeating rhythm grew more urgent. The thump of a bass drum accompanied every third repetition, the snare drums building to a crescendo before Ron Goodwin's main theme blasted through the stalls. The balcony seating overhead would have the same effect, but McNulty liked to sit downstairs. He liked looking up at the screen.

The throb of the bass drums intermingled with the snares, as a small shape grew bigger in the distance. The camouflaged airplane flew right at the camera, and the Germanic lettering of the title filled the screen. *Where Eagles Dare* had begun, and it made McNulty as giddy with excitement as the first time he'd seen it. McNulty was lost in a childhood that hadn't really existed, his trips to the cinema being the only distraction from life in Crag View Orphanage and the brutality of the headmaster, Mr Cruckshank.

The film played on. McNulty shrank in his seat. Richard Burton foiled the Nazis, and Clint Eastwood blew everything up. There was a fight on a cable car, a journey through the castle, and a race to the airfield, all accompanied by Ron Goodwin's best score since *633 Squadron*. It wasn't until the final confrontation on the camouflaged Junker and the end credits theme began to roll that McNulty returned to the present and scanned the handful of customers from his seat in the back row. Donkey Flowers hadn't stopped coming to the Friday night screenings of classic films. He hadn't stopped waiting until the very end before standing up either. McNulty watched the back of Donk's head for a few moments, then went through the door into the foyer.

* * *

Donkey flowers felt the same wave of sadness that he always

felt when the film was over. He stayed in his seat while the end credits rolled and wished he could start the film all over again. The house lights came up, and Donk stretched his legs. He turned and surveyed the auditorium as he did every time he came to the late-night show, awash with nostalgia for all the times he'd watched a classic film here. The red velvet curtains looked brand new, and there were three crystal chandeliers hanging above the stalls. It was a real picture palace, and *Where Eagles Dare* was the latest throwback film.

Donk put his coat on and walked up the aisle to the foyer. He pushed open the doors. The foyer was still adorned with classic film posters and a concessions stand that sold Sunkist popcorn and Kia-Ora orange squash. He didn't think it was actually Sunkist anymore, but some do-it-yourself popcorn maker. The posters were classics. *Casablanca* still took center stage between vintage James Bond, *From Russia With Love,* and Eastwood's breakout film, *A Fistful of Dollars.* There was also *It's A Wonderful Life* and Donk's favourite, *The Dirty Dozen.* He was looking at *The Dirty Dozen* when a hand clamped on his shoulder and spun him around.

"What the fuck?"

* * *

Pat Tubah felt a wave of relief as he watched the ex-policeman and another man come out of the cinema and cross the road to the pub. The pair were in deep conversation and didn't notice the stolen Subaru parked up a side street facing the Hyde Park Picture House. The car behind Tubah was too small for the three men squeezed inside it. Tubah couldn't tell if they were relieved as well.

Tubah waved for the leader to follow his gaze, then nodded. Target acquired. The leader didn't respond. Tubah wasn't sure if his relief had been premature, but it was still better that he'd found McNulty, despite having lost him in the first place. The downside was that The King's Arms was too public a place to break McNulty's legs, so they'd have to wait for him to finish his drink. The other complication was the man McNulty was drinking with. Tubah didn't think that would be a problem for the three men sitting in the car behind him. Two legs or four, it was all the same to them.

Chapter Fifteen

T he King's arms was a little busier with the after-show crowd, but calling the rush of customers a crowd was stretching it a bit. The snug was the smaller of the two bars, most of the cinemagoers having gravitated toward the lounge, so McNulty and Donk had no trouble finding a table.

"You still on Carlsberg?"

"You still on Pepsi?"

McNulty smiled. "'*What the fuck?*' What kind of greeting is that?"

Donk pulled out a chair and sat at the scarred wooden table. "The same greeting you gave me when you nearly twisted my arm off for tapping you on the shoulder."

"I told you about sneaking up on a cop."

"Cop? Have you gone all-American now?"

McNulty laughed. "Copper. Still shouldn't have snuck up on me."

"You overreacted."

"I was prime suspect for the missing girls."

"Not when you watched *Von Ryan's Express*."

"True. Carlsberg?"

* * *

Donk was right, McNulty hadn't been prime suspect in the missing girls case when he'd bumped into Donk at the late-night screening of *Von Ryan's Express,* but it hadn't been long before he was. It had been McNulty's bad luck that the underage girls had all worked at the massage parlours he used to frequent in a vain attempt to still feel like an undercover Vice Squad cop. It had been even more unfortunate when one of the girls turned up dead in an oil drum on waste ground behind Kwik Save, and McNulty had been identified as one of her last customers.

That had sparked a whole chain of events, including McNulty having his flat blown up, rescuing another girl from Northern X's torture sex spinoff, and getting Donk beaten to within an inch of his life when the girl had been recaptured. It had also led to DC Tynan offering McNulty salvation by putting him back undercover to locate Northern X's torture chamber, which had been hidden in a derelict factory on the Southside Industrial Park. A dawn raid among the dismembered bodies of the underage girls had finally closed Northern X down, Telfon Speed getting blown to smithereens by the gas leak McNulty had created and the metal plate that had sparked in the microwave.

All that after the "What the fuck?" moment at Hyde Park Picture House when Donk had caught McNulty by surprise, and McNulty had goose-necked Donk's wrist in a self-defence move that almost broke Donk's arm. The fallout of the Northern X saga had been that McNulty was flavour of the month, his fame allowing him to join the Savage Police Department in Maryland, USA, and continue the search for his sister, who had been sold into adoption in America. In the end, it had been his sister who had found him, after another child sex ring had hit the news when Titanic Productions had been filming in Quincy, Massachusetts. Being technical advisor for Larry Unger had given the movie plenty of publicity. Susan had seen that publicity, and little sister had been reunited with her big brother.

McNulty was thinking about his sister when he brought a Carlsberg and a Pepsi to the table. He pushed the thought aside and sat down opposite Donk. It was better to ignore the reason he was back in Yorkshire and talk about *Where Eagles Dare* instead.

Donk didn't give McNulty the chance. "What you doing back in Yorkshire?"

* * *

Pat Tubah sat in the Subaru and waited. The three men in the car behind him had climbed out and were standing in the shadows beneath a broken streetlamp. One thing Tubah had decided, he wasn't getting involved in breaking McNulty's legs. He hadn't been squeamish when he'd worked for Telfon Speed, but this fella; he was brutal for the sake of it. Tubah had been a more tactical heavy, only breaking bones when threats hadn't worked. Tonight wasn't about threats; it was about retribution. Tubah just didn't want to see how far that retribution would go.

Am I going soft? Tubah thought about that for a moment, then shook his head. Phoning the new boss had simply been a way of getting back in the game. He didn't need to be a leg-breaker anymore, but his experience gave him insights that other heavies did not have. Like when to rush in and when to stand back, for instance. Let somebody else break the legs and go to jail.

He kept his eyes on the King's Arms. A trickle of after-cinema drinkers was beginning to drift away from the dingy pub. The trickle was becoming a flow as the landlord called last orders. It wouldn't be long now. Part of him hoped the man and McNulty went their separate ways, but another part wanted to see the three heavies tested. Three against one wasn't a test.

A bell sounded inside the pub, and the lights were dimmed twice before coming back on. The landlord was reinforcing his message. Time to go home. Tubah watched the front door. There was no rear exit. McNulty wasn't going to slip out the back this time.

* * *

McNulty wasn't ready to talk about his mother yet, so he prevaricated. "I'm just back for a few days."

"To do what?"

"Take a break."

"From what? I'd have thought working in the pictures would be right up your street. Making your own, *Where Eagles Dare.*"

McNulty snorted a laugh. "Larry making *Where Eagles Dare?* More like, *Where Chickens Roost.*"

Donk wouldn't let go. "But still. Got to be better than getting stabbed or petrol bombed."

"I never got petrol bombed."

"You got your flat blown up."

80

McNulty thought about some of the stuff he'd been through in America. There had been the boat chase in Quincy, the mass shooting on the film set in Waltham, the gun battle in Colorado, and the wildfire at Piru Canyon. He didn't think any of that was better than getting stabbed or petrol bombed. On a technical point, it had been Donk who had turned the lights on to spark the explosion in McNulty's flat.

"It was *you* blew my flat up."

"Now you're getting picky. It was *you* they were after."

"True. Another Carlsberg?"

The last orders bell rang, and the landlord dimmed the lights twice to reinforce the message. It was almost kicking out time. McNulty bought another Carlsberg and a Pepsi and rejoined Donk. Donk nodded his thanks but still wouldn't let go.

"A trip down memory lane, then? The reason you came back."

McNulty still didn't want to talk about his mother. "I guess. Yeah."

"So, your first stop will have been Ecclesfield nick."

"I did pass it on the way over."

"From Manchester? That's quite a detour."

McNulty shrugged. "I did most of my service there."

"You did most of my arrests there."

"I only arrested you because taking you home with a few harsh words wasn't working."

It was Donk's turn to shrug. "I was young and foolish."

"You were an idiot. Your mum saw your potential, though. That's why she agreed a night in the cells would do you some good."

Donk raised his eyebrows. "My mum signed off on that?"

"She told me to lock you up and throw away the key. I kept the key."

Donk let out a sigh. "Short, sharp shock. She never told me that."

"Mothers don't tell you everything."

And that brought McNulty right back to why he'd come home. His mother hadn't just not told him everything; she had dumped him in an orphanage. Donk seemed to have his finger on the pulse of that as well.

"You been to Crag View yet?"

"I heard it had burned down."

"You don't want to believe everything you hear. There was a fire. Not big."

"They haven't knocked it down?"

"No."

"They should have knocked it down."

The last time McNulty had visited Crag View Orphanage was when he had been on the run from the police. The building had stood empty for years since a scandal closed it down. McNulty felt like he had been chained to Crag View Orphanage his entire life.

"They should definitely have knocked it down."

Donk showed surprising insight. "You can't knock down your past. It's what shapes your present." Then he brought it back down to earth. "It's knocking down the present could brighten things up."

McNulty gave Donk a questioning look. "Isn't your present bright enough?"

Donk realised he sounded maudlin and picked up his Carlsberg. "Nothing a late night showing of *Where Eagles Dare* can't cure."

McNulty raised his Pepsi, and the pair clinked glasses. "Broadsword calling Danny Boy."

Donk smiled at the memory of Richard Burton trying to get through on the radio while death and destruction rained down on him. He held up his glass. "Broadsword, this is Danny Boy. Receiving you loud and clear."

The final bell sounded even louder and clearer, the landlord losing patience with the stragglers. Donk and McNulty were the stragglers. They finished their drinks and stood up. McNulty took the empties to the bar, waved an apology, then stepped out into the night.

Chapter Sixteen

Death and destruction waited in the shadows beneath a broken streetlamp. Tubah watched through the steamed-up windows of the Subaru. Three men built like brick shithouses waited to pounce. Two men came out of The King's Arms. It was a confluence of circumstances that was about to clash in the bloodiest way possible.

The lights went out in the pub. The shutters were brought down over the front door. The two men stood talking, then they both turned right and took a shortcut through a cobbled alley that had no streetlamps at all. The worst possible choice. Or the best if you were the three brick shithouses. The brick shithouses crossed the road and followed.

* * *

"How come you're taking the bus?"

"Because I don't have a car."

"Me neither. You staying in town?"

"The Station Hotel."

"Urgh. Not exactly Hollywood style."

"Larry doesn't do Hollywood style. I'm on a budget."

Donk watched the last of the cinemagoers melt into the

night, then jerked a thumb toward a cobbled backstreet behind the cinema. "My bus goes through town. Short cut to the bus stop."

McNulty glanced at the bus stop where he'd gotten off. "That's my bus."

Donk shook his head. "Goes all around the houses. Mine takes the main road."

"And drops off in town?"

"Every bus drops off in town. They changed the routes to save on drivers. Instead of just going from the bus station to the outskirts, each route goes from one side of town to the other. Driving right through the middle."

McNulty turned his collar up against the cold. His breath bloomed around him. He looked at the cobbled street, then back at the relative light of Brudenell Road. There was no moon to glint off the cobbles. There was no light at all. He thought about waiting for the bus he'd come on, but didn't want to hurt Donk's feelings. It had been Donk he'd come to see anyway, not just Clint Eastwood.

"I hope they fixed the potholes."

Donk laughed. "Don't worry. If you fall down one, I'll send a search party."

* * *

The three men watched from the mouth of the alley and waited until McNulty disappeared around a bend in the cobbled street. There was no footpath, just cobbles and walled backyards with wooden gates and cubbyholes for the dustbins. The leader glanced at the overcast sky, not so much black and grey as orange from the city lights that polluted the clouds.

There was only enough light to see twenty feet along the alley, but he knew that once they blended into the darkness, his night vision would show him the way.

He listened to the sound of footsteps in the distance. Once he was sure they were far enough away, he nodded to his men. All three edged toward the darkest side of the alley and followed the line of the redbrick wall, careful not to kick the broken bottles that spilled out of the dustbin cubbyholes.

The leader slipped a brass knuckleduster over his already formidable fist. Number Two let a lead pipe slide out of his sleeve while Number Three pressed the button on his flick knife. The blade clicked into place, making a threatening noise in the quiet of the alley. The leader stopped and gave him a dirty look. He held a finger to his lips. Quiet. Then he led the way, as light on his feet as a dancer.

A cat squealed, and a dog barked. There was no traffic noise. Some of the back gates were splintered, paint flaking off like dead skin. Some of the cubbyholes smelled of rotten vegetables and something else. Somebody had taken a shit in the relative shelter of a bin store. There was the sound of TV show laughter from an open window. A man shouted at his wife, and his wife shouted back.

The further they went along the alley, the more life crept into the silence. Nobody would report the noise they would soon be hearing. Nobody in Hyde Park ever called the police.

* * *

McNulty walked along the cobbled backstreet and remembered being a uniform patrol officer walking a footbeat at night.

He took a deep breath of cool night air, avoiding the rotting garbage smells from the dustbins by walking down the middle of the alley. That's what he used to do on the night shift; walk down the middle of the road, because that way you could see more of the buildings on either side of you. If you walked close to the edge, back walls and hedgerows obscured your view. As a cop, you needed to see everything. The other thing you needed to do was hear everything. McNulty let his breath plume around his head and listened to the night sounds.

A cat squealed, and a dog barked. There was no traffic noise. There was the sound of TV show laughter from an open window. A man shouted at his wife, and his wife shouted back. Somebody kicked a bottle, and it skittered over the cobbles. The only thing missing was the occasional squawk from the police radio that would have been clipped to his collar.

Donk concentrated more on his footwork than the sounds of the alley, looking out for potholes or missing cobbles. McNulty scanned the back walls and flaking gates as he passed them. Broken glass and discarded pizza boxes spilled out from some of the dustbin cubbyholes. A ginnel crossed the alley just after a slight bend in the road, the narrow footpath even darker than the alley because the gable ends of the terrace houses blocked out the orange light reflecting off the clouds. The ginnel was an even narrower passageway that cut through each row of terrace houses and would have been a nightmare for any cop chasing a suspect. The network of passageways could take you anywhere on the housing estate and avoid you being seen on the main roads.

The figure watching McNulty from the shadows was avoiding the main roads.

* * *

The leader kept to the side of the alley as he rounded the bend, scanning ahead to make sure he didn't run into McNulty before he was ready. It was scanning ahead that meant he wasn't watching the ground. His foot clipped a bottle that had spilled out from the dustbin cubbyhole and sent it skittering across the cobbles. He froze and waited for the echo to stop. Number Two and Number Three bumped into the back of him and kicked the bottle again.

The bottle smashed and stopped skittering. The TV show laughter became a burst of applause. The dog barked in frustration at having lost the cat. Number Three wanted to hold a finger to his lips—quiet—but didn't have the nerve. He might have been the one with the flick knife, but the leader's fist was like a side of ham. He'd seen what that fist could do, even without the knuckleduster.

The alley fell silent.

The leader checked his footing, then rounded the corner. McNulty and his friend had taken the second bend in the dogleg turn and were out of sight. The leader picked up the pace as he passed a ginnel that cut across the alley. His two colleagues caught up with him. None of them checked the shadows of the left-hand passage. None of them saw the man with the cold, hard eyes step out behind them until it was too late.

Chapter Seventeen

McNulty made it to the last stretch of the dogleg alleyway before he heard the sound that should have set alarm bells ringing. Sounds, because there was more than one. Back when he'd been a uniform patrol officer, he used to stand in the dark and listen to the night. Often, those sounds were just like tonight, televisions through open windows, dogs barking, and couples arguing. There was often distant traffic noise, but what he had been listening for were noises that were out of the ordinary. Anything that wasn't normal.

Of course, normal meant different things depending on what beat you were walking. If you were in Ecclesfield or Idle, then raised voices would signal trouble. If you were on Ravenscliffe or Thorpe Edge, then silence was more threatening; raised voices you got every day. The noises he'd just heard in the midsection of the dogleg alleyway weren't everyday noises.

There had been what sounded like three slaps across the face, followed by a scuffle and commotion, then three more slaps. Back in the day, the noise would have turned McNulty around and had him walking toward trouble, not away from it. But as much as he still thought of himself as a cop, he'd been out of the game too long. He heard the fight in the alley but felt no urge to get involved. People around here had fights in alleys all the time. If he'd heard a woman scream for help, it would have been different, but street gangs fighting in the street, that was a shrug the shoulders and move on situation. McNulty shrugged his shoulders and moved on.

* * *

The leader was the first one to turn at the sound of another kicked bottle. This one didn't skitter across the cobbles; it clunked against a dustbin in the nearest cubbyhole, but it was enough to raise the hackles on the leader's neck. He knew he was the one who had kicked the first bottle, but damn it, his wingmen should have learned from his mistake.

He turned to glare at his cohorts and stared straight into the deadest-looking eyes he'd ever seen. Number Two and Number Three turned to see what the leader was looking at, then the silenced gun fired three times. Square in the chest. One, two, three. The suppressor dulled the sound but didn't silence it, the muffled gunshots sounding like three slaps across the face.

Number Two was the only one who managed to lunge at his killer, but he stood on the bottle and slipped, making a grab for his friends to stop himself from falling. His friends were already dead, and the three bodies hit the ground in a tangle of arms and legs and at least two groans of pain.

The scuffle ended with three bodies on the ground. The gunman stood over them and fired three more shots, one each in the head for good measure. The small-calibre bullets entered the left eye socket, then rattled around the skull, mashing the brains and soft tissue of the already dead men.

The gunman knelt to pick up the shell casings, then melted into the shadows. He kept his eyes on the second dogleg and listened. The night was filled with nothing. Even the dog had stopped barking. There was no sound of approaching footsteps. There was no sudden rush along the alley or a shout for him to drop the gun. There was silence, followed a few moments later by the sound of a double-decker pulling up at the bus stop.

Chapter Eighteen

cNulty got off the bus outside Leeds Town Hall, so he had to walk down Park Row to reach City Square. The roads were quiet, with hardly any cars and no pedestrians at all. Conversation had dried up on the bus ride; Donk looking like he thought it was his fault. McNulty wanted to tell him it wasn't, but then he'd have to not only explain why he was here but also why he felt less than himself. The noise in the alley had been the start of it.

McNulty had recognised the sound of a scuffle, of course, he had, and he would normally have gone back to make sure nobody was hurt. That was what cops do: protect and serve. The prime directive of being a police officer was to protect life and property. After that, there was, prevent crime, and finally detect and arrest offenders. The fight in the alley would have covered two out of those three: protect life and arrest offenders.

Except he wasn't a cop anymore. That was why he felt so low when he got off the bus. That and the fact he was staying in a shithole hotel and visiting a woman he didn't want to visit. He stood in the dark for a moment in City Square and stared at the front of the railway station. Despite it being almost two o'clock in the morning, he considered catching a train to Manchester Airport and flying back to America. That was where his real family was, both surrogate and flesh and blood. Larry Unger and Titanic Productions felt more like a family to him than the woman who had dumped him at Crag View Orphanage. Susan *was* family to him, his sister being the only blood kin he had.

Susan. He had been avoiding thinking about his sister ever since he'd boarded the ill-fated flight from Boston. Not his sister, per se, but her reaction when McNulty had told her about their mother.

* * *

"She can rot in hell as far as I'm concerned."

"She can rot in hell for me as well."

"But you're still going to see her."

This hadn't felt like a conversation for over the phone, so McNulty had used the Titanic Productions official car and driven to Marblehead, fifteen miles northeast of Boston. Susan had moved out of the clapboard bungalow on the corner of Kirkstall Road after a cartel hitman had tried to kidnap her and her daughter there. Ever since then, Newtonville just hadn't felt safe. That had been more Jim Grant's fault than McNulty's, but Susan still blamed her brother.

McNulty was fighting an uphill battle. "She's family."

Susan stamped her foot under the kitchen table. "I'm family. And so is Tilly."

McNulty looked out across Boden Sound through the kitchen window. The western shore of Marblehead Neck was lined with yacht clubs and marinas, and the sheltered bay was dotted with small boats that were moored in the shallow waters. A distant bell sounded more foreboding than it should have, but McNulty reckoned that said more about his state of mind than the dangers of open water sailing.

"I know," was all he could come up with.

"Then think about us instead of her."

McNulty was shocked that Susan even thought that. "I think about you every single day. I'd lost you for the first half of my life. I'm not going to lose you again."

"You can't lose what you never had. Back then. At Crag View. Neither of us had the other. I was just a girl in Mr Cruckshank's office. You were just the boy who broke his nose with a Bible. We weren't brother and sister. We were nothing."

McNulty felt emotion welling up inside him. "You were never nothing."

Susan toned down the harshness in her voice. "Neither were you. But we weren't family. Not then. And that's all because of her."

She made *her* sound like a bad taste. Her face couldn't hide the disgust she felt for the woman who had abandoned not just one child but two. The picturesque New England coastal town couldn't paint over the cracks in a childhood that had been anything but childlike. Living in peace and serenity didn't mean you could forget the past, when things were the opposite of peaceful and serene.

McNulty felt her pain. He had been living with that pain his entire life. But he needed answers. Despite burying the questions beneath a work ethic that prioritised arresting bad people for doing bad things, he couldn't hide from them now. The man in the black suit had opened a can of worms, and the worms were crawling free.

"I want to look her in the eyes and ask her why?"

Susan shook her head. "No. You want to look her in the eyes and see the monster you've built her up to be."

"You've built her up to be that as well."

"And I want to keep that fire. It keeps me warm."

"Fire burns."

Susan let out a sigh. "I'm not flying all the way to Yorkshire to see a little old lady with dementia. I need the monster to be a monster."

McNulty turned away from the beauty of Boden Sound and spoke softly. "I need to slay the monster. Dementia or not."

* * *

Slay the monster? Sitting in City Square at two in the morning, he thought, "What was I thinking?" He was back in Yorkshire. He was one day away from facing his demons. Why did he feel like running away and hiding under the pillow? There were so many questions he wanted to ask, but wasn't sure if he could put them into words. He'd heard the stories about single girls having their babies taken away at birth by the Church. He'd seen that movie with Judi Dench. He knew that kind of thing used to happen all the time in the not-too-distant past. What if his mother had had no choice and been forced to give up her son?

He stood up with such force that he banged the back of his legs against the bench. Leeds Railway Station looked dark and foreboding. The Queens Hotel didn't look much better. Apart from the entrance lobby, the windows were dark and empty across the ornate façade. McNulty's face was dark and empty, too.

Being forced to give up one child might be unfortunate. Giving up a second five years later was unforgivable. His mother would have been five years older and five years wiser. The Church couldn't get away with stealing her baby twice. No, that was a lifestyle choice, and his mother had made it.

McNulty crossed City Square and walked into the tunnel that passed beneath the railway platforms. His footsteps echoed in the dark. His thoughts rattled around his brain. He came out of the other side none the wiser and crossed the road. The dingy façade of the Station Hotel did nothing to lift his spirits. The fear in the eyes of the desk clerk and the broken nose did even less.

Chapter Nineteen

Donk was surprised to get a call from McNulty so soon after seeing him get off the bus at the Town Hall. Three o'clock in the morning. Donk had only just got home himself, spending half the bus journey wondering how he'd upset McNulty and the other half replaying *Where Eagles Dare* in his mind. *Where Eagles Dare* was endlessly replayable, as were *The Dirty Dozen* and *Von Ryan's Express*, except it had a more upbeat ending than Frank Sinatra not reaching the train or eleven of the dozen getting killed.

"I thought you were staying in town."

"I was."

"So what's wrong with the hotel?"

"I'll tell you when I get there."

* * *

What was wrong with the hotel was this. Everything. McNulty sensed it more than saw it when he stepped out of the shadows of the tunnel and crossed the road. Station Hotel was a throwback to the age of the steam train. It was dark and smoke-stained, with cracked brickwork and dirty windows.

The letters E and L in the neon sign above the front door kept blinking, making it Station Hot. At this time of the year and in the early hours of the morning, it felt anything but hot. It felt cold and dark and threatening. Threatening came more into focus when McNulty entered the lobby.

The night clerk shrank away from the sound when the front door opened. The man behind the reception desk wasn't the person who had checked McNulty in so McNulty wasn't sure if the bruises were there when the clerk came on duty but the look in his eyes told McNulty they were new.

"You okay?"

McNulty stepped up to the counter and noticed the blood splatters on the wall. The clerk had stuffed pieces of tissue up his nose to stop the bleeding, but it still looked bent out of shape. Dark rings showed under both eyes, and his lip was split and swollen.

"You get robbed?"

The man blinked and shook his head.

McNulty put added compassion into his tone. "Has any-body looked at that for you?"

Another shake of the head followed by a weak voice. "I'm all right."

"If that's all right, I'd hate to see you when you're not."

The man seemed to be struggling with a decision, then rested both hands on the counter. He fixed McNulty with a questioning look and appeared to be satisfied with what he saw. "They were looking for you."

He pointed toward the stairs. "Went up to your room."

McNulty squared his shoulders. "They still there?"

The man shook his head and obviously wished he hadn't. "Said they were going to the pictures."

* * *

Even though the night manager had said the heavies had left, McNulty was still being cautious as he approached Room 302. He had taken the stairs for the same reason the heavies had, to avoid the noise of the lift warning anyone that might be waiting for him. The stairs creaked. The floorboard in front of his room creaked. McNulty paused and listened at the door. There were no trains pulling into the station to disguise any noises inside the hotel room. The only thing McNulty heard was the monotonous dripping of the tap in the bathroom.

McNulty took out his room key—it was that kind of hotel—but then he saw that there was no keyhole. There was no lock at all. No handle either. He nudged the door open with the toe of his shoe, then stepped back and to one side. The same way he had taught Alfonse Bayard about cops approaching a door. The actor had learned fast; a cop never knows what's on the other side of a door, so he always knocks, then steps aside. McNulty didn't knock; he just paused for a beat, then rushed in with his forearms up to protect his head.

Nobody attacked his head. The room was empty.

McNulty checked the bathroom and tried tightening the tap. The dripping stopped for a moment, then continued its annoying drip, drip, drip. His toiletries were still on the glass shelf below the mirror. His clothes had been strewn across the bed. At least they hadn't ripped the overnight bag open or torn his clothes. He sat on the bed and puffed out his cheeks.

Why would anyone be interested in him? He'd been out of the country for almost five years. Before then, he'd been a wandering ex-cop with no job and no prospects, visiting massage parlours to get his kicks and still feel connected to the life he'd left behind. He thought about the map and the little red dots as he'd plotted his way around the north.

He took a deep breath. Of course, that was a narrow view. He had only been a wandering ex-cop until DC Tynan had put him back to work, inserting him into the Northern X chain undercover. He had been the big story on the national news for three weeks, and then he'd moved to America. First day back, and somebody had broken the night manager's nose and ransacked his room. What did that tell him?

It tells me some people have long memories. It was the only possible explanation. Destroying Northern X was his only claim to fame. He remembered that kerfuffle at the Los Gatos Movie Ranch near Jacumba Hot Springs. The drug cartel that Jim Grant had pissed off at Snake Pass and Montecito Heights had had long memories, too. Bad guys are not only bad; they don't like the good guys that shut them down. McNulty had shut Northern X down.

He rubbed his face with both hands, then stood up. He began to fold his clothes and pack his overnight bag, all the while trying to figure how they'd known he was back so soon. He paused when he picked up the complimentary American Airlines travel pack he'd been given after the crash landing at Manchester Airport.

He remembered the evacuation slides and the media scramble. He pictured the spilled luggage, the child's shoe, and the teddy bear. More importantly, he remembered the intrusive reporter shoving a camera in his face and McNulty telling the cameraman to fuck off. He nodded as the realisation set in. He guessed the *fuck off* had made the Six O'clock News.

McNulty swept his toiletries into the travel pack and

dropped it in his overnight bag. He closed the wardrobe and the bedside cabinet, then picked up the crushed Evening Post off the floor. A shiver ran down his spine, and the hairs stood up on the back of his neck. He straightened the newspaper, which was still open at the entertainments page. *"Said they were going to the pictures."* The scribbled circle stood out around the late-night showing of *Where Eagles Dare.*

"Shit."

McNulty's mind immediately went to the only thing that had seemed untoward during the entire evening. The scuffle and slaps in the alley on the way to the bus stop. He didn't know what the commotion meant, but he'd bet a pound to a pinch of shit it had something to do with this. He finished packing his bag, then opened his phone and called Donk.

Chapter Twenty

oday's the day! That was the first thought to go through McNulty's mind when he woke up the following morning in the spare room at Donk's house. The second thought was, *I don't want this to be the day. I don't want to do this at all.* The third thought was, *Donk really needs to clean the house.*

McNulty slept late, hardly surprising since the taxi hadn't dropped him at Donk's house until half past three in the morning. Grey light through the threadbare curtains tried to wake him early, but it was the rain on the windows that finally dragged him out of the land of nod.

Donk knocked politely and stuck his head through the door. "Do you want Full English or have you gone completely American?"

McNulty yawned. "Bacon and eggs. Americans can't do bacon for shit."

* * *

The semi-detached house was the same as all the other semis on Mean Wood council estate, tired old and in need of a little TLC. The front door faced onto the T-shaped turnaround at the end of the cul-de-sac, but nobody could turn their car around because the council hadn't repainted the double-yellow lines, and the residents of Mean Wood ignored them anyway. The stubby street was crammed with parked cars, pushbikes, and junkers that stood on piles of bricks because the wheels had been stolen. Donk's front lawn was neat and trimmed, a testament to the woman who had raised him and the love he still felt for his mother. The testament didn't extend to airing the bedroom, which McNulty did by throwing the window wide open when he got out of bed.

"Smells like a dead rat in here."

Donk peered around the room. "There is a dead rat in here. Haven't been able to find it yet, though."

McNulty wasn't sure if Donk was joking or not. He drew the curtains back to let what little light there was brighten the bedroom. It didn't brighten it much since the grey clouds that were bringing the rain were also sucking up the daylight. McNulty looked down at the dirt track that ran behind the houses and remembered parking his Astra there after his flat had blown up. Donk had helped carry the girl McNulty had saved from Northern X. The overhanging apple tree he had parked under was even bigger and more overhanging.

"Well apart from the dead rat, it's good to see you've kept the place tidy."

Donk nodded. "Mum was all about being clean and tidy."

McNulty smiled. "And straight and honest."

Donk looked offended. "I was always straight and honest. You never had to arrest me for thieving."

"And even if I had, the navy knocked it out of you."

Donk wagged a finger. "You knocked it out of me. That's why the navy took me in the first place."

McNulty got dressed. "Sorry that didn't work out for you."

"The navy?"

"The marriage."

Donk shrugged. "I had a bit of a temper back then. Despite her being a drug addict, she still got the kids and took them back to America. Mum was glad to have me back. For as long as she lasted. Died happy. She deserved that much for putting up with me."

"Like you said, you were straight and honest. She knew that."

"She knew I was keeping you up to date with the local thievery. Reckoned I was the next best thing to an undercover brother."

McNulty let out a sigh. "Undercover isn't all it's cracked up to be."

"A lot of girls got out because of you."

"A lot didn't."

Donk put on a deep voice. "If one gets out, it's a victory."

McNulty laughed. "Trevor Howard said it better."

Donk smiled. "Frank Sinatra was a better foil."

They were both lost in thought for a moment while they remembered Howard's Major Fincham telling Sinatra's Colonel Ryan, "I once told you Von Ryan. If only one gets out, it's a victory." It had been such an important line it even played out in voiceover on the end credits and *Von Ryan's Express* rode into the tunnel.

Donk got serious. "And here you are. Thugs turning over your hotel room and me having to pick up the pieces."

McNulty got serious, too. "More than the hotel room. I think they wanted to turn us over at the pictures."

"They were at Hyde Park?"

McNulty shrugged. "I didn't see them. But that was the plan."

He didn't mention the kerfuffle in the alley or who he thought was behind it. Northern X was a thing of the past, but the thing about the past is it doesn't always stay there. Even when you didn't know about your past. He didn't tell Donk about that either. Visiting a mother McNulty didn't know would be no consolation to a man who would give anything to have *his* mother back.

"I'm not smelling that bacon."

Donk winked. "But you're not smelling the rat either. Look on the bright side."

* * *

Pat Tubah had put off making the phone call until he was sure he had something to report. Now that he had something to report, he put it off even longer. This was one phone call he didn't want to make. After identifying the target coming out of The King's Arms, he had told himself that was his part done. He had waited in the Subaru for twenty minutes out of a sense of duty, but when the three heavies didn't come back out of the alley, he got worried. Surely McNulty and his friend hadn't bested the man with fists like sides of ham and his thugs.

Tubah had waited another ten minutes, then got out of the car. He had listened at the mouth of the alley, but there was nothing to hear. It was late, even the warring couples had stopped shouting, or they had shut the windows. There was no TV noise and no barking dogs. The residents of the terrace houses had gone to bed and left the backstreets to night owls, thugs, and criminals. In this instance, all three amounted to the same, underworld hoodlums with an axe to grind on behalf of their boss.

Tubah considered going down the alley to check, but decided that discretion was the better part of valour. If the three heavies couldn't handle a has-been ex-cop and his podgy friend, it wasn't Tubah's fault. Let them phone it in. He had got back in the car and left them to it. No phone call. No report. Until he saw the news this morning. Tubah picked up his phone as soon as he saw the Look North headlines on BBC Breakfast.

BODIES FOUND IN ALLEY BEHIND HYDE PARK PICTURE HOUSE

Then he made the call and prepared to duck.

Chapter Twenty-One

"No. Seal it off fifty yards either side of the alley."

"The entire road? It's a bus route."

"Not any more. It's a crime scene."

Detective Sergeant Jimmy Tynan stepped under the crime scene tape that the uniform patrol officer had strung across the mouth of the alley and made sure that the officer updating the scene log spelled his name right.

"T-Y-N-A-N. Major Crime Unit." That last part was in case the fresh-faced constable thought MCU was the Marvel Cinematic Universe. The night detective had got the call half an hour before she was due off duty and had called the Detective Superintendent and the MCU after a quick examination of the scene. Three dead. Gunshot wounds to the chest and head. People didn't get double-tapped in West Yorkshire. This was definitely a case for the Marvel Cinematic Universe.

* * *

DS Tynan set up an incident room at Brotherton House, the outreach police building that used to house CID, the communications centre, and the Scenes of Crime Office. SOCO still had a photographic studio on the third floor, but the rest had moved to Millgarth when the Police Headquarters had expanded four years ago. Brotherton House was scheduled for demolition, but until then, the CID office was used for police operations and major incidents. Three men shot in the head was a major incident.

Tynan had been promoted to Detective Sergeant after being instrumental in closing down the Northern X underage sex ring and still worked from Ecclesfield Police Station in Bradford, but that was just his base. He would deploy wherever and whenever the MCU was needed. Hyde Park was part of Weetwood Division, the modern steel and glass building having replaced the old Ireland Wood Police Station decades ago, but Weetwood PS was at the opposite end of the division, so Tynan opted for Brotherton House near Leeds Town Hall.

He had called his office to set the ball rolling; an incident room required staff and equipment, and a radio operator that knew the area. DC Bill Baildon could start organising that while Tynan did what he always did, walked the crime scene.

"Have you marked the common approach?"

The constable with the scene log indicated the right-hand side of the alley. "I didn't want to disturb anything by sticking flags in the cobbles, but the paramedics and first officer stayed to the right."

Despite the night detective reporting three GSW bodies, protocol dictated that medical staff verified that the gunshot wound bodies were dead. That started with an ambulance crew and ended with the police surgeon. The on-call police surgeon pronounced life extinct and then handed the scene over to the police. SOCO had been put on standby but hadn't been allowed access to the scene yet, so Tynan used the common approach to prevent disturbing any trace evidence.

"Record the time. DS Tynan. Examines scene." He waved a hand along the street at the top of the alley. "Tape it off from the next street, either side of the alley. Nobody in or out. And leave the parked cars in situ. Nobody gets their car back until they're documented and photographed."

Tynan stood for a moment in the middle of the street and scanned both ways, looking for lines of sight and security cameras. This being Hyde Park, most people's idea of security was a big dog with little food. The cinema had a camera mounted high above the advertising awning, but judging by the angle and the fact that it was hanging loose, Tynan didn't hold out much hope for usable security footage. None of the other buildings on the street, including The King's Arms, appeared to have cameras, but Tynan would have detectives canvas the neighbourhood in case anyone had a camera in their living room.

Once he was satisfied he'd identified possible lines of enquiry, he walked slowly down the alley, keeping to the common approach. He used soft eyes to look ahead while his peripheral vision noted the dustbin cubbyholes and garden gates. There were broken bottles and spilled garbage, but there was nothing of note until he reached the ginnel that cut across the alley. Another uniform constable stood guard at the intersection.

"Halt, who goes there?"

Tynan stopped and threw the officer a quizzical look. "Did you really just say that? You're not a sentry."

The constable looked close to retirement, his uniform as creased and tired as the face of the night patrol officer who hadn't been relieved yet. "I'm not the day shift either. Got to do something to amuse myself."

"You're not supposed to be amused."

"Come on, Jimmy. We're always amused. Why do you think they call it gallows humour?"

Tynan remembered working with Tim Cranston at Ecclesfield, the ex-military veteran cop being famous for not only his gallows humour but for his blitzkrieg approach to community policing. Tynan smiled and changed the quizzical look to an understanding nod. "I'll get you relieved as soon as I can. Meanwhile, what have we got?"

Cranston stepped aside from the police tape that sealed the immediate area around the crime scene. "Dead people that deserve to be dead."

"How d'you figure that?"

Cranston snorted a laugh. "Grazed fists, knuckledusters and flick knives. Weren't out here collecting for charity."

Tynan glanced around, again checking for sight lines and cameras. This was a cobbled back alley, there weren't going to be any cameras, but the upstairs windows that overlooked the alley would need checking. At least the bodies were against the brick wall of somebody's back yard, so the rubberneckers hadn't started craning their necks for a look yet.

"Crime scene tent will be coming with SOCO. Until then, can you block the view from across the alley? Pretend you're a flasher and open your coat."

"I am a flasher. But only on my days off. Which this should be."

* * *

Twenty minutes later, Tynan had seen all he was going to see without disturbing the scene. He tucked his tie into his shirt so it wouldn't dangle in the blood and fastened his jacket. Dropping to one knee, he checked the low angle, and standing up, he got the overview. Keeping his distance from the three corpses, he viewed the scene from three angles; the fourth was the back wall of a house with a monkey-puzzle tree in the yard. The twisted branches peeked over the wall like a demented triffid.

Tynan marshalled his thoughts without committing them to paper. That would come later when SOCO confirmed what he had seen by photographing the scene. The first thing to stand out was the injuries. GSW to the chest with scorch marks on the clothing, but not close enough for powder burns. That was reserved for the kill shot to the eye, which was much closer. There were no shell casings that he could see, so either the killer had picked them up or used a revolver.

The next thing he noticed was the blood. There wasn't any. Well, not much anyway. That suggested that the first shot had been the kill shot and the second was insurance. There was some seepage, but not the pool of blood you saw in the movies. The heart had stopped pumping immediately, so the blood hadn't leaked much beyond the initial spill.

The bodies were laid at awkward angles where they had fallen, all twisted arms and legs with their faces pressed against the cobbles, one on his right and the other two on their left. The faces had already begun to flatten against the ground with a deep bruise showing where the blood had settled after the heart stopped pumping. That told him this hadn't happened recently and that they were shot sometime in the middle of the night. It also told him that nobody had come down the alley after the shooting, so it was probably the early hours of the morning, not midnight. He couldn't tell which direction they had come from, but it didn't take a genius to guess.

There was no sign of disturbance in the ginnel either side of the alley and there were no cigarette butts showing on which side the attacker had been waiting. That didn't prove anything; the attacker might have been a non-smoker, or he might not have been waiting long. He might have seen the three men come into the alley and run down the parallel street to head them off from the ginnel.

All that was conjecture and wouldn't be proved until his team started knocking on doors. Probably wouldn't be proved even then. This had happened in the wee small hours. Even in Hyde Park that was past most people's bedtime.

What wasn't conjecture was the arsenal the three men had brought with them. Only one of them was holding a weapon—the knuckleduster still wrapped in a giant fist—but the others were near enough to suggest who had been carrying them. A grubby lead pipe lay next to one man, and daylight glinted off the evil blade of a flick knife that lay beside the other. These fellas had followed somebody into the alley with the purpose of causing serious damage. This was going to be GBH or attempted murder. In the end, the grievous bodily harm and the murder had been theirs. That suggested that the person they were following had hidden in the ginnel and flanked them, stepping out behind them before spinning them around and shooting them. One shot in the chest followed by the insurance shot in the eye socket.

Somebody was a serious bad ass, and these three bad asses had picked the wrong person to mess with. Nobody had walked down the alley after the deed had been done until an early morning worker had taken a shortcut to the bus stop at the bottom of the alley. It was unlikely these three had come on the bus, so their car was probably still parked in one of the side streets.

Tynan made a mental note to have uniform patrol PNC all the cars in a three-street radius to find out which didn't belong where they were parked. That might be easier once Tynan could check for wallets after SOCO had photographed the bodies. These three hadn't driven it away. He stepped away from the scene and untucked his tie.

"Tim. What time did the cinema close last night?"

"The Hyde Park?"

Tynan let out a sigh. "What other cinema is around here?"

Cranston shrugged, then dipped into his local knowledge. "Late-night show on a Friday. Classic war films. After midnight."

Tynan nodded. "So the last people taking a shortcut to the bus stop would have been half an hour after that."

Cranston shook his head. "Hour and a half. The King's Arms stays open for the after-show drinkers."

Tynan nodded again but didn't speak. He was thinking that the Hyde Park Picture House might not have a working camera outside, but everywhere had CCTV inside. That meant the cinema and the pub just leapfrogged the list of things to do.

Chapter Twenty-Two

Halcyon Court Care Home wasn't anything like McNulty had expected. His only experience of care homes had been back in his uniform days when the occasional resident went missing and sparked a division-wide search. One of those had been a dementia care home before dementia was widely known; an elderly male had gone missing during the night, prompting a search of all the nearby wasteland, including the allotments between the care home and the cemetery. It had been a cold and frosty night, and the consensus of opinion was that they would find him frozen to the ground in a cabbage patch. It turned out he'd gone into the wrong room after going to the toilet and was found fast asleep with an elderly woman who didn't even know he was there.

That care home had been a small family-run business. Halcyon Court was part of a chain that had bought impressive old buildings that were too big for private ownership and made them even bigger. The extensions were tastefully done but even so, red brick and modern windows to the rear degraded the impressive architecture at the front. The doors had keypad locks and an intercom, turning the place into Colditz rather than home. In this prisoner of war camp, if one got out, it was not a victory.

"You going to do this now?" Donk had been shocked when McNulty told him why he was back in England. Despite losing his own mother, he was very supportive. Probably because he *had* lost his own mother.

"Yeah." McNulty wasn't ready to open up any more than he already had. "Bus to Woodhouse Moor, then left up Cliff Road?"

And that's what McNulty did, getting off the bus at Hyde Park Corner then crossing Woodhouse Moor, which wasn't so much a moor as a public park with tennis courts and tree-lined walkways. Cliff Road wasn't on a cliff either, but McNulty was just nitpicking. Halcyon Court wasn't Colditz, but it still felt like a prison, except the prisoner was McNulty's childhood. He stood at the main gate, then turned around and went to sit in the park. He needed time to get his mind straight before going in to slay the monster.

* * *

Doreen Wills wasn't a monster as far as the care home staff was concerned; she was a frail old woman with a debilitating disease. Not as old as some of the residents, but there was a lot of mileage on the clock and not enough brain cells to keep track of it. Alzheimer's was only part of the problem; her body was letting her down, and cancer was eating the rest. Add to that she had chronic heart disease, emphysema, and acute something-or-other. Basically everything.

"There you go, Doreen. Make yourself comfy."

"I will."

Doreen settled into the easy chair in the private reception

room, then a confused look settled over her face. "Where am I?"

The nursing staff knew better than to overexplain. "You're in the visitors' room, Doreen."

"Why?"

"Because you've got a visitor."

Doreen looked excited, like a child at Christmas. "Ooh, that's nice."

"Yes, it is, isn't it? He should be here soon."

"He?"

"Your son."

The look of confusion took over again. "I have a son?"

* * *

McNulty took a deep breath, then pressed the buzzer. The visitors' entrance was in the car park around the back, the front door being mainly for show since it was completely impractical for dementia residents. The main entrance looked like Downton Abbey with its ornate glass and carved pillars. The back door was much more utilitarian.

The intercom buzzed, then a harsh voice spoke. "Yes?"

McNulty leaned closer as if talking to a deaf person. "Vince McNulty."

The receptionist's tone didn't soften. "Yes?"

"To see…" He had to think for a minute. "Doreen Wills."

The door lock clicked, and McNulty pushed it open. He stepped into a vestibule, but the internal door didn't unlock until the outside door closed. He felt like he was in an airlock waiting to be decontaminated. When he was finally allowed in, he wondered where the receptionist was because he couldn't see her over the chest-high counter.

"Sign in. Time and date and registration number."

McNulty peered over the counter and saw a small, fat woman with a face that sucked lemons. She reminded him of the woman at Golden Touch massage parlour when he'd been enquiring about the missing girls, except without the figure. Manning the Halcyon Court reception desk obviously wasn't the highlight of her day.

McNulty cut her some slack. "I don't have a car."

"Time and date then. And who you're visiting."

McNulty found the register on a small table beside the door. He almost wrote Doreen McNulty, but stopped himself just in time. When he'd finished signing in, he stood at the counter. "Is she okay?"

The woman arched an eyebrow. "This is a dementia care home. Nobody here is okay."

McNulty stopped cutting her some slack. "Then maybe she should be in a care home that actually cares."

The woman sat upright as if slapped in the face. "Maybe Doreen should have a son that actually cares. First time in, what? Ten years?"

It was McNulty's turn to be slapped in the face, but he hid it well. "First time ever. Since I only found out she was here four days ago."

The receptionist knew that already, since she was the one who sent the man-in-black to visit McNulty. Passed the message on anyway, the manageress sent the man.

"I'll get somebody to take you through. It's Doreen's first time as well."

* * *

Doreen sat with a blank expression on her face. Some days she had a better idea of what was going on, and other days she just drifted along in a fog. Today was a foggy day. She knew she was sitting in a pale blue and pastel pink room with three comfy chairs and a coffee table. She vaguely recognised the young woman who was sitting with her, but the polite conversation about the weather and what Doreen wanted for dinner did nothing to enlighten her. The girl had said lunch, but Doreen knew she meant dinner. Doreen wasn't so far gone that she didn't understand the Yorkshire way of breakfast, dinner, and tea. Sometimes supper as well, but not since she'd been staying here. Bedtime was too early to leave time for supper. Posh people had breakfast, lunch, and dinner. Doreen didn't know much, but she knew she wasn't posh.

A bing-bong electronic chime made Doreen jump, then a disembodied voice said, "Maggie to reception."

The young woman stood up and patted Doreen's hand. "Here he comes."

Doreen wracked her brain but could only come up with, "Who?"

Maggie gave a gentle smile. "Your son."

Doreen had already forgotten. "I have a son?"

Chapter Twenty-Three

An elderly woman with a walking stick shuffled past McNulty and stood looking out of the front door. She smelled of flowery perfume and talcum powder. Her face was creased with the kind of lines that come from smiling a lot. She smiled at the window in the door, then a look of concern crept across her face. She craned her neck for a better view, first to the left and then to the right. McNulty tried to see what she was looking at.

"Waiting for somebody?"

The woman seemed to notice McNulty for the first time. "No. Somebody moved my car. It was parked right there."

The receptionist stood up, looked at McNulty, and shook her head with a sad little smile. It was the first time he'd seen her smile. It changed her entire face. The woman stamped the walking stick on the ground.

"I bet the builders have moved it again."

McNulty hadn't seen any builders. He hadn't seen anyone outside at all. There was no scaffolding, or building site, or builders' van. There were a couple of cars, but he assumed they belonged to the nursing staff since they were parked in plain view of the door.

The lemon-sucker's face became overly friendly. "Do you

want tea and biscuits in your room, Gladys? Or upstairs with everyone else?"

Gladys blinked and came back to reality. "Thank you. I believe I will take it in my room." She turned and walked to the lift. The doors opened straight away, and the woman disappeared, along with the flowery perfume, leaving Mc-Nulty to breathe in the natural care home smell. Despite the judicious use of air freshener, that smell was the same as the small family-run care home in his uniform days: voided bowels and antiseptic.

The receptionist rested her elbows on the counter. "She still thinks her husband comes to see her and parks right outside."

"Doesn't he?"

"Doesn't have a husband. He died before she joined us. That's why she's here. He was her only carer."

A young woman in hospital scrubs came down a corridor behind the counter, her name badge glinting in the light. Maggie. Written in the friendly curls of Comic Sans MS. He presumed that was meant to exude an air of warmth and friendliness. It also disguised the fact that almost everything she said was a lie. The woman smiled when she saw McNulty.

"Vincent. Your mum is looking forward to seeing you."

* * *

McNulty stood in the doorway but couldn't cross the threshold. He was frozen to the spot despite the welcoming colours of the visitors' room. The pastel shades were calming and friendly, but McNulty felt anything but calm. The nondescript pictures on the walls and a faux tearoom vibe did nothing to alleviate the growing sense of dread. He had dreamed of this moment his entire life, the same as every child at Crag View Orphanage; the day when your parents come to take you away from life in prison. The day when you are no longer abandoned. Damaged goods. McNulty still felt like damaged goods.

"You can go in and sit down." Maggie fussed around McNulty as if he was a resident. "I'll bring tea and biscuits. Unless you prefer coffee. We've only got instant, I'm afraid."

McNulty didn't move. He looked at the white-haired old lady. "I'll have what she's having."

"Tea then. Make yourself at home."

But McNulty wasn't at home. He hadn't had a home – at least not one he could remember – before Crag View Orphanage. And the reason he hadn't had a home was sitting in front of him right now. He felt his hands begin to sweat. His mouth was dry. The woman sat patiently with a faint smile on her lips. He wasn't sure if she even knew he was there. He waved a hand to see if she noticed the movement. Doreen blinked and looked at McNulty.

"Have you come about Susie?"

Asking about his sister caught McNulty by surprise. "What about her?"

"She's gone missing."

She hasn't gone missing, McNulty thought. *You gave her away. Me as well. So don't give me that innocent smile; tell me why.* That's what he wanted to say. What he said was, "Where did you last see her?"

"Under the table after dinner. We feed her scraps."

McNulty felt anger bubbling up inside him, but couldn't bring himself to express it to this little old lady. Feeding

Susan scraps under the table was something Susan had never mentioned. McNulty stood in the doorway and balled his fists. He couldn't bring himself to speak, so he kept quiet.

Doreen pointed to the door with a wavering hand. "Somebody left the back door open, and she must have got out. Wasn't wearing a lead, but her name was on the collar."

McNulty let out a sigh but still couldn't speak.

Doreen's voice trembled. "Frank will be so angry. Susie was his favourite. Best dog we ever had." She appeared close to tears. "I don't want to get Frank angry."

McNulty found his voice. "I'm not here about the dog."

He heard the tinkle of crockery behind him and stepped into the room. Maggie put a tray on the coffee table and waved for McNulty to sit. He pulled up a chair and sat opposite the little old woman he still couldn't bring himself to call Doreen. He definitely couldn't call her mum.

Maggie indicated the tray with a wave of the hand. "You've got milk and sugar and a selection of biscuits. If you need anything else, press the buzzer." The buzzer was a chunky control unit hardwired to the wall. It only had one button, a big orange one with the silhouette of a smiling face on it.

"Thank you."

"You're welcome. You have a good catch-up now."

McNulty didn't want to catch up; he wanted to get out. He was beginning to think Susan had been right not to come. He wished he hadn't come either, but sitting here opposite the woman who had given him up, the tension began to unwind. The knot in his stomach began to ease. Maybe it was the biscuits. He loved custard creams.

Doreen leaned over the coffee table, her hands steady now, and picked up the milk jug. "Shall I be mother?"

The simple phrase knotted his stomach again. He wanted to ask why she hadn't been a mother when he'd needed her. He wanted to say a lot more, but how could you get angry with a little old lady who was pouring milk in your tea?

Doreen poured the milk. "Do you take sugar?"

"Two, please." He put two custard creams on the saucer.

Doreen dropped two cubes into his cup and stirred. She stopped in mid-stir, her face suddenly blank. She blinked twice, then looked at McNulty. "Have you come about Susie?"

McNulty distracted himself by dunking a custard cream in his tea, then eating it. The conversation was going round in circles. He forced a smile and drank his tea. Part of him was wondering if she really did have a dog called Susie? Another part wondered what Frank did when he got angry.

Chapter Twenty-Four

Frank Gardner wasn't angry, he was worried. When he was worried, he hurt people. Today, he was hurting Pat Tubah. He stood over the cowering henchman and pressed his foot down on Tubah's neck.

"So you're telling me he took out three of my best men. On his own?"

Tubah tried to speak, but the foot was crushing his throat. Gardner released the pressure. "Speak up."

Tubah croaked, "He wasn't on his own."

"Donkey Flowers? Don't tell me you think that lowlife snitch is SAS trained?"

"He likes his war movies."

Gardner's foot crushed his throat again. "Films. War films. We're British. We're not fuckin' American."

"Just saying. He might have picked up a few things. From the war films."

Frank Gardner hadn't picked up things from war films; he had picked up things from war itself. Despite being seventy-two, he was as hard as nails and trained to use them. Fighting for his country wasn't nearly as rewarding as fighting for himself, though. The downside was the company he was forced to keep. He lifted his foot off Tubah's neck and gestured for him to get up.

"What he's picked up is a few things from America. Namely, bringing a gun to a knife fight."

Tubah rubbed his neck. "A gun? On the plane? It crashed. Kid's toys were spread all over the runway."

"In his luggage. Which obviously wasn't spread all over the runway."

Gardner linked his fingers and flexed them until they cracked. He turned hard eyes on Tubah. "And what were you thinking, bringing a knife in the first place? I wanted payback, not dead."

Tubah didn't think this was the time to mention it was Gardner's men who brought the knife; all Tubah had done was find the target. He tried a bit of careful back-pedalling. "They were only going to rough him up."

"Somebody flashes a knife, you're entitled to believe you're going to get more than roughed up."

Tubah back-pedalled some more. "But Hyde Park Picture House. Nobody takes a gun to the pictures."

Gardner's glare intensified. "McNulty isn't nobody. He's the fella that blew up Telfon Speed with a gas leak and a microwave."

Gardner's phone vibrated in his pocket. He checked the screen and recognised the number. His tone brooked no argument. "This better not be what I think it is."

* * *

What it was, was the watcher getting a call from Halcyon Court for the watcher to get his arse over there pronto. There had been a development. The watcher could hardly believe it;

he'd been pulling surveillance duty for six months, rotating with two other watchers, and thought the only news he would be giving was the untimely demise of Doreen Wills. Not all that untimely since she was almost eighty, was riddled with cancer, and couldn't hold a thought for more than ten minutes.

Still, the care home worker had insisted, and the watcher had dashed across Woodhouse Moor, parking in Back Montpelier Terrace with a view across Cliff Road. Halcyon Court stood out above the trees like a Gothic mansion. The watcher had to settle on a view of the driveway since the school grounds and the houses on Cliff Side Gardens blocked the rear. The caller had identified the visitor as Vince McNulty and given his description. He hadn't come in a car, so McNulty would either call a taxi or use the bus. The watcher had both eventualities covered.

He settled down to wait and took out his phone. He paused for a moment to gather himself. Calling the boss was a daunting proposition. The watcher had heard stories of what Gardner did to people who displeased him. He wasn't sure if this was good news or bad, so he took a deep breath and made the call.

* * *

"What do you mean, you don't know." Gardner had to be careful not to grip the phone too tight. He had crushed two phones already this month.

The voice down the line was obviously trying not to sound nervous, but Gardner knew that making people nervous was his bread and butter. "I can't see the visitors' room from out here."

Gardner stated the obvious. "The insider is inside."

The watcher was managing his nerves well. "She saw one of the care workers take McNulty to the visitors' room and bring tea and biscuits."

"What kind?"

The voice down the line sounded confused. "I don't know. I can ask."

Gardner exploded with anger. "I don't fuckin' care what biscuits he had. Has he talked to her yet?"

"The care worker?"

"Doreen Wills. Who the fuck are you supposed to be watching?"

"They're in the room together, so I'm guessing yes, they're talking."

"Can you guess what they're saying?"

Again, the confusion down the line. "You told us to see if she went out or had any visitors. We're not set up for sound. The place is too big, and we'd never know which room she'd be in."

Gardner was losing what little patience he had. "If she had a visitor, you mean?"

"Yes."

"How many visitors' rooms are there?"

The voice sounded like he knew where this was going. "One."

"Then if she gets a visitor, you know exactly which room she's going to be in."

The watcher tried to explain. "It's a dementia care home. They've got restrictions up the wazoo. We can't just wander in a wire it for sound."

"The cleaner's got ears, hasn't she?"

Even though that was a rhetorical question, the watcher answered. "Yes."

"Then get her to spill something outside the room and clean it up."

The voice sounded relieved that there was finally something he could do. "I'll call her and let you know what she hears."

"Good."

Gardner ended the call. This didn't feel good at all. He knew that Doreen Wills had dementia and couldn't hold two thoughts in her head, but he also knew that dementia sufferers had periods of clarity. If she had a moment of clarity with McNulty, this could go downhill fast. Gardner was sitting atop a very big hill. Downhill from there was a long way down.

Chapter Twenty-Five

McNulty sat on a park bench and watched the world go by. It felt like there was a lot of world to watch, and it distracted him from the world he felt closing in around him. His world. A world that, up until finding his sister, had been a party of one. Then it had been a party of two with Susan, and then three with her daughter, Tilly. That was as big as the world was ever going to get, especially after he'd pissed off Amy back in Boston. Being unable to commit was something he reckoned was set in stone, and the reason for that was eating custard creams at Halcyon Court. Doreen Wills. She didn't even have the decency to be called McNulty.

Two children laughed and giggled as they ploughed through fallen leaves on the way to Woodhouse Moor playground. The attraction of swings and roundabouts outweighed the warnings to slow down from their mother. A pair of teenagers walked arm in arm until the boy slipped his arm around her waist, and the girl smiled.

McNulty wasn't smiling. He was forcing himself to hang on to the hate, but it was hard to hate a woman who couldn't even remember losing her dog. It was hard not to smile when her custard cream broke in half after dunking it in her tea. It was hard not to like a soggy custard cream that melts in your mouth.

An angry motorist sounded his horn on the main road. Music from a radio drifted across the park. McNulty closed his eyes and soaked it all up. What he was really soaking up was the first visit with his mother. That and the smell of fish and chips in the dining room.

* * *

"Would you like to join her for dinner?"

That Yorkshire thing again, breakfast, dinner, and tea. Maggie had returned to the visitors' room after a polite delay to let Doreen get to know her son. Getting to know anybody was difficult for a woman with dementia. Remembering them after was even harder. Maggie obviously thought joining Doreen for lunch would increase the odds of some kind of breakthrough.

McNulty was still getting over the custard cream incident. "I thought visitors had to avoid meal times."

Doreen appeared to be oblivious to the conversation. Maggie gave Doreen's back a gentle rub. "There are exceptions. Mealtime brings the residents together. It opens the receptors." She tapped her temple with one finger. "Reawakens the mind. A new face might seem friendlier when she's eating."

McNulty checked his watch as if he had an appointment.

Maggie noticed. "Unless you don't have time."

Her tone of voice was admonishment enough. *If you don't have time for your mother on your first visit.* McNulty glanced at the woman who was still fishing bits of soggy custard cream out of her tea and made a decision he hadn't thought possible on the bus over here.

"Okay." Not *that would be nice,* or *that's great.* He hadn't made that much progress.

Maggie rubbed Doreen's back a little faster. "Hear that, Doreen? Vincent is going to join you for dinner."

Doreen looked up from her recovery efforts. "Vincent?"

Maggie smiled. "Your son."

"Oh yes. That would be nice." It seemed Doreen was making all the progress.

Maggie helped Doreen to her feet. "It's fish and chips today. You know how much you like fish and chips."

"I do?"

McNulty followed them both to the lift, wondering if Maggie was expecting him to take over helping Doreen. They stood in silence as the lift hummed its way up to the third-floor dining room, then McNulty stepped right into *One Flew Over the Cuckoo's Nest.*

* * *

McNulty found himself smiling as he sat on the park bench, not at the children laughing in the playground or the teenagers touching each other, but at the scene that had greeted him when he'd stepped out of the lift. When he realised he was smiling, he forced his mouth into a frown. He hadn't made that much progress.

The lift had opened onto a wide landing that was laid with industrial linoleum. The lino was coated with little pimples to stop anybody slipping if it got wet. Since it continued beyond the landing into the dining room, there was plenty of opportunity for the floor to get wet. Spillages were a common occurrence at mealtime.

Eight round tables with wooden chairs were dotted around the dining room, and there were two smaller tables with easy chairs for those who needed help feeding themselves. The colour scheme was the same as the visitors' room downstairs; the pastel shades enhanced the calming sounds of the fifties crooners coming from the radio. Val Doonican told the audience to walk tall, walk straight, and look the world right in the eye. His soft, friendly voice reminded the residents of better times, if any of them could remember beyond yesterday.

The woman who had been looking for her car had obviously decided to join the rest of the residents for dinner instead of eating in her room. Her face lit up when she saw McNulty. "Have you found my car?"

McNulty took his cue from Maggie, who gave him an encouraging look. "You were right. The builders moved it. Said they didn't want it getting damaged."

Gladys waved an admonishing finger. "Those rascals. They should have asked first. I almost had a heart attack."

Maggie led Doreen to the middle of the room. "Where do you want to sit, Doreen?"

Two other old ladies waved for Doreen to join them at a table on the left. One of them was grinning so wide McNulty could see the gums all the way to the back of her mouth. She had three teeth that looked like twisted tombstones.

McNulty nodded. "I guess we're over there."

Maggie helped Doreen into a chair at the table and indicated the next seat for McNulty. "She'll need help cutting her food."

"Does she need help eating it?" He pointed at the woman

with the tombstone teeth. "Teeth or gums is what I mean."

Maggie gave him a sideways look. "Did she eat her custard creams?"

"After it was floating in her tea."

"Don't let her drop fish in her tea. Apart from that, she'll be fine."

Tombstone and her friend joined Doreen at the table. Gladys came over and took the last chair. There was a smattering of conversation around the tables, a few entreaties and complaints, and one or two raised voices. A woman with a gravelly voice told a carer to fuck off, causing a flurry of gasps and disapproving looks.

Tombstone leaned close to McNulty. "She's a nasty one. Never happy."

Doreen smiled contentedly. "Fish and chips today."

McNulty glanced at the mobile catering trolley being wheeled from the lift. Steam drifted from the hotplates. "Yes."

"I like fish and chips."

"Me too."

McNulty wasn't lying. He couldn't remember the last time he'd had decent fish and chips. Along with bacon and tea, fish and chips was something else the Americans didn't know how to make.

The server started filling plates with battered cod while the carers went round the tables asking who wanted chips and mushy peas. Not everyone ordered chips, but sensitive gums meant everybody wanted mushy peas. McNulty was surprised to be offered a plate himself and said yes to everything.

Maggie had been right; Doreen did need help cutting her food into manageable portions. McNulty leaned over and played mother, an irony that wasn't lost on the man who had grown up in an orphanage. Feeding the woman who had put him there felt strangely therapeutic, his hands moving smoothly as he cut the fish. The batter was soft after being transported in the steamer, but considering the number of gummy mouths being fed that was probably intentional.

"Salt and vinegar?"

"Vinegar, please. No salt. Your father used to drown his food in salt."

Tiny electric shocks ran up the back of McNulty's neck. He dropped his knife, and it clattered off the side of his plate. He wiped it with a napkin to give himself time to absorb that last piece of information. His father used to drown his food in salt? He actually had a father?

"My dad?"

Doreen's expression became clear and present, her eyes boring into her son's. "The less you know about him, the better."

"Well, that's easy since I don't know anything."

"He liked salt. You know that."

* * *

The children in the playground were still laughing, finding more pleasure in wading through the drifts of leaves than playing on the swings and roundabouts. McNulty wasn't interested in the swings and roundabouts either; he was thinking about seesaws. If you sat on one end, you were either all the way up or all the way down. McNulty was all the way down.

Salt was the only thing Doreen had told him about his

father before her face had gone blank again and she had concentrated on eating. Forking food into her mouth took a lot of concentration. McNulty had considered asking her outright, who was his father, but he wasn't sure he wanted to know. He didn't particularly want to know about his mother either, this entire trip being more about closure than discovering his roots. As far as he was concerned, his roots were in Crag View Orphanage.

But still, his father? That was one tidbit he hadn't seen coming. Doreen had needed a nap after dinner, so Maggie took her back to her room. McNulty didn't want to see Doreen's room. He knew from past experience that care home bedrooms were small and basic. He didn't want to feel sorry for her; he was having a hard enough time feeling sorry for himself. He stood up from the park bench and kicked the drift of leaves that had gathered around his feet. The dead leaves flew like bats in the night. Or branches tapping against the dormitory window.

Chapter Twenty-Six

There weren't many leaves outside the Hyde Park Picture House because there weren't many trees. The rows of back-to-back terrace houses opened straight onto the road with only three stone steps to buffer them from the pavement. The bigger, through-terrace houses had backyards, but even they backed straight onto the cobbled alleys between streets. The only trees were the ones that residents had planted, but most of them were either dead or exotic, like the monkey-puzzle tree along the way to the bus stop.

Tynan checked his watch, then peered through the front doors of the cinema foyer. There was no Saturday matinee, but there was some activity in the manager's office. Tynan scanned the foyer looking for CCTV cameras. He found what he wanted above the concession stand and knocked on the door. Hard.

* * *

"That thing? THAT hasn't worked since the popcorn machine blew the wiring."

"Not having much luck, are you? Since the one outside is

hanging like a limp dick."

"Limp dicks is how we want to keep it. After we went classic instead of porn."

Tynan gave the manager a double-take. "You used to show porn?"

The manager waved a hand over his shoulder to indicate the past. "Way back. Wasn't just a fleapit cinema; used to get your typical dirty mac brigade."

"Was that why they installed CCTV?"

"No. We used to get kids stealing the posters. That was before you could buy them on the Internet. We kept the camera when we started having late-night shows. Helps keep the fighting to a minimum."

Tynan indicated the neutered camera in the foyer. "Not if it isn't working."

"They don't know that. The one outside." He shrugged. "Just makes this one here look even more functional."

"So you can't show me any footage?"

"Not unless you want to watch *Where Eagles Dare*."

Tynan let out a sigh. "And I don't suppose you can remember who was in the late show last night."

The manager laughed and shook his head. "We had a good crowd last night. The classic war films are always popular. That's why we keep running them. Three or four times a year."

"That's a no then?"

"Not exactly."

"No?"

The manager puffed out his chest with pride. "We get our regulars. Some come and see the same films every time we show them. *Von Ryan's Express. Dirty Dozen.* And this one.

That's why we call it Classic Night. A good film never dies."

Tynan felt a glimmer of hope. "And you know the regulars?"

"Some of them. Not all by name."

"Try."

The manager puffed out his cheeks and scratched his head. "There's an old couple, Mr and Mrs Pearson. Said he proposed to her after Frank Sinatra didn't make it to the train."

Tynan jotted it down in his notebook. "First names?"

"George, I think. Don't know hers."

Tynan was thinking about the carnage in the alley. "Any big fellas? Look like they could handle themselves?"

"We don't get troublemakers in war film night. Vicarious excitement."

"Vicarious?"

"They watch it, don't live it."

"Anyone unusual, then?"

The manager changed from scratching his head to rubbing his chin. He had all the ticks when it came to focussing his mind. "One fella that always comes. On his own most times. Had a friend with him last night. Didn't look like trouble, though."

Tynan waited, pen poised. "Name?"

"I don't know his friend's name."

"The loner."

"I think it's just a nickname."

"What's his nickname?"

"Donkey. Donkey Flowers."

Tynan looked up from his notebook. It had been a long time since he'd run across Donkey Flowers. "What did his friend look like?"

The manager held up his hands. "I can't remember. Go see

for yourself. They went over the road to The King's Arms. His cameras work."

* * *

The landlord of The King's Arms had needed more persuading than the Hyde Park Picture House manager across the road.

"You got a court order?"

"That's in America. Over here, it's a search warrant."

"You got a search warrant?"

Tynan kept his tone light. "I'm not searching, I'm asking."

The landlord wasn't fooled. "Asking to search my CCTV."

Tynan gave up on the light tone and leaned closer for added menace. "I'm asking you to cooperate in the murder of three men down the alley behind the cinema. Because those three men might have been customers last night. And the person that killed them might have been in here as well."

"Didn't see nothin' suspicious."

"Define suspicious."

The landlord looked nonplussed.

Tynan held up a hand. "Let me tell you what's suspicious. A landlord not wanting a murder detective to see his security footage."

The landlord was about to speak, but Tynan extended a finger for him to be quiet. "Makes me wonder what you don't want me to see."

The landlord tried to speak again, but Tynan turned the hand into a fist. "If I have to get a court order, I'm going to shut you down until it arrives, and when it does arrive, I'm going to be looking at a lot more than who was in here last night."

The landlord raised his eyebrows for permission to speak. Tynan nodded. The landlord let out a sigh. "I thought a court order was in America."

Tynan relaxed the fist. "What we've got in Yorkshire is the Ways and Means Act. That gives me permission to fuck you six ways from Sunday. And believe me, I will."

The landlord held his hands up in surrender. "If you put it like that. What do you want to see?"

* * *

The security camera on the wall behind the bar looked fairly modern but the recording device was a long way from state-of-the-art. The King's Arms must have been the only pub in Yorkshire that still used VHS with time-lapse photography, meaning that Tynan had to find the right place by rewinding or fast-forwarding the tape until he was viewing from ten minutes before the cinema turned out.

"Is The King's Arms a free house or a brewery chain?"

"Independent."

"Then somebody should have told you VHS went bust years ago."

"Lots of cheap tapes then, isn't there?"

"Just the one camera?"

The landlord shook his head. "Two. One in the snug and one in the lounge."

Tynan sat back, exasperated. "How do I view them both?"

The landlord indicated a second video recorder. "Separate tape for each bar."

"Show me the lounge first."

140

The landlord switched the feeds to the single monitor, cued the right place, then pressed play and half speed. Static images jerked across the screen, customers coming to the bar or sitting down. Tynan kept soft eyes on the screen, same technique as examining a crime scene.

"Do you know your regulars?"

"Some of 'em."

Tynan pressed normal speed to skip through the images. The three dead men hadn't been in the lounge bar, and nobody left just before the cinema crowd came in. "Do you know Donkey Flowers?"

"Donk? Yeah, I know Donk."

"Which bar was he in?"

"Snug."

Tynan waved for the landlord to change the tapes and cue ten minutes before the cinema turned out again. Normal speed until a familiar figure came through the door. Half speed to slow the movement. Two men entered the snug, Donk in the lead. The door closed behind them. Tynan pressed pause and looked at the grainy image. Tynan hadn't had much to do with Flowers when he'd busted Northern X, but there was no mistaking Vince McNulty.

Chapter Twenty-Seven

"Did you see her then?"

"I saw her."

Donk held out his hands, palms up, as McNulty slumped into a chair at the kitchen table. "Well?"

McNulty felt drained. "Well, what?"

Donk pulled up a chair. "How'd it go?"

McNulty didn't feel like talking, so he looked out through the kitchen window. The curtains were the same as before, a red and white chequered pattern that matched the tablecloth. The sky was the same dull grey, only without the rain this afternoon.

Donk persisted. "Well?"

McNulty turned tired eyes on his friend. "She dropped a custard cream in her tea and doesn't like salt with her mushy peas."

* * *

McNulty replayed the visit in his mind and kept most of it to himself. Apart from that brief moment of clarity, Doreen Wills had been the same confused old lady he'd met in the visitors' tearoom. McNulty still couldn't bring himself to consider her a McNulty but had to accept that the man who loved salt probably was. That one little snippet threw his life into a tailspin. That, and the stern look his mother had given him when she'd said, "The less you know about him, the better." The stern look was anything but confused. It was hard and cruel and the very epitome of a woman who had not only given up one child but two.

That was the part that hurt. This sweet little old lady had once been tough enough to give away her children, not once but twice. Or had they been taken away from her? Was there something else at play here that McNulty didn't understand? That wouldn't be difficult. He didn't understand any of it, except his mother was bad with custard creams and didn't like salt with her mushy peas.

The rest of the dinner had proceeded without incident apart from the noisy woman telling her carer to fuck off and the other ladies muttering about how nasty she was. McNulty wondered if she was nasty enough to abandon her children, but kept that to himself. He helped cut Doreen's fish and made sure she didn't drop any down her skirt. Judging by the stains on her blouse, spillage was par for the course at mealtimes. He ate his own fish and chips in silence, only responding to the occasional comment from the other ladies around the table and reflecting on how much he missed Yorkshire's premier food source.

"Your father used to drown his food in salt."

That was the thought that kept going through his mind as he ate. He even experimented with a little mound of chips, turning them into a snow-covered peak. Was that how his father used to eat? Was that why he had a predilection for extra salt himself? He'd never thought about it before, but he did have a tendency to add flavour with plenty of shakes of the salt pot. Mostly, it was a salt grater in America, and Amy was always screwing up her face in disgust.

Amy, another thought that was always on his mind. He missed her and wished she were here so he could talk about the jumble of emotions rolling around in his head. He dusted the salt off the twin peaks and added extra vinegar. The fish and chips were good. Halcyon Court must have paid top dollar for a decent chef. That meant the residents must be paying top dollar for their care. McNulty wondered who was paying for Doreen's.

The staff cleared the plates and offered ice cream for dessert. Most of the ladies had eaten enough. Doreen was as clumsy with ice cream as she had been with custard creams. McNulty didn't want to touch her to wipe it off her blouse, so he gave her a napkin and told her to do it herself. Maggie came over and used a damp cloth to clean the spillage.

"She's not as steady as she used to be."

McNulty glanced at the woman who couldn't stop her hands from shaking. "She used to be steady?"

Maggie nodded. "Safest hands at Halcyon Court. She could hold a cup of tea without a tremor."

McNulty let out a sigh. "Except the tremors in her head."

"Except for those. Yes. But they're better today. She was looking forward to seeing you."

Another lie, and this time McNulty recognised it as such. A little white lie to make McNulty feel better. McNulty didn't feel better. He had a ton of questions and no one to ask. Unless his mother had another moment of clarity.

"She said something about my dad."

Maggie stopped what she was doing. "Really? That's

progress."

"She didn't say much. Then it was gone."

"It's a good sign, though. I told you mealtime opens the receptors."

"You also told me she was looking forward to seeing me. She doesn't know me from Adam."

Maggie turned steady eyes on McNulty. "Mostly. Yes. But she knew you enough to talk about your father. Fish and chips has a way of doing that."

"I can't keep feeding her fish and chips."

Maggie smiled. "You could take her out for a coffee. She used to love going to Costa in Horsforth. Coffee and a cake might jog her memory some more."

"Not custard creams?"

"Costa doesn't serve custard creams."

* * *

Donk ordered takeaway pizza for tea. McNulty didn't argue; he'd had enough fish and chips for one day, and he didn't like Chinese. The table didn't take much setting since pizza was pretty much an eat-with-your-fingers kind of meal, but Donk did offer beer or Coca-Cola from the fridge. McNulty chose a Coke.

"You don't feel like celebrating?"

"Celebrating what?"

Donk put a can of Coke on the table. "You just met your mum. That's got to count for something."

McNulty stared at the Coke. "It counts for nothing."

Donk slammed his beer on the table. "Well, it should. I'd give anything to see my mum again."

The noise made McNulty jump. He'd never seen Donk angry. But it didn't change how he felt. "I'd give anything to not be dumped at Crag View."

"Maybe you weren't dumped. Maybe you were taken."

McNulty snorted a laugh. "If they were going to kidnap me, it would have been for something better than sticking another kid in the orphanage."

"Taken from her. You know, like that film with Judi Dench."

"*Philomena* was about Judi Dench trying to find her son. My mum didn't try to find anybody."

"How do you know?"

"I don't want to know." That was a lie, and he knew it. McNulty desperately wanted to know. He wanted to know what was behind the hard look his mother had given him during that moment of clarity. And he wanted to know about his father. It seemed that the road to unlocking those secrets was a trip to Costa Coffee in Horsforth. He didn't think the best way to do that was by taking the bus.

"Can you get me a car?"

Chapter Twenty-Eight

Pat Tubah was shocked to hear the noise on the other side of the door. It sounded like somebody was smashing his way through the wall. The roar of anger suggested it was something else. The prim and proper woman sitting behind the reception desk looked unperturbed. She was obviously used to the mood swings of the man who had taken over Northern X.

The noise stopped echoing around the wood-panelled antechamber, and the room fell quiet. After a few more moments, a light flashed on her intercom. The woman pressed a button to turn it off, then looked at Tubah.

"He will see you now."

* * *

Frank Gardner didn't think of himself as an angry man but knew the value of instilling fear in those who worked for him. Since taking over and expanding Northern X, he had instilled more than his share of fear. What he hadn't done was feel fear himself, and it was that new sensation that had provoked his latest outburst. He took a deep breath, brushed the smashed telephone into the waste bin, and pushed a button on his desk.

There were three: red, green, and amber. A kind of traffic light system. Red meant do not disturb. Green meant come in. Amber, he never used. In his estimation, you only ever needed go or stop. His next decision was a go.

He took several deep breaths to calm himself, then put on his game face. The door opened, and Pat Tubah came in. Gardner shouted through the open door. "I need a new phone."

"Yes, Mr G."

Gardner nodded for Tubah to close the door, then waved him to a seat in front of the desk. "Have you found his friend yet?"

"I'm working on it." Actually, Tubah was doing nothing of the sort because he hadn't been asked. He was being asked now. The noise was enough motivation for him to give his best effort. That and the chance to move up the food chain.

"What was his name?"

"Vince McNulty."

Gardner managed to contain his impatience. "The friend."

"Oh. Donkey Flowers."

That part had been easy. All Tubah had to do was nip into The King's Arms and ask about the man who had been with McNulty. After the three heavies had gone down the alley and before they hadn't returned.

"Donkey?"

"Everybody calls him Donk."

* * *

Tynan had replayed the footage three times, drawing the landlord's attention to the man with Donkey Flowers.

"And you haven't seen him before?"

The landlord prodded a finger at the screen. "Him, no. Donk's in all the time."

"But they left together."

The landlord nodded. "Right after the final bell. They were the last to leave."

"Anybody follow them?"

"What part of *last* don't you understand?"

Tynan gave him a hard look. "I could still pull your licence."

The landlord held up his hands. "Nobody followed them. Not from in here."

"Meaning what?"

The landlord was treading on thin ice, but he couldn't resist. "Meaning whoever followed them came from outside after the fella came in asking about them."

"What fella?"

* * *

The what fella was nervous as he sat opposite the man who had not only taken over from Telfon Speed but rebranded Northern X into something bigger than simply a massage chain with a side order of torture porn. Xtreme North had gone international, importing girls from all over the world and using their exotic nature to give its clients more than just a hand job. The massage parlours might have closed down, but the online presence meant Xtreme North boasted locations all over the country. Gardner had kept the North and the X in the name for sentimental reasons. The girls were specially chosen for their tolerance of pain, and those with a low tolerance were transferred to the single-use side of the industry. None of them complained. None of them were around to complain after a single-use session.

Gardner turned steady eyes on Tubah. "McNulty moved out of the hotel after your team botched the room search."

Tubah chose the better part of valour and didn't remind the boss that it was *his* team, not Tubah's. Tubah was just the spotter.

Gardner continued. "I'm guessing he's staying with this Donk. When you find out where he lives, call me straight away and set up an observation post."

Tubah swallowed to moisten his mouth. "The police will be looking for him as well."

Gardner stiffened. "They know about him?"

"They will by now. Tynan is like a dog with a bone." That part had been easy too, watching the police operation on the news and recognising the lead detective. "He was at the scene this morning and will have asked the same questions I did."

Gardner lowered his voice. "Then you'd better use your connections to find him before they do."

Tubah gulped. "Connections?"

Gardner tapped the side of his nose. "Nose to the ground. And remember, when you're up to your neck in shit, don't open your mouth."

* * *

Miss prim and proper was ready with a replacement telephone by the time Tubah left. She had a stock of them in the cupboard behind her desk. Destroying telephones was a regular occurrence. Gardner nodded his thanks and waited for her to close the door, then he puffed out his cheeks and let out a long, deep sigh.

The information that had prompted him to destroy the landline was still fresh in his mind, but the anger had subsided. The watcher at Halcyon Court had called as soon as McNulty had finished his visit. The news wasn't good. McNulty had been invited to stay for fish and chips and had sat with his mother during dinner. There had been a lot of talking. There had been a few smiles. More importantly, there had been at least one moment of clarity when Doreen Wills had talked with her son.

That moment of clarity was the problem. Gardner couldn't afford to let the old woman spill the beans about what she knew, even if she couldn't understand that she knew anything at all. Even the slightest slip could be dangerous. And now there was the news that McNulty had been given permission to take her out for coffee tomorrow morning. Gardner couldn't wait until tomorrow morning. He had to make a decision now. He picked up the phone and called his secretary.

"Get me Salino."

Chapter Twenty-Nine

"Ham and pineapple?"

"I like pineapple."

"On fruit salad, yes. But on pizza?"

"It's great. Brings out the flavour. Like cranberry sauce on turkey."

"That's because turkey has no flavour."

Donk opened the other box and pushed it across the table to McNulty. "I got a spicy meat feast as well. Thought we'd go half-and-half. But you take it. Jesus, you're grumpy today."

McNulty held up a placating hand. "No. Half each is fine. I'm sorry. It's been a hard day."

Donk accepted the olive branch. "Yeah, well. Look on the bright side. Coffee with your mum in the morning."

McNulty wasn't sure that was the bright side, but he appreciated Donk making the effort. "Yes."

Donk checked his watch, then turned on the kitchen TV. "Let's see what the forecast is tomorrow."

McNulty reckoned he knew what the forecast was tomorrow, dull, grey, and miserable. No amount of Donk enthusiasm was going to change that. McNulty pointed at the TV with a slice of pizza. "Your mum never used to like the TV on at mealtime."

Donk angled his chair so he could watch the news. "It's not mealtime, it's a takeaway."

"We're eating."

"Not with a knife and fork."

"I don't think your mum would agree."

Donk looked at McNulty. "And if she was here, I'd happily turn it off. But she isn't. Yours is. So eat your pizza and enjoy a coffee tomorrow."

McNulty nodded and took a bite of spicy meat feast. Donk's enthusiasm was starting to rub off on him, but he wasn't ready to admit it. He settled down with his pizza and a Coke and waited for the weather forecast.

*　*　*

Television newsreaders in England were completely different from the saccharine news reporters in America. In the US, TV news was entertainment delivered by powder-puffed presenters with perfect teeth and day-glow tans. The BBC was more down-to-earth. Sky News was somewhere between.

As McNulty sat at the kitchen table, he was transported back to a grubby hotel room in Halifax after a massage that had turned violent. He remembered poring over the Ordnance Survey map of the north of England with its red dots denoting massage parlours he had visited before heading back to his old stomping ground, and his confrontation with Northern X. He had flicked through the TV channels and settled on Sky News. He could even remember the stories.

International news had washed over him in the background. Famine. Terrorism. An eight-lane motorway bridge that had collapsed into the Mississippi. Big stories with zero impact on the seedy hotel room in the northern mill town. Rescue workers in fluorescent jackets had tried to winch survivors to safety. The info bar scrolling across the bottom of the screen had said seven were confirmed dead, but the death toll was expected to rise. To remind viewers how tragic this was, they had kept replaying footage of the dramatic collapse.

The TV had caught his eye again, and he'd known even before looking up that it was local news. Two police officers in fluorescent jackets had been wrapping crime scene tape around a lamppost and across a road. Blue lights on their patrol car had flashed, and in the distance, a three-car pileup had revealed it was a fatal accident. Boys in blue. The thin blue line. He had watched with the sound down and had felt he was part of them. Still did, despite having been an ex-cop for many years now.

"Vince." At first, the voice was faint and distant, then Donk shook McNulty's shoulder. "VINCE."

McNulty came out of his reverie. "What?"

Donk jabbed a finger toward the TV. "Look."

The BBC was more professional than Sky News, but they still had very nice teeth. The current story wasn't about famine or terrorism or a collapsed bridge in Mississippi, and it wasn't about the boys in blue dealing with a three-car pileup. It was the boys in blue, though, wrapping crime scene tape around a lamppost to seal off the road. Not a road, a cobbled alley.

"Shit."

Donk nodded. "Yes, shit."

The newsreader described how three bodies had been found halfway down the alley. All male. All shot to death. A plain-clothes officer ducked under the crime scene tape and waved the reporters away as they shouted questions at him. Jimmy Tynan had aged since the last time McNulty had met him, and he seemed to carry more authority. The identifier below the image explained why. Detective Sergeant Tynan, Major Crime Unit, West Yorkshire Police. The DC had been promoted, but he was still dealing with major crimes. In Yorkshire, three men shot to death was a major crime.

McNulty's mind replayed the sounds he'd heard in the alley. Three slaps across the face, followed by a scuffle and commotion, then three more slaps. On the TV, a wide shot showed the alley in relation to a nearby building, the Hyde Park Picture House on Brudenell Road. The movie poster was still in its frame beside the entrance canopy. *Where Eagles Dare*. It wasn't the film he was thinking about, though. The alley was the shortcut to the bus stop. The men who were killed could just as easily have been Donk and McNulty.

II

PART TWO

MOTIVE
The reason the defendant committed the crime.
—Blackstone's

Chapter Thirty

The car was a yellow two-door FIAT 500 hatchback with accident damage to the nearside door. McNulty checked to make sure the door still opened. It did, but with a creak that sounded like it was going to fall off at any moment. After the shock of seeing the murder on the news, it wouldn't have surprised McNulty if it *had* fallen off. It felt like that kind of day. First, there had been the meeting with his mother and the revelation about his father, then there had been the murder at the cinema, and now this, a car so small McNulty could barely fit behind the wheel. He would normally have said something sarcastic, but now wasn't the time.

"Thanks."

Donk was leaning against the only lamppost in the cul-de-sac that worked. "Is that all you've got to say?"

* * *

McNulty had to admit that saying nothing wasn't an option anymore. After all, his friend had pulled out all the stops to find a car that wasn't a rental at extremely short notice and had given McNulty a bed after his hotel room had been trashed. It was having his hotel room trashed that was the main topic of conversation when they went back in the kitchen.

"So, three fellas search your hotel room and end up dead in an alley."

"We don't know they're the same three fellas."

Donk held up a hand because he wasn't finished. "An alley round the back of the cinema where you, the person whose hotel room got searched, just happened to be watching *Where Eagles Dare*."

McNulty shrugged. "Nobody ever got killed for watching *Where Eagles Dare*."

"They weren't watching it. You were. They were watching you."

"Allegedly."

"Well, allegedly this. If they were waiting in the alley for you, what do you think they'd have done with me?"

"They didn't do anything. They got it done to them."

"Is that supposed to make me feel better?"

McNulty let out a sigh. He had run out of arguments, but he hadn't given up. "I know it looks bad, but look on the bright side. We aren't suspects. We didn't do anything. We were just at the pictures like everyone else."

Donk hadn't given up either. "When three men who searched your room just happened to get shot."

"Allegedly searched my room."

"Yeah, well, I allegedly shit my pants when I saw the news."

McNulty sniffed the air. "False allegation."

Donk slapped the table. "It's not funny."

McNulty finally gave up. "I know. I'm sorry. But if these were bad fellas, then bad people were after *them*. Not us. We walked down that alley. Nobody ambushed us. They were the target."

"Do you think that's what the police will think?"

"They can think what they want. They can't prove anything because we didn't do anything."

It was Donk's turn to let out a sigh. "You remember all the times you arrested me?"

McNulty nodded but didn't speak.

"Did you need proof to arrest me?"

"I had proof."

"But you didn't need it to make the arrest. To charge me and take me to court, yes. But to arrest me? All you needed was your nose."

Donk might have been exaggerating about the nose, but he was right. Depending on the offence. If an arrestable offence has been committed, any police officer may arrest anyone suspected of committing that offence. The same rule applies even if the police officer suspects that an arrestable offence has been committed. If the police wanted to bring you in for questioning, all they had to do was meet the above criteria. Donk and McNulty fit that criteria.

"Their nose isn't sniffing at us. It's sniffing at everybody in the area. That's the pictures and the pub. We're not even top of their list."

"Until the faces hit the news."

McNulty shook his head. "Even then."

Donk was right again, though. "When they put mugshots on the news, their faces will go public. How long before the hotel guy recognises the fella who broke his nose?"

McNulty was swimming against the tide. "So?"

"So? So, Vince McNulty is the name on the register. It's

Vince McNulty they were looking for when they broke into your room. And Vince McNulty will be on camera at The King's Arms."

"The King's Arms has cameras?" He wasn't even swimming now. He knew there were cameras in the snug bar. It was the first thing he'd noticed when he was ordering the drinks. Christ, he'd even smiled at the camera as a joke.

Donk continued. "And the landlord knows me. I've been going in there after the pictures for years. So when two and two makes four, guess whose door the police will be knocking on next?"

"You didn't do anything either."

"A cell is still a cell. Even when you're innocent."

"Don't be so melodramatic."

"Fuck melodramatic. You've never been locked in a cell. You were always the one doing the locking."

That was true, but McNulty still had some wriggle room. "Your mum wanted you locked up. To straighten you out. It worked. Look at you now. An upstanding citizen."

"An upstanding citizen that's in the shit."

"Not even close." McNulty was trying to be upbeat, but he knew there were other considerations. He hoped Donk hadn't got around to thinking about them yet.

Donk had. "Here's something else to think about. Whoever killed those three can ask the same questions as the police. Probably with more weight. So, if our fellas were looking for you, then the fella who killed them will have known they were looking for you. And he'll know you were with me. Do you think the landlord is going to keep quiet about that while he's having his fingernails pulled out?"

McNulty waved a placating hand. "He knows you drink

there. He doesn't know where you live."

Donk snorted a laugh. "Donkey Flowers. How long do you think it'll take to track that name?"

McNulty looked out of the kitchen window at the getaway car. Having the wrong people knock on Donk's door was a consideration, but McNulty didn't think it would be the hitman. If Donk's suspicions were correct, then the hitman hadn't been after McNulty he had been protecting him. No, since the police didn't know about the hitman, all they would have to go on was the hotel search and the fact that the three men had been looking for McNulty. From there, it wasn't a stretch to think that McNulty had been the real target in the alley and had defended himself with lethal force.

"The fella who leant you the car. Does he have a spare room?"

Chapter Thirty-One

The police raid on the house at Mean Wood was all about timing. It was important to not only get all your ducks in a row by making sure the target was on the premises, but Tynan also had to coordinate an armed incursion with the local division and hide the build-up from nosy neighbours. Since Mean Wood was almost as bad as Mos Eisley spaceport when it came to wretched hives of scum and villainy, nosy neighbours were at a premium.

"Three in the morning is the best time to sneak past these motherfuckers." That was the local division sergeant liaising with the MCU.

"We can't wait until three in the morning. We go now." That was Detective Sergeant Jimmy Tynan. Not of the Marvel Cinematic Universe.

*　*　*

Events leading to the house at Mean Wood were typically procedural. Police work isn't like the movies; it isn't all car chases and shootouts, especially in Yorkshire, where gunfights were practically unheard of. Of course, there was that battle at the diner on Snake Pass a few years ago, but that was the exception rather than the rule. In general, police work is all about joining the dots and filling in forms. Joining the dots that led to Vince McNulty involved hours of enquiries and a few minutes of luck. The luck was Jimmy Tynan knowing where Donkey Flowers lived. The enquiries started with a call from The Station Hotel.

"Are you going to circulate him?" That was Bill Baildon, Tynan's lead detective, who had been working at the MCU ever since Tynan brought down Northern X.

"I don't want his name hitting the news until we've got him in custody." That was Tynan, who was still having trouble believing that Vince McNulty was a trained killer who could take out three men with a single shot to the chest and a double-tap to the head.

Baildon gave his sergeant a sympathetic look. "People change, you know."

Tynan shook his head. "He works in the movies. Titanic Productions doesn't train you in marksmanship and give you a silencer."

"How do you know he used a silencer?"

"Because six gunshots in the middle of the night would even have the people at Hyde Park calling the police."

Baildon sipped coffee in the conference room at Brotherton House. "You like him. That's your problem."

Tynan ate a doughnut. "It's not a problem if he didn't do it."

More coffee. "We can't ask him until we've got him."

No more doughnut. "I just don't want to be going in heavy-handed."

"Six gunshots in the night needs heavy-handed."

Tynan had to admit it didn't look good for McNulty. The ex-Vice Squad cop had been seen near the scene of the crime at about the time of the crime, time of death having been confirmed as not long after McNulty had left the King's Arms. The three men had been identified as the same men who were looking for McNulty at The Station Hotel in Leeds. They were also known associates of Frank Gardner, the businessman in charge of Xtreme North, the shady reboot of Northern X. Another McNulty connection. So, two and two making four suggested Gardner had an axe to grind, and his three henchmen were doing the grinding. Except McNulty had got the drop on them and done some grinding of his own. QED. Two add two. Four.

There was no avoiding bringing McNulty in for questioning, and since firearms were involved, going in heavy-handed was the order of the day. Or night, since it was a long way after dark. Late evening, if you were splitting hairs. Tynan didn't like splitting hairs.

"Heavy-handed it is then. Get me Firearms and PSU."

Baildon already had a Police Support Unit on standby and only needed to call the Firearms Department to get two mobile firearms units. "Do you want X-Ray Nine-Nine?"

Tynan snapped a reply. "Of course I want the fucking helicopter. If we're going in heavy-handed we might as well go the whole hog."

* * *

The whole hog was deployed to a Forward Operating Post three streets away from the house on Mean Wood. Tynan knew it was Donk's house. The lights were on in the kitchen and the back bedroom, so one of them was still up. The cul-de-sac was crammed nose to tail with parked cars, so the PSU van would have to offload in the middle of the street while the firearms officers would park on the main road. The only giveaway was the noise of X-ray 99 hovering over the edge of the estate, but Mean Wood was used to the police chasing car thieves and burglars with the Force helicopter.

Tynan gave a refresher briefing at the back of the PSU van, then told everyone to wait for his signal. He looked at each person individually until they had all nodded their acknowledgement. Tynan nodded in return, then set off down the road. His radio was set to earpiece so there would be no noise pollution to give away his approach. He walked slowly and calmly. Quiet as a mouse.

Mean Wood wasn't quiet. There was the distant noise of a motorbike racing around the playing field in the middle of the estate. Several dogs barked like a rabid pack. There were at least two domestic arguments and a lot of noisy televisions through a lot of open windows. Tynan flapped his arms across his chest to keep warm. His breath plumed around his head in the cold. What the fuck were they doing with their windows open?

He paused at the mouth of the cul-de-sac. The lights were still on in the kitchen and the back bedroom. The street was still crammed nose to tail with parked cars, at least two of them on stacks of bricks since somebody had stolen their wheels. There was one narrow gap outside the target premises that he hadn't noticed the first time he'd checked. Good. That would be the offload point.

Tynan took a deep breath and let it out slowly. There were two other plumes of breath in the darkness either side of the house. The divisional units that had been watching the house ever since Tynan had identified the address. Nobody had come in or out. All the ducks were in a row.

* * *

"Go, go, go…"

The door crashed open with one swing of the battering ram, and PSU officers swarmed into the kitchen. Not Tynan's preferred option, but his softly, softly approach hadn't worked. He had tried looking through the windows and knocking on the door. He had even tried shouting through the letterbox, asking McNulty if he could come in for a chat. There had been no signs of movement in the house. There had been no welcoming reply. It was crash bang wallop time. The PSU crashed banged and walloped.

The mobile firearms units leapfrogged the PSU, each unit consisting of a response driver and a firearms officer. The drivers stayed with their vehicles. The firearms officers went in with shotguns. This was an enclosed space search and containment operation. Shotguns gave maximum spread at close range.

"Clear." That was the lead officer, having secured the kitchen.

"Clear." That was the second officer, continuing the leapfrog tactic, having cleared the hallway.

PSU officers secured the perimeter while the firearms units searched the semi-detached house, one room at a time. The lights were on, but nobody was home. By the time they'd searched the entire house, all the lights were on. "All clear."

Tynan gave the order to stand down, and the officers in riot gear grumbled at the lack of action as they shuffled into the garden. The firearms officers were more pragmatic. Any day they didn't have to shoot anybody was a good day. Guns were the last line of defence, never offence. PSU thrived on offence.

Tynan got on the radio and asked for talk-through with X-ray 99. "Can you sweep the gardens for heat signatures?"

The observer raised his voice over the thudding rotor blades. "Affirmative. Infrared sweep."

Tynan stood in the street and watched the helicopter hover over the gardens either side of Donk's house. He didn't hold out much hope, even with infrared. The pilot instructed his observer to use the powerful searchlight just to make sure. Blazing white light speared the gardens. Tynan stood in the narrow gap between the parked cars and already knew what the gap meant. It wasn't bad parking by the adjacent vehicles; it was the space left by a very small car. The birds had flown the coop.

Chapter Thirty-Two

McNulty listened to the throbbing beat of the helicopter and couldn't help feeling guilty. He had been a policeman for most of his adult life, and it went completely against the grain to let the police waste their time searching an empty house. Donk was feeling less guilty.

"Yippee, look at them fuckers go."

They were standing in the back garden of Donk's friend, half a mile from Donk's house, watching the light show as if it were a fireworks display. All the neighbours were out in the street as well, some of them cheering, most of them jeering. Mean Wood always rejoiced when the police fucked things up.

"They used to be my colleagues."

Donk hugged himself to keep warm. "Yeah, well, your colleagues are trying to lock you up. Now you know what it feels like."

* * *

What it felt like was, shit. McNulty had been in more than a couple of tight scrapes with the police since he'd been forced to resign over Daniel Roach, the child molester who had been diddling his little sister since she was four years old. Some had been scrapes of his own making, but most had simply been a case of wrong place, wrong time. One had even involved Jimmy Tynan, back when McNulty had been a suspect for the missing girls from the Northern X massage parlours. That time it had worked out fine after McNulty helped Tynan find the torture sex ring and close down Northern X. This time felt completely different.

"Let's go inside."

Donk gave McNulty a concerned look. "You okay?"

McNulty indicated the helicopter with a wave of the hand. "Does it look like I'm okay? They just went Iwo Jima all over your house."

"They'll tidy up when they're finished."

McNulty tilted his head and raised his eyebrows. "They'll nail the door shut and post an invoice through the letterbox."

"What? They weren't looking for me. Not my fault they got the wrong house."

"They got the right house. Because you were seen with me at the pictures."

Donk tried to lighten the mood. "Broadsword calling Danny Boy."

"Broadsword is in deeper shit than Richard Burton at the Schloss Adler."

Donk snorted a laugh. "Half the German army were trying to kill him."

"What do you think they were trying to do in the alley?"

That shut Donk up. McNulty felt guilty all over again. Shouting at Donk was like kicking a puppy. The soulful eyes broke McNulty's heart. He let out a sigh that plumed more breath around his head, then patted Donk on the back. "Sorry. It's got nothing to do with you, but you're mixed up in it now."

Donk looked offended. "What makes you think they weren't after me?"

McNulty rubbed Donk's shoulder. "Because they're not bothered about council house tenants going to the pictures. They're after the man who killed Telfon Speed and closed down Northern X."

Donk sucked in his breath. "This is about the massage parlours?"

"They're the only people I've pissed off. Unless Daniel Roach has finally grown some balls."

"Daniel Roach?"

"Long story. Bottom line. Speed's crew are after payback."

It was Donk's turn to indicate the police helicopter. "Then go tell Tynan. Let him sort it out."

McNulty nodded. "I will. Just not yet. I've got a coffee date in the morning. Remember?"

"Maybe you should go see Tynan first. You don't want the police storming Costa Coffee when you're with your mum. That won't help jog her memory."

McNulty remembered the serious look on his mother's face when she'd said, "The less you know about him, the better," and thought maybe a short, sharp shock might do just that. Police kicking in doors has a way of focussing the mind.

"Let's go see if your friend has a bigger bed than he has a car."

"Fuck the bed. You're on the sofa."

* * *

While McNulty curled up on a sofa that was the Fiat 500 of home furnishings, somebody else was staying up all night. "Get me Salino," might have seemed like an innocent request to his secretary, but Frank Gardner knew exactly what calling in the A Team would entail. The repercussions would be enormous, but there was no avoiding them.

Salino worked through the night. The results of her work wouldn't be discovered until the following morning. The fallout would spread much further.

Chapter Thirty-Three

The first phone call came just after breakfast. The second blew McNulty's world apart. But first there was breakfast. Just not cooked in the basement kitchen.

"How come you put the kitchen in the basement?"

"Because if I burn the toast, it won't set off the fire alarm."

"So don't burn the toast."

Eric Hugunin looked at McNulty. "Donk said you were a sarcastic bastard."

McNulty held up his hands. "Sorry. Not on purpose."

Eric shrugged. "That's okay. They say sarcasm is the lowest form of wit. But it's still funny."

"You think I'm funny?"

"I think you're fucking hilarious. But I'm still ordering takeaway."

"In case you burn the toast?"

"Because I only have a kitchen because it came with the house."

McNulty doubted it came in the basement, but then nothing about Eric Hugunin was where it should have been. The ex-circus performer stood four-foot-six with short legs and a wide forehead. That explained why he didn't need a bigger car and why the sofa was plenty big enough as a spare bed. He had settled in Mean Wood after the Big Top had burned down on Woodhouse Moor, the cinder moor section that played host to the Christmas Market, the circus, and the Headingley Feast, a mobile fair that included dodgems, a ghost train, and every shade of candyfloss. As long as it came in pink.

"Well, thanks for putting me up at short notice."

Eric put the kettle on. "Should I expect a helicopter any time soon?"

McNulty sat at the kitchen table. "I'm going to sort it out today."

"Before they arrest you?"

"They're going to arrest somebody else. I just don't know who yet."

Footsteps sounded on the garden path, followed by a knock on the front door. Eric threw his hands up in exasperation. "I keep telling Donk to just come straight in. He thinks his mum is watching from above if he doesn't mind his manners."

McNulty checked his watch. It was barely half past eight. "What's he doing out this early?"

Eric shouted up the stairs for Donk to come in, then turned back to McNulty. "Getting breakfast."

* * *

Breakfast was a Sausage, egg, and bacon flat cake the size of a dinner plate. Each. McNulty wondered where Hugunin managed to put it, the little man not seeming to have enough room in his tiny body. Donk had no problem wolfing his sandwich down. McNulty took a bit longer. It had been a long time since he'd had a Full English in a bread cake.

"You sure you've got enough sauce on that?" McNulty pointed at the brown sauce leaking out of Donk's sandwich.

Hugunin glanced at Donk, then looked at McNulty. "Donk said you'd been in America too long. Bacon and eggs cries out for brown sauce. Not like across the pond, where they smother pancakes with syrup for breakfast."

McNulty waited until he'd swallowed. "It is pretty sickly. What they eat over there." He considered mentioning the size of the portions, but that didn't seem appropriate while eating a ten-inch flat cake. He swilled down the latest mouthful with a drink of tea instead.

His phone began to vibrate in his pocket, and the James Bond Theme filled the room. He gave an embarrassed smile, wiped his mouth, then answered the call. He didn't recognise the number, so he simply said, "Hello?"

"Hello? Is that all you've got to say after leading us down the garden path?"

"I'm not down the garden path."

Tynan laughed down the phone. "You're not at the Hyde Park Picture House either, but you were there the other night."

McNulty took a deep breath and let it out slowly. "So were you. I saw you on the telly."

"Seems like we've both been on the news. I just saw your grand entrance at Manchester Airport. What *did* you say to the cameraman?"

"Can't you lip-read?"

"No, but I can guess."

"What if I was to say the same to you? I'm having breakfast."

"Telling me to fuck off wouldn't be your best idea right now."

McNulty let out a sigh. "I haven't had a best idea for

years. But I'm going to come over and see you. You still at Ecclesfield?"

"No. Incident room at Brotherton House. Leeds."

"Okay. There's something I've got to do first, though."

"You know I'm still going to come after you."

McNulty nodded. "I know." Then he hung up.

** * **

Bill Baildon watched Tynan's shoulders sag. "Well?"

"He told me to fuck off."

"Really?"

"Not in so many words, but yes."

"It was the right number then."

Tynan had spent most of the night debriefing the PSU and firearms officers and the rest of the night making calls across the Atlantic. Finding Titanic Productions had been easy enough, but getting hold of Larry Unger was a whole other level of difficult. Tynan had finally got through to the movie producer half an hour ago, Tynan doing calculations in his head to subtract five hours for US East Coast time. It turned out that movie producers never sleep. Unger even tried to recruit Tynan as technical advisor in case McNulty didn't make it back. Then he gave McNulty's number.

"That Larry Unger is a piece of work."

Baildon shrugged. "Maybe you should take him up on it."

"I don't want to be a technical advisor. I want to arrest villains."

"So does McNulty."

Tynan nodded. "That's the problem. He still thinks he's a cop."

"Cop? You've been talking to Hollywood too long."

"Titanic Productions is a long way from Hollywood."

Baildon was on coffee and doughnuts again. "So we're still looking for McNulty then."

Tynan shook his head at the offered doughnut. "He's in Mean Wood somewhere. I'll bet my pension on that. But nobody in Mean Wood is going to tell us where."

Baildon licked his fingers. "I'll start with Donkey Flowers' known associates."

Tynan thought about the small gap between the parked cars outside Donk's house. "Yes. And see if you can find out how many small cars are registered on the estate."

* * *

McNulty got in the Fiat 500 and was amazed that even Eric Hugunin could fit behind the wheel. The car was so small you'd have to open the door to change gear. McNulty thanked Donk again and told him to keep a low profile. The police wouldn't be the only people looking for them.

Donk rested a hand on the roof of the car. "No worries. People on the estate have an aversion to anybody asking questions."

McNulty craned his neck to look up from the driver's seat. "They have an aversion to broken fingers, too. These fellas don't play nice."

"Noted. I won't go out for any more sandwiches."

McNulty closed the door and felt even more cramped. The Fiat started on the first go, and McNulty plotted a course toward Halcyon Court. It had been a long time since he'd done any driving in England, but he adjusted to driving on the left fairly quickly. What he didn't adjust to was the route to Cliff Road. He had taken two wrong turns and one dead end before he was on the Ring Road heading west. He was about to turn left toward Headingley when his phone buzzed again. James Bond was muted by his seatbelt. Another number he didn't know.

"Yes?"

"Is that Vincent McNulty?"

McNulty recognised the voice from the care home. It was Maggie. "Yes."

There was a pause down the line and a sigh. Maggie's voice quivered. "I'm sorry to have to say this over the phone. Doreen passed away in her sleep."

Chapter Thirty-Four

The Fiat skidded to a stop in a bus layby opposite Lawnswood Grammar School. Three days ago, McNulty couldn't have given a tuppeny fuck if Doreen Wills had died in her sleep, but having shared fish and chips with the woman, she was now more real than anything he had known before. Up until now, he hadn't had a mother. Up until now, he'd known nothing about his father. Now that those doors were beginning to open, they were slammed shut in the cruellest possible way. On his way for a chat at Costa Coffee.

McNulty turned the engine off and listened to the ticking as the metal cooled. McNulty didn't cool. He was hot and angry and close to tears. He squeezed the steering wheel until his knuckles were white. What was he going to do now? He let out a sigh and made the only sensible choice. He started the car and set off for a coffee. Minus the chat.

* * *

Costa Coffee Horsforth was sandwiched between Greggs Bakery and Daniel Hayton Opticians on Horsforth Town Street. The parade of shops was only part of a shopping street that included a Morrison's Supermarket, a Bet Fred, two toyshops, and every other kind of independent shop you'd expect to see on a village High Street. Horsforth wasn't so much a village as a suburb of Leeds, but it maintained the village feel by having a country park and tables outside the restaurants. Costa wasn't a restaurant, but there were still tables under the familiar red canopy despite it being autumn. This was Yorkshire. People were used to cold weather.

McNulty paused at a slanted parking bay outside Costa, but the faded lettering marked it as a Disabled space. He continued down the one-way street until he found an empty spot just past the Post Office. During his time in uniform, he had driven through Horsforth but never worked there. It had always seemed like a low-crime area compared to Bradford or Leeds. He had wanted to catch criminals, so he'd gravitated toward the busier places. Thieves and shitbags didn't populate Horsforth Town Street.

McNulty sat in the car and wondered why he was there. Without his mother, there was no reason to walk the street he had never visited and no information to be gleaned from the woman who wasn't here. There was nothing to be gained at all. Apart from an understanding of what made his mother tick. The things that made her smile, apart from fish and chips. Maggie had told him Doreen always smiled when she talked about having coffee at Costa.

McNulty let out a sigh and got out of the car.

A single-decker bus eased down the street, mindful of the ageing pedestrians crossing the road. It waited patiently while a car with a disabled badge made hard work of reversing into the parking space McNulty had ignored. A barista wearing the same colours as the Costa canopy cleared the outside tables.

McNulty waited for the bus to pass, then set off walking up the street. Every other shop on his side was a charity shop until he passed the toy shop. He glanced at the window displays to distract himself from the place he was really heading for. Eventually, there were no more shops, just restaurants and a dance gym. He stood with his back to the gym, then crossed the road.

Soft music and friendly faces welcomed him into Costa. McNulty stood in the doorway and scanned the interior. There were tables along the right-hand wall and a serving station and display counter along the left. There were three tables in the window, two along the front and one wedged up against the display counter. The one in the left-hand corner was beneath a circular laurel leaf sign on the wall.

A VERY

WARM WELCOME

TO

HORSFORTH

It was the very warm welcome that Doreen used to enjoy, according to Maggie. The table under the sign was her favourite seat. As if by destiny, the seat was empty, so McNulty draped his coat over the chair and went to the counter. The barista took his order and said she'd bring the latte and tiffin to the table. McNulty had only ordered the chocolate-coated biscuit because he remembered the scene in *Carry On Up The Khyber* where Sid James had tiffin in the afternoon, tiffin being something else altogether. He had never seen tiffin on offer in a coffee shop.

He sat in his mother's seat and looked out of the window. For some reason, he felt a warm glow inside, as if he were revisiting a familiar haunt from a past that didn't exist. He had never been here with his mother. He had never felt the very warm welcome to Horsforth, but he did now. The barista smiled and put the tray on the table. McNulty stirred three sugars into his latte, a weak milky coffee he only ordered because he didn't drink coffee. At least with three sugars, this just tasted like a hot, sweet drink.

"Doreen passed away in her sleep." The words washed over him like a receding echo. He took a drink of coffee and didn't taste anything. He looked out of the window and didn't see anything. He felt lost and alone, like a boy in an orphanage who had just had his lifeline withdrawn. Every child at Crag View had secretly held the hope that their mother would come for them one day. It was never the father, always the mother. Like keeping a candle in the window, it was hope that fanned the eternal flame. And now the candle had gone out.

Pull yourself together, man, McNulty told himself. *Grow up.* But McNulty had never really grown up; he would always be the lost boy in the orphanage. He watched the world go by outside the window and felt completely disconnected from it. Little old ladies pulled wheelie shopping bags. Pre-school age children held their parents' hands. Retired couples smiled or argued, but were always together.

McNulty took a bite of tiffin just so he could feel something. The chocolate melted in his mouth. The biscuit crumbled, and the raisins chewed. He wondered if Sid James had ever realised what he was missing by having afternoon sex instead of chocolate. He swilled the biscuit down with milky coffee, then repeated the routine. He could understand why his mother enjoyed sitting here. She would have felt less alone. As McNulty ate and drank, he began to feel less alone himself.

Whatever he had hoped to learn was lost forever. Whoever his father had been would be a mystery. Maybe he'd find a few things out at Halcyon Court. He still couldn't believe he was expected to go there again since he hardly knew his mother. But Maggie had insisted, after apologising again for breaking the news over the phone.

"You can come and collect her things whenever you're ready."

"Collect them, why?"

Maggie had sounded affronted. "Because you're her next of kin."

McNulty had struggled to talk and drive, the Fiat 500 seeming to have a mind of its own. "I hardly knew her. How can I be next of kin?"

Maggie huffed down the line. "Well, she knew you. She made you next of kin years ago. Before dementia took away her faculties."

Chapter Thirty-Five

"Why the fuck is he going back there?"

"Because one of the staff phoned him."

Frank Gardner tried to be rational. "The woman died in her sleep."

The watcher was only passing on what he'd been told. "Apparently, she made McNulty her next of kin."

"She's got dementia. She can't sign shit."

The watcher was glad he was doing this over the phone. "A few years ago. Before she lost her marbles."

"She knew about McNulty all the way back then?"

"She knew about him always. Kept a diary and everything. For when she wasn't around anymore."

"A diary?"

The watcher played the dementia card. "It's not up to date."

"It's not the now I'm worried about. It's the before."

The watcher kept quiet. Before the line went dead, he reckoned he could hear Gardner's phone being thrown across the office.

* * *

Frank Gardner told himself once again that he wasn't an

angry man, and once again, he wasn't convincing anybody. He also told himself that there was nothing to worry about. He wasn't convinced about that either. If Doreen Wills had written anything important in her diary, then the fact that she'd passed away before letting anything slip to McNulty was the least of Gardner's worries. He pressed the green light. The door opened.

"I need a new phone."

His secretary nodded and went to the stationery cupboard. Five minutes later, Gardner had a new phone and somebody else to call. A couple of somebody else's. The first call was to Gardner's eyes and ears on Mean Wood. He knew that the police had drawn a blank trying to find McNulty last night, but the police didn't have Gardner's resources. Or his intimidation factor. Twenty minutes later, he knew where McNulty was staying and what car Donkey Flowers had procured for him. Gardner was surprised that the circus midget was still living in Leeds after his short-lived career as a porn star in Xtreme North's torture videos. Being a witness to some of Gardner's excesses wasn't good for your health. Now that Hugunin was helping McNulty, it gave Gardner another reason to terminate the midget's contract. Permanently. Pity. They had been good videos.

The second call was more succinct.

"Yellow Fiat 500. Registration number…" He read out the number.

"Cliff Road, Headingley."

* * *

McNulty left a healthy tip on the table and nodded at the

barista so she knew it was there. He was surprised how therapeutic watching the world go by from his mother's favourite seat had been. Some of that was the unthreatening nature of a milky coffee and a chocolate tiffin. Some of it was the relaxed way in which the shoppers on Town Street went about their business. But mostly it was sitting under the WARM WELCOME TO HORSFORTH sign with his back to the wall.

The sun had moved across the sky by the time he crossed the road, and the Fiat was in the shadows. Stepping out of bright sunlight into the shade made the interior feel even smaller and darker. McNulty was carrying enough darkness himself. He didn't need any more. He started the engine and pulled into the light. The gleaming yellow bonnet almost blinded him when he reached the sunny side of the street. The joyous colour made him feel even more relaxed. It felt strange, feeling glad to be alive on such a terrible day, but something Maggie had said touched him in a place he was rarely touched. In his heart.

"Well, she knew you."

After all these years of feeling abandoned, McNulty felt a touch of hope. Not hope that his mother would take him away from Crag View, that boat had sailed long ago, but a possibility that he hadn't been completely abandoned after all. He was a long way from reconciling his feelings about that, but coffee and tiffin was a start.

He reached the bottom of Town Street and turned left toward the Ring Road. Left again at the lights and he was heading back to where he'd started, West Park roundabout and a right turn toward Headingley. Halcyon Court was a short hop from Headingley. It was a short hop that McNulty wasn't going to make.

* * *

Ninety per cent of road traffic accidents are caused by driver error. The rest are either mechanical failure or road conditions: potholes, snow, ice or fog. Since Police Driver Training said you should only drive according to the conditions, that meant even those accidents were actually driver error. You should have seen the pothole, snow, ice, or fog and driven accordingly. That's why the police had reclassified RTAs to RTCs, Road Traffic Collisions, since every accident involved a vehicle on a road colliding with something. The Fiat 500 didn't collide with anything it was collided into. Even then, it wasn't driver error. It was driver intension.

McNulty took the turn at the bottom of Cliff Road nice and slow. The little yellow car didn't like taking corners too fast. He always felt like it was going to tip over. McNulty didn't want to tip over, so he'd driven through Headingley at a snail's pace, taking every corner like an old woman. He wasn't embarrassed. Old women seemed to be his raison d'etre at the moment.

The trees were bare at the bottom of the road, the naked branches reminding McNulty that he still had the tattoo on his neck, the wicked black fingers of the tree that in turn reminded McNulty of Crag View. He had had the tattoo done when he was young so he wouldn't forget the hellhole of his childhood. He was unlikely to forget that. Mr Cruckshank and the Bible would always be in the back of his mind.

It wasn't in the forefront of his mind as he drove the final lap to Halcyon Court, he was thinking about the leaves on the road. Another example of road conditions was wet leaves reducing your breaking distance. Kids loved wading through fallen leaves when they were dry, but leaves become slippery when wet. McNulty slowed even more as he passed Endecliff Mews, a modern development on the spare land opposite Woodhouse Moor. He was concentrating on the leaves, not Endecliff Mews. That might have constituted driver error since Endecliff Mews was where the big yellow bulldozer was parked.

The Fiat 500 waded through the leaves. McNulty kept his eyes on the ground to make sure there weren't any dead branches amid the debris. A delivery truck reversed out of Cross Cliff Road and blocked the road. So fast and unexpected that McNulty had to slam on the brakes. The Fiat skidded. The delivery truck kept reversing, closing the distance. The Fiat slid into the bulky tailgate and stopped. Right opposite Endecliff Mews.

The bulldozer didn't wait for McNulty to get out and argue with the driver. It shot straight out of the Mews and slammed the Fiat with its dozer blade. The teeth cut through the already damaged passenger door. The leaves gave McNulty no traction. The delivery truck reversed some more. The bulldozer pushed the Fiat across the road into a huge oak tree. The solid tree trunk trapped McNulty between a rock and a hard place. It didn't matter which was which. The Fiat was crushed. McNulty's lights went out.

Chapter Thirty-Six

The beeping noises sounded like they were coming from a long way away. They were almost as distant as the voices that were so faded McNulty couldn't make out any words, only the urgent tone. The world was dark and full of pain. The beeping was a dull, regular beat. It matched the slow pulse of pain, which seemed to rise and fall with each breath he took.

Breath? At least I'm breathing. That's got to be a good thing, right? He tried to open his eyes, but the lids felt like they were gummed shut. That would account for the darkness but not the pain. Then he remembered the accident, and his eyes flew open. The world was only marginally brighter. He was in a darkened room with a single light coming through the blinds from the corridor. The hospital curtains weren't drawn, but it was dark outside. There was no sign of a clock to see what time it was, but it was obviously a long time after coffee and tiffin.

McNulty tried to sit up. The pain told him to stay down. And something else. He lifted his left wrist. He was handcuffed to the bed.

* * *

"You're a wanted man." That was in response to McNulty asking about the handcuffs.

"I reckon I'm right popular." That was McNulty not giving Tynan an inch.

"Yeah, but you're not Josie Wales."

"And you're not the weaselly rat-fuck who tried to shoot him in the saloon either."

"Oh, I can be a rat-fuck if I need to be. Do I need to be?"

McNulty had been rushed to A&E at Leeds General Infirmary after the fire brigade had cut him out of the car. The delivery truck had fled the scene of the accident, but the bulldozer was still wedged into the side of the Fiat 500. It had taken half an hour to ease the bulldozer backwards and another forty minutes to uncrush the crushed Fiat. That had entailed removing both doors, then cutting the roof off. The steering column hadn't been forced into the driver space quite as much as it would have with a front-end collision. Since the car had been smashed from the side, it was just a narrower version of the already narrow Fiat.

The ambulance had blue-lighted to the nearest Accident & Emergency at the LGI, which was barely three miles away in the city centre. The helicopter pad on the roof was noisy as another accident victim was airlifted in. McNulty had been unaware of any of it. He had been conscious but not exactly compos mentis. Things were happening around him, but not to him. Except it was. And it hurt. They say that pain focuses the mind. For McNulty, it closed his mind down.

The next thing he remembered was waking up in the darkened room. Handcuffed to the bed. With DS Tynan leaning over him. Josie Wales had never been handcuffed to a bed. Clint Eastwood had never been handcuffed anywhere.

"Are you going to read me my rights?"

"You already know your rights."

"I know you've still got to caution me."

"If you were under arrest."

McNulty rattled the handcuffs.

Tynan smiled. "Let's talk about that."

* * *

Talking about that took almost an hour, Tynan doing most of the talking. McNulty trying his best not to react. His best wasn't very good. "You've got to be fucking kidding."

"It's not a boilerplate plan. One size fits all."

"It's not a plan at all. It's suicide."

"Only if the fellas in the alley had really wanted to do you harm."

McNulty gave Tynan a knowing look. "They had a knuckleduster and a flick knife."

Tynan wagged a finger. "The other fella had a gun. And he was very good with it."

"Not helping."

Tynan slipped the handcuffs in his pocket. "Look at it this way. It means I don't think you were the man with the gun."

That was a positive, McNulty couldn't deny it, but the downside was far more dangerous. The basic outline was this. The three men in the alley had been identified as known associates of Frank Gardner. Gardner had taken over and expanded Northern X, rebranding it as Xtreme North but doing much the same, only on a bigger scale. There had been rumours, but very little intelligence to prove the link between Xtreme North and the string of exotic girls being imported from abroad. The sex industry had moved away from bricks-and-mortar massage parlours and gone online. It was a case of supply and demand. Demand hadn't gone away, just the means of fulfilling it. Gardner was filling a void. And taking it underground.

Until now, Gardner hadn't raised his head above the parapet, keeping such a low profile that bankers in the city thought he was a legitimate businessman. He had investors from every walk of life, from pension funds to royalty. Some said he even had an heir to the throne on his books. Bottom line was, Gardner was untouchable. A man of the moment making big money from other people's suffering. The suffering belonged to the exotic girls imported from abroad. There would be no missing person reports because nobody knew they were in the country.

Tynan circled back to the low-profile part. The parapet. Gardner hadn't so much as got a parking ticket since taking over from Telfon Speed. He had been keeping his head down. Until McNulty had been seen on the news telling a cameraman to fuck off, and Gardner's known associates had trashed McNulty's hotel room looking for the ex-vice squad cop. The associates had come up short when they'd cornered McNulty in the alley behind Hyde Park Picture House.

"They didn't corner me. I caught a bus."

Tynan nodded. "You're the only person knows that."

"Donk knows."

"We're looking for Donk."

McNulty smiled. "You haven't found him, though."

"That's not a smiling matter. I doubt we're the only people looking for him."

McNulty stopped smiling. "And me?"

"Full circle. Gardner sticks his head up. We cut it off. QED."

"More heads will spring up."

"Not if we shut down the body."

"Xtreme North sounds like a bigger body."

"The bigger they are, the harder they fall."

McNulty let out a sigh. The sigh hurt his ribs, which were tightly strapped to avoid the cracks from flexing. He also had numerous cuts and bruises to his face and shoulders, and stitches in at least three cuts that were too big for butterfly dressings.

"And you want to stake me out as bait."

"For Gardner, you're very enticing bait. You're the man who killed his boss and shut down his business."

"Doesn't seem like it's shut down."

"It went from Cool Runnings to Titanic hits an iceberg. That's a huge bump in the road. Believe me. He's pissed off at you."

"Yeah, well, I'm thinking more Jurassic Park."

"Jurassic Park?"

"The goat they staked out for the T-rex."

"Haven't seen it."

"Well, when you do. Pay attention to what happened to the goat. Because I'm the goat."

* * *

The T-rex took the call but didn't smash his phone this time. This time, the news was exactly what he wanted.

"He isn't dead?"

"No. Jubilee Wing at the LGI."

"Good."

Gardner had his own reasons for not wanting McNulty to read the old woman's diary, but having McNulty killed wasn't part of the plan. People got injured in car crashes all the time, but fatal accidents always drew more attention. There would be road safety forums and bereavement counselling, and in a high-profile case like McNulty—who could still be considered a minor celebrity after the news coverage of Northern X— there would be unwanted media attention. Gardner didn't want any media attention. He wanted to keep this on the hush-hush.

"Let me know when they discharge him."

Then he hung up and sat looking out of his window.

Chapter Thirty-Seven

The real fly in Frank Gardner's ointment was a tenacious Detective Sergeant. Tynan might have been setting McNulty up for the fall, but it was a fall with purpose. McNulty had been a detective himself in a former life; he would understand. That was Tynan's justification for tethering the goat. That all changed when he heard the bad news from the goat himself.

"I thought you were an orphan."

"Even orphans have mothers." McNulty hadn't always believed that, but if the last few days had proved anything, it was that change was possible.

Tynan's demeanour went from hard-nosed detective to concerned citizen in a flash. "I'm sorry for your loss."

"Did you get that from an American cop show?"

"Cop?"

"Police."

"Get what?"

"I'm sorry for your loss. I thought over here it was, 'My condolences.'"

"The news didn't break you up then?"

"Like you said. I'm an orphan. I'm already broken."

Tynan let out a sigh. "Well, anyway. I'm sorry. Overnight,

you say?"

"Died in her sleep."

Tynan nodded. "I'll take that. When it's my time."

"Sex on a beach for me."

Tynan snorted a laugh. "Not watching Where Eagles Dare?"

"After watching Where Eagles Dare."

* * *

That was as sensitive as it got. After a few more questions about whether McNulty was okay, Tynan showed he was a true detective.

"So you spent some time with her yesterday?"

"Fish and chips and a brief moment of clarity."

"Clarity, how?"

McNulty shrugged. "My dad used too much salt on his food."

"I thought you were an orphan." Tynan repeating himself. "And all of a sudden you've got a mother *and* a father.

"They usually come in pairs. I just didn't know who mine were."

"But you do now."

"I know one died in her sleep, and the other likes salt."

"That's a bit insensitive."

"I'm feeling insensitive. I get a message out of the blue that my mum's in a care home, then before she can say why she abandoned me, she passes away."

Tynan was still thinking like a detective. "You were on your way to see her this morning?"

"I got the news halfway there."

"But you were still going to Halcyon Court."

"Yes."

"When a stolen bulldozer rams into the side of your car."

"It was stolen?"

Tynan nodded. "Building site at West Park. The delivery truck didn't hang around for the police."

"Hit and run?"

"Block the road to wedge you in, then hit and run."

McNulty was beginning to think like a detective, too. "On the way to clear my mum's effects."

"Which are still at Halcyon Court."

McNulty straightened up in bed. The pain and the strapping meant it wasn't very straight. "She was a little old lady."

"She wasn't always. And you don't believe in coincidence any more than I do."

McNulty did some thinking of his own. Out loud. "I get run off the road the day after three men follow me into the alley. Somebody shoots the three men in the alley, but nobody saves me from the bulldozer."

Tynan continued the thread. "The three men in the alley weren't trying to stop you getting to Halcyon Court."

"They might have been."

Tynan shook his head. "No. They were after you because of Northern X."

McNulty nodded. "Which has nothing to do with my mum."

"But the bulldozer was."

McNulty let out a sigh. "Seems like a bit of a stretch."

"Stretch is what we do."

"And you want me to stretch my neck out."

"That would be, stick your neck out. But yes."

"Because you don't believe in coincidences any more than I do. And we both know the shooting and the bulldozer are connected."

"We just don't know how."

"Except somebody didn't want me seeing my mum's things."

"So you need to go see your mum's things. ASAP."

"I'm in hospital."

"You'll live."

"Not if somebody else tries to shoot me."

"They didn't try to shoot you. They shot the people who wanted to shoot you."

"With a flick knife and a knuckleduster?"

"Figure of speech. Bottom line. You're drawing a lot of heat."

McNulty shifted his position. The worst of the pain seemed to be easing, but he was still stiff and sore. "I know."

"No way Gardner isn't connected."

"No way."

"So we need to do some more stretching."

McNulty tested his stretching. That didn't seem to be easing. "Ouch."

Tynan looked at the whiteboard above McNulty's bed. The template had, The Leeds Teaching Hospitals NHS across the top, then sections for, Patient's Name, Preferred Name, Consultant, and Named Nurse. He read the information.

Patient's Name: Vincent McNulty

Preferred Name: Vince

Consultant: T2

Named Nurse: Green Team

It didn't give any details about the timescale, so Tynan had to ask. "When's the next doctor's rounds?"

McNulty flexed a little more and sat up straight. He pressed the call button on the side of the bed. "I'm not waiting for the next doctor's rounds."

Chapter Thirty-Eight

Cliff Road was dark and foreboding, the streetlamps spaced out and mostly hidden by giant oak and ash trees that should have been trimmed years ago. McNulty wasn't sure if it was pressure about the environment or laziness from the council, but the trees were perfect cover for anybody lying in wait. Halcyon Court was a beacon of light at the end of the tunnel. McNulty didn't feel like he was anywhere near the end of the tunnel.

"You sure you don't want a lift?"

McNulty appreciated the offer but had turned Tynan down. "If Gardner's going to come out from under his rock, he isn't going to do it if I'm in a police car."

"He isn't going to come out tonight. He's going to have somebody come out for him."

"Same thing applies. Not if they see you dropping me off."

McNulty had met Tynan halfway, accepting a lift to Woodhouse Moor but then walking the rest of the way. It was almost ten o'clock and long past visiting time, but Maggie had made an exception over the phone. Doreen's room hadn't been sanitized yet. They hadn't bagged her belongings.

Tynan had tried one last time. "You sure you don't want me to come with you?"

McNulty hadn't wanted to tell Tynan the real reason he needed to do this alone; he wasn't sure how he was going to feel seeing his mother's room. The last thing he needed was a witness to his discomfort. "I'll be fine."

Then he had closed the car door, tapped the roof, and crossed Woodhouse Moor toward the dark and foreboding street.

* * *

McNulty stood in the shadows beneath one of the untrimmed oak trees and watched Halcyon court. The frontage was even more impressive after dark, discreet spotlights highlighting the ornate carvings and intricate architecture of a bygone era. The front door was locked and bolted. Nobody used the main gates of Colditz. Nobody was lying in wait among the trees.

McNulty scanned the windows along the front and down the side toward the rear car park. The lights were on in almost every room. The corridors were brightly lit. The only movement was staff putting the residents to bed or clearing the dining room after supper. There was no traffic in Cliff Road. Nobody was visiting the Wat Buddharam Temple across the road or the detached houses at the end of the cul-de-sac. McNulty had the street to himself. It felt peaceful.

There was very little peace in McNulty's head. His heart thumped in his chest, and his mind was racing. Whatever Frank Gardner hadn't wanted McNulty to see was secondary to what McNulty himself didn't want to see. His mother's final resting place. The poky little bedroom where she had spent her dying years. He took a deep breath, checked the shadows one last time, then walked down the side of the building to the visitors' entrance round the back.

* * *

Frank Gardner didn't throw his phone across the room this time, not because he was happy about the news but because he was at home. Nobody ever called him at home unless it was urgent. He didn't have a mobile phone. Security. Too many opportunities for eavesdropping. This was urgent.

"He's back." The watcher sounded nervous despite having apologised for calling so late. The last couple of phone calls hadn't been well-received.

Gardner stood in the entrance hall of a house that could rival Halcyon Court for its ornate frontage but far surpassed it with its plush interior. The telephone was the old-fashioned Bakelite type, wired to the wall and designed to replicate the 1930s style with a separate receiver cradled on the neck of the handset. If he was in a playful mood, he would flick the earpiece off the stalk and catch it before saying, "City desk." Paying homage to those black and white newspaper movies where everyone had a snappy retort. He wasn't feeling playful.

"Alone?"

"Yes. He walked up from Hyde Park Corner."

"No car?"

"His car got totalled."

Gardner gripped the handset until the whites of his knuckles showed, but kept his voice calm. "Did anybody drop him off?"

"No."

"Good. Tell me when he leaves. Whatever the time."

Gardner hung the earpiece on the cradle and put the phone down. His only concern was why the hospital watcher hadn't reported McNulty being discharged. McNulty visiting Halcyon Court was inevitable, and, in a way, necessary. He wouldn't fly back to America until he'd settled his mother's estate. Now that Salino had retrieved the diary, Doreen Wills' estate didn't amount to much. There was certainly no threat any more.

Gardner let out a sigh then flicked the cradle. The phone pinged then fell silent. He smiled and whispered, "City desk. Hold the front page."

* * *

The judicious use of air freshener was still fighting a losing battle against the smell of voided bowels and antiseptic. A different receptionist told McNulty to sign in and list who he was visiting.

"Doreen Wills."

The woman looked up and gave McNulty a sad little smile. "Oh, I'm so sorry. Doreen was a lovely woman. We're going to miss her."

McNulty tried to keep his breathing smooth and even. "Thank you."

The woman picked up the phone. "Maggie is expecting you. I'll just give her a call."

McNulty stood at the glass door looking out at the car park. He wondered if Gladys had given up looking for her car or if it was a recurring scenario, a kind of Groundhog Day in a care home. Then he realised he looked just as dazed and confused standing at the window looking into the night. He turned back but was confronted with the corridor that led to the pink room, the Tea Room that was designed to make visitors and residents feel at ease in the pastel colours. McNulty didn't feel at ease. He felt like turning tail and running.

The lift gave a musical bing-bong like a microwave, and the doors slid open. Maggie kept her foot against the door and waved McNulty over. She didn't speak. She looked as if she'd been crying. McNulty felt like putting an arm around her, but knew that was highly inappropriate. He'd never consoled a bereaved care home worker before.

Maggie stepped aside to let McNulty enter, then let the doors close. She pressed the button for the second floor and let out a sigh. "I'm sorry you didn't get more time with her. She was looking forward to a coffee at Costa."

McNulty nodded. "I was, too."

"It's always hard. Letting them go."

"You must get that a lot."

"Too much. I sometimes think I'm in the wrong line of work."

McNulty still wanted to put his arms around her. "You make people's lives better. And you're good at it. I could see that with mum. She might not have understood what was going on, but she knew how to smile. I'd say you're in the right line of work."

"Thank you. This part is always the worst. Clearing the room. I'll never get used to it."

"You should never get used to it. That would mean you've stopped caring."

The lift jerked to a stop even though it had been travelling so slow McNulty felt he wasn't moving at all. It gave the little bing-bong, and the doors slid open. Maggie led the way along the corridor. It was long and straight with doors on either side. Each door had a nametag in a pastel coloured frame. Most of the doors were open, lights shining into the corridor.

Maggie saw McNulty's curious look. "They aren't allowed to close their doors on this floor. The night staff need to be able to see inside. Until lights out." She checked her watch. "Which isn't long now."

They walked along the corridor, McNulty glancing into each room as he passed. The rooms were small and narrow with a sash window against the outside wall. There was a door in the far corner, presumably a bathroom, and a television cabinet on the right. The televisions were blaring out inane quiz shows or soap operas on repeat. The beds were partly hidden behind the door. Some of the rooms smelled stronger than others. None of them smelled nice.

McNulty felt his shoulders begin to sag the further he walked. His breath was coming in short, shallow breaths. Borderline hyperventilating. He tried to slow his breathing to regulate his heartbeat. His pulse sounded loud in his ears. Maggie stopped outside the last room on the right. It was the only room with a closed door. The pastel frame still had the nametag.

DOREEN WILLS

McNulty was struggling to breathe. His chin trembled. Maggie stepped in close and put her arm around him, and gave him a little squeeze. Role reversal, only she did a better job than McNulty, who hadn't done anything at all to comfort Maggie. She rubbed his back, then stepped aside.

"I'll let you have some time to yourself. When you're ready press the call button. I'll bring you some bin liners."

Maggie turned and walked back along the corridor. Mc-

Nulty found himself wishing she would stay with him, but then pulled himself together. He didn't want anyone with him. He didn't want anyone to see him cry. He took a deep breath and prepared himself for the narrow cubicle where his mother had spent her final years. He opened the door and stepped inside.

He froze in the doorway. His breath came in one big gulp. This wasn't a narrow little cubicle. This was a mink-lined prison.

Chapter Thirty-Nine

McNulty had had this feeling before, stepping out of one world into a completely different one. When he had entered the derelict factory on Southside Industrial Estate, only to find the plush interior of Northern X's torture sex reception. This wasn't quite as dramatic, but it was equally disconcerting. The rooms along the corridor had been small and rundown. There was barely enough room to swing a cat around. Doreen Wills had been living in a palace.

McNulty closed the door behind him and let out a long, slow breath. The room was the same length as the other bedrooms but three times as wide. There were two big windows instead of the single sash window, and the bathroom door was smoked glass and chrome. There were built-in wardrobes, floor-to-ceiling bookshelves, and enough fitted furniture to make IKEA jealous. The smooth edges and sand coloured worktops belonged in a high-end hotel suite.

There were two easy chairs and a coffee table, as well as a drop-leaf dining table near the window. A wicker laundry basket stood in one corner, and a matching wastepaper basket stood in the other. The bed was an expensive orthopaedic version, not the basic models used in hospitals and care homes.

It was the bed that made McNulty gasp.

The room was clean and tidy, but the bed was unmade. The duvet was half off to one side, and the pillows were strewn across the mattress. This was his mother's last resting place, and it looked anything but restful. McNulty had dealt with plenty of sudden deaths and death warnings during his uniform days; he recognised the last-minute urgency that surrounded such occasions. The only difference here was there were no discarded medical supplies or emergency dressings. Doreen had died in her sleep. There had been no attempt to resuscitate her. She was probably on a DNR order anyway. No, this was what dying in your sleep looked like. One minute you're breathing, and the next minute you're not. The dishevelled bed was just the result of removing the body.

McNulty slumped into one of the chairs and closed his eyes. He took several deep breaths, then opened them again. Something glinted under the bed. Several somethings. He got down on one knee for a closer look. There were half a dozen golden Twix wrappers and two or three Werther's Original toffee wrappers. A couple of screwed up tissues. A gold locket and chain was mixed in with the wrappers. He reached out and scooped it up with several Twix wrappers. He sifted the wrappers aside and dropped them in the wastepaper basket, then held the locket up to the light. It was heavy, with a thick-link chain. Solid gold, not plated. Eighteen-carat, not rolled gold.

He flicked the locket open and gasped again.

Neither of the two faces that stared back at him bore any resemblance to the woman he'd had fish and chips with yesterday. The other face he didn't recognise anyway. A man. Possibly a salt lover. His father? McNulty scrutinised the slim, handsome face to see if there was any family likeness. He tried to remember what he looked like at that age, around thirty. The photo was black and white, so he couldn't tell if the man had blue eyes. He did share the chiselled jaw and prominent cheekbones, and the hairline was similar, but in a combed-back style, not a side parting. A straight nose and full lips.

McNulty shook his head. He wasn't ready to accept a father so soon after losing the mother he'd only just met. It probably wasn't him anyway. Salt or no salt. He clicked the locket shut and stood up. To distract himself, he began to tidy the bed. He remembered somebody telling him about an American admiral giving a speech about bed making; it might have been Jim Grant. The admiral had said that if you wanted to change the world, first you had to make your bed. Having accomplished that task, you could then complete another task. And another.

McNulty set out to accomplish that first task. He smoothed out the bottom sheet and straightened the duvet. He tucked the bottom of the duvet into the foot of the bed. He picked up the first pillow and placed it carefully against the headboard, then picked up the second. He paused for a moment, looking at the indentation in the middle of the first pillow. The pillows were made of memory foam, and the shape of his mother's head was clearly visible. The place where she had slept every night. He thought about smoothing the pillow out, but didn't want to remove the last sign of her existence.

He took a deep breath, the second pillow dangling from one hand. He let out a sigh and was about to lay the second pillow on the first when he noticed that the second pillow had an indentation in exactly the same place. He placed it over the lower pillow, indentation face down, and the dents matched. There were also two smaller indentations on the top of the pillow, either side of the main dent, but on the opposite side.

A shiver ran down McNulty's spine. He scanned the duvet. There were several scuffmarks on the wall beside the bed, most of them old and faded. Three of them looked fresh, three parallel scratch marks that had scraped the paint off. He flipped the duvet open and ran his hands over the bottom sheet. Nothing. He pulled the bed away from the wall and leaned forward. There was something else down there among the Twix wrappers and Werther's Originals.

He pulled the bed out further and reached down. The three broken fingernails were small and neatly trimmed. The nail polish was plain and pink, not garish or showy. An old woman's colour. McNulty didn't remake the bed. He failed at the first task and took out his phone instead.

Tynan answered at the first ring.

McNulty struggled to keep his voice from trembling. "She didn't die in her sleep."

Chapter Forty

Some decisions are easy, and some are not so obvious. Generally, when you're a cop, you get the easy decisions. The obvious choices. Bad people do bad things. It's fairly straightforward to bring those bad people to justice. Sometimes there is a lot of hard work involved, a lot of man hours and a lot of effort, but the decisions are easy. They did bad things. They're going to pay, one way or another. Sometimes justice was within the system. Sometimes you had to take a roundabout route. Summary justice. A bang on the head when the prisoner is getting into the car. A few bumps and bruises when the prisoner is resisting arrest.

Sometimes sacrifices had to be made for the greater good. To catch the bigger fish. Sometimes you had to wait for the bigger fish to stick its head above the parapet. But sometimes you had to force it.

* * *

"A massage? You think I'm interested in having a fucking massage?"

"He'll be watching you. He's been watching ever since you got off the plane."

"And you want him to see me have a massage?"

"He'll see you booking one of his girls as a threat. He'll have to respond."

This was after a lengthy and heated discussion about why McNulty shouldn't call the police. Tynan's argument being, "I am the police." His stronger argument was that if Gardner knew the police were looking into the death of Doreen Wills, he would go underground. He was already underground enough; Tynan didn't want him disappearing altogether. That didn't sit well with McNulty.

"They smashed me off the road so I wouldn't see her room. Because they knew I was a cop once and I'd see the clues."

"I don't think that was the reason. As far as they knew, the care home staff would have cleaned the room. Dented pillows would have been restored. The floor would have been vacuumed. Whatever they didn't want you to see, I think they took it while you were in hospital."

They were sitting in the easy chairs either side of the coffee table. Tynan had been smuggled in through the fire exit after McNulty had asked Maggie to keep it quiet, the fact that a detective wanted to see Doreen Wills' bedroom. They hadn't mentioned their suspicions about her death. As far as Maggie was concerned, this was a fraudulent claim case stemming from the fact that a little old lady had been able to afford such an expensive room.

"She wasn't paying for it herself."

That was the first fly in the ointment.

Tynan had asked the obvious question. "Who was paying?"

Maggie had looked embarrassed. "I can't tell you."

McNulty had put on his gentlest voice and patted Maggie's hand. "She's gone, Maggie. You can tell me anything."

"No, I mean it's privileged information. We can only give that information to the power of attorney."

"She made me next of kin before I even knew her."

"But she didn't give you power of attorney. You would both have had to sign."

"It's important."

Maggie had looked at the detective, then McNulty. "It's a police investigation. Can't you get a court order or something? I want to tell you, but I'd lose my job."

"Didn't she write it down somewhere? When she named me next of kin?"

Maggie had shrugged. "Maybe in her diary. When she could still remember things. She hasn't written in it for years."

That had prompted a frantic search of the cupboards and drawers. Apparently, the diary was always in the top drawer, but Doreen had been increasingly lax of late. She had even started throwing her rubbish under the bed instead of in the wastepaper basket. After checking all the usual places, they had searched the bathroom, the wardrobe, and the laundry basket. The diary wasn't there.

Tynan's comment later reflected that. *"Whatever they didn't want you to see, I think they took it while you were in hospital."*

Tynan's comment at the time had been more succinct. "She lost it?"

Maggie had shrugged again. "She lost a lot of things. We could never keep track of her clothes or her handbag or her…" Another embarrassed look. "Her underwear."

McNulty was beginning to have his own suspicions about who had been paying for his mother's upgraded care. He remembered sitting in the pastel coloured tearoom; Doreen saying, *"Frank will be so angry. Susie was his favourite. Best dog we ever had. I don't want to get Frank angry."* Something else popped into his mind as well. Something he hadn't thought of before.

He looked at Tynan. "She knew Frank Gardner."

Tynan gave McNulty a blank look. "That's a bit of a stretch."

"Stretch is what we do."

Tynan had considered that. "He'd be the right age. A few years older than your mum."

That had thrown McNulty into a tailspin. The thing that had been staring him in the face this whole time suddenly blinked, flashing lights at him. Doreen Wills had known Frank Gardner. Gardner was a few years older than her, the traditional age gap for men and women of that era. Ergo, Gardner was paying for Halcyon Court because of their relationship. McNulty wondered if Gardner liked salt on his fish and chips.

* * *

"A massage? You think I'm interested in having a fucking massage?"

And that brought them right back to the present.

Tynan said, "He'll be watching you. He's been watching ever since you got off the plane."

McNulty snorted a laugh. "And you want him to see me have a massage?"

"He'll see you booking one of his girls as a threat. He'll have to respond."

McNulty was still thinking about excessive salt with fish and chips, about a father who was complicit in dumping his son in an orphanage. His mind was still reeling even after

Maggie had left. He clawed his way back to the surface and tried to make the argument against booking another massage. It had been years since he used to visit massage parlours, so he could still feel like a vice squad cop. Once a cop, always a cop. It had worked for a while. Until Telfon Speed and Northern X.

"How do we know which girls are his?"

Tynan gave McNulty a look that said, *what kind of detective were you?* He lowered his voice as if the bedroom had ears. "Because it's all over the internet. The profiles, booking forms, everything. Xtreme North. Book an appointment here."

Chapter Forty-One

The door buzzed, then the lock clicked. McNulty opened the tinted glass door and stepped into a brightly lit entrance hall. There were mailboxes on the left-hand wall and a staircase on the right. A second door led to a corridor that ran the full length of the ground floor. The door clicked shut behind him.

McNulty had never booked a massage this late—it was way past midnight—he had always been a daytime customer. Massage parlours had long since given way to online escort services. He missed the comfort of having bricks-and-mortar premises, like visiting a store instead of shopping online. Standing here in the tiled entrance hall felt anything but comfortable. It felt more illicit somehow, not like visiting a professional masseuse.

He checked the text message for the apartment number, then pushed through the inner door.

* * *

Frank Gardner was way ahead of the caller, not the watcher at Halcyon Court this time, but one of his other staff. He had reconciled himself to the fact that he wasn't going to get much sleep tonight. McNulty's booking had flagged up on two of Gardner's online security programs and one Internet guru. Gardner had set the wheels in motion before the second watcher made the call.

"I know." In response to McNulty arriving at the apartment building.

"Salino's got it covered." In response to the query about what to do next.

Pat Tubah was just glad to be part of the organisation again and was surprised how quickly he had been brought up to speed. He already knew the main players he might have to work with and had a fair understanding of how Gardner worked. He felt emboldened to ask a rather cheeky question. "Is Salino okay doing this?"

Gardner knew exactly what Salino was okay doing. "Salino is a professional."

Tubah sat in the stolen Subaru Impreza and watched the front entrance. The Subaru was discreetly tucked away in the far corner of the car park, facing the main building and the vehicular exit. He didn't feel emboldened anymore. "Of course. Sorry."

Gardner didn't flick the handset and say, "*City desk.*" He sat in the telephone chair with his feet on a velvet footstool. "Keep watching in case McNulty comes out before Salino gets the job done."

That was Gardner's first acknowledgement of doubt about Salino's ability after having to revisit Halcyon Court to get the diary. The diary hadn't been Salino's fault; Gardner hadn't known there was a diary when he'd ordered the hit.

Tubah considered what he knew about McNulty. "He won't come back out. McNulty can't resist a naked woman."

* * *

McNulty didn't want to see the naked woman, but there was no avoiding it if this was to work. He never thought he'd hear those words in his head; naked women were God's gift to mankind. If He didn't want men looking at them, He shouldn't have made them so good to look at. McNulty never thought he'd be having this debate with God either. He was a long way short of being a religious person; Crag View Orphanage had a way of knocking that out of you at an early age.

He walked along the corridor checking the apartment numbers, even numbers on the right facing the front of the building and odd numbers on the left facing the back. Number 21 faced the back. Good. There would be no traffic noise. The door to the apartment opened before McNulty had a chance to knock. It opened inwards, and a hand from behind the door invited him in. The woman closed the door and slid the peephole shut. She was maybe thirty years old, and she was definitely worth looking at, tall, slim, and shapely in all the right places. The high cheekbones and thin lips made her eyes look even bigger, but couldn't hide the soulful look she gave McNulty. Even the hint of a smile didn't make her look happy.

"Good evening. This way."

The accent was even more enticing than her looks. McNulty couldn't place it but reckoned it was somewhere between Italian and Polish. Maybe Eastern Bloc or Russian. There were so many countries with a similar accent and high cheekbones. The white nurse's smock was more practical than titillating. It showed off her flat stomach and firm breasts while keeping them under wraps. There was no attempt to make the smock look more like a fantasy nurse's outfit. She wore plain flat slip-on shoes and no stockings. This was a business outfit. There was no name badge or medical accessories. No stethoscope or nurse's hat. The long, thin legs looked strong, muscle definition standing out against the smooth, hairless skin.

But McNulty still didn't want to see the naked woman.

"You're working late." A lame attempt at conversation.

"I work when I'm needed. You made the appointment. I must be needed."

The woman led McNulty to an en suite bedroom, the smoked glass and chrome bathroom door reminding him of his mother's room. That didn't help his libido, which was already rock bottom. If Gardner was going to stick his head over the parapet, McNulty wished he'd do it soon.

The woman indicated the bathroom. "Shower?"

"I had one before I came out thanks."

She straightened the fluffy white towel that covered the bed. "Get undressed then. Lay face down, please."

McNulty got undressed and lay face down on the bed. He had never felt so awkward getting ready for a massage. The woman checked the temperature of the heated massage oil on the bedside cabinet, then turned to face the bed. She slowly undid her smock, one button at a time. Starting at the top.

First button. The bottom of her throat was revealed.

Second button. Her collarbones were sharp and detailed below her throat.

Third button. The smock began to open wider, revealing her cleavage.

Fourth button. Now her smooth flat stomach.

CHAPTER FORTY-ONE

Fifth button. More stomach as her breasts pushed the smock open.

Last button. The smock fell completely open, revealing a toned body with good muscle definition and small, firm breasts. The nipples were dark and hard, suggesting he might have been right about her heritage. Somewhere warm and exotic. She let the smock slide to the floor and turned toward the bedside cabinet. Her stomach muscles tightened as she leaned forward. The muscles in her back looked even stronger. Her buttocks were round and solid. When she stood up, she cradled a small wooden bowl in both hands, her arms drawing her breasts together to give a false cleavage. This woman didn't need a cleavage; what she had was perfect. What wasn't perfect were the three scars on her lower back and the two jagged lines just below her ribcage. She might well be smooth and well-muscled but she had got there through the school of hard knocks. She poured warm oil along McNulty's spine.

McNulty let out a contented moan. It had been a long time. "My name's Vince, by the way."

The woman nodded. "McNulty. I know. It was on the booking."

"I don't suppose your name is Trixie. Like on the booking."

She began to smooth the oil across his waist and shoulders. "You don't think I look like a Trixie?"

"I don't think anybody looks like a Trixie."

The woman kneaded the muscles down McNulty's side. "I knew somebody had a poodle called Trixie Bell."

"You don't look like a poodle either. What should I call you?"

The woman swung one leg over McNulty's waist so she

could straddle him and work his spine. "You can call me Salino."

Chapter Forty-Two

The ambulance caught Tynan by surprise. He had been keeping an eye on the scuzzy-looking fella in the stolen Subaru Impreza that was parked in the far corner away from the front entrance. He couldn't tell from his vantage point across the road, but he thought it was Pat Tubah, former lieutenant to Telfon Speed before his boss had his chestnuts roasted in the fireball that closed Northern X.

The blue lights flashed across the front of the building, but there was no siren and no squeal of tyres as it pulled up outside and reversed to the front door. The strobe lights bounced off the windows and glinted off the cars in the car park, highlighting the shock on Tubah's face. The low-rent crook looked as surprised as the detective. Despite the emergency lights, the paramedic showed no sense of urgency as he used a key card to open the main door. That should have raised the alarm for Tynan. Since when did ambulance drivers have a key card to their emergencies?

* * *

Once a cop, always a cop. McNulty thought about that as Salino massaged scented oil into his shoulders, leaning so close that her naked breasts teased his shoulder blades. It was a thought he used to have when he'd visited the massage parlours of Northern X, but now he felt a long way from being a cop. He felt unclean, letting an East European who was probably part of a human trafficking ring strip away his defences. He wondered how much of this life was her choice and how much was threats and intimidation.

Salino's hands slid up the inside of McNulty's thighs, and all thoughts of threats and intimidation went right out the window. Soft fingers caressed what they found at the top of his thighs, then withdrew. Hard nipples on spongy breasts gently played across his shoulders and neck. He could feel her breath close to his ear. It was warm and friendly. McNulty remembered reading about advanced interrogation techniques at Guantanamo Bay, the first thing being to strip your subject naked because a naked man feels completely defenceless. McNulty wasn't being interrogated, but he did feel completely defenceless. He was beginning to doubt the wisdom of hoping the massage would draw Gardner out. It was drawing McNulty out instead. He shifted on his love muscle to make himself more comfortable. McNulty was beginning to feel very comfortable.

He heard the main door to the entrance lobby slam shut, followed by the sound of the door to the corridor opening and closing. Footsteps sounded in the tiled passage. McNulty remembered the noises that had distracted him during a massage at The Sauna Kabin all those years ago. The front door. The female voice escorting another punter upstairs to the lounge. The muffled words from upstairs. Something banging in the bar. A gruff voice followed by a stifled scream. Noises that had prompted McNulty to abort the massage and pretend he was a policeman again, despite not having a warrant card or a badge wallet. There was no stifled scream this time, just somebody coming along the corridor. To an apartment further along the passage maybe. Even so, the sound distracted him, and the pulse down in the engine room subsided.

Salino didn't try and revive it. Still straddling McNulty's waist, she leaned across to the bedside cabinet. For more scented oil, he reckoned. He felt her weight settle on him as she centred herself. He turned his head to one side and let out a sigh. It was all you could do when a naked woman was tickling your tackle. When he didn't feel the reassuring warmth of fresh oil, he opened his eyes to glance over his shoulder. Salino wasn't holding the wooden bowl.

Defenceless; the main reason they stripped prisoners naked at Guantanamo Bay. Defenceless; the main thought to go through McNulty's head as he saw the glint of the hypodermic needle. Strong thighs pinned him down. There was nothing soft about the skin anymore. The breasts jiggled slightly as Salino leaned forward. McNulty felt a slight scratch in the side of his neck, and he tried to jerk away from the needle. Strong hands held his head until she was finished.

McNulty had just enough time to wonder if all those sedatives he'd seen in the movies were realistic. Did they really work that fast. Then the sedative really worked that fast, and McNulty's world went dark.

* * *

Tynan was out of the car and sprinting across the road before the ambulance doors closed. He had radioed for his backup team to cover the fire exit at the rear and told his driver to block the Subaru. The phone tracker showed that McNulty was still in the flat. Police are hardwired to work in conjunction with paramedics, and Tynan had no reason to change now, but an ambulance blue-lighting to a location where an undercover cop was trying to draw out a vicious criminal was cause for concern.

A nurse in a white smock had joined the paramedic as they wheeled the gurney into the back of the ambulance and collapsed the legs. She jumped in the back, and the paramedic closed the doors. He got in the passenger seat, and his driver fired up the blue lights again. And the siren this time. Tynan stepped to one side as the ambulance sped forward. He didn't try to bypass the key card and simply kicked the glass door just above the handle.

The ambulance made it to the road before Tynan had a chance to check who the casualty was. He shouted down the radio for his operator to check with 999 and get back to him. The door took three kicks before the flimsy lock gave way, cracking the laminated glass as it flew open.

He dashed through the inner door and checked the numbers on the wall. Numbers 1 to 15 were to the left. Numbers 16 to 30 were to the right. McNulty had texted him the apartment number. Tynan turned right and sprinted along the corridor to Number 21. The apartment faced the back of the building, away from the car park, so McNulty wouldn't have seen the blue flashing lights. That set more alarm bells ringing. Tynan shouted at the ACR operator to expedite the ambulance enquiry and immediately felt guilty. If there was one thing that 999 operators never did, it was shout down the radio. The Area Control Room operator was calmness personified as she acknowledged Tynan's request.

Number 21 was partly open, the door snagged against the deep-pile carpet. The detective didn't wait to check behind the door. He already knew where McNulty was. He walked to the only other open door, a bedroom with an unmade bed. McNulty's clothes were neatly folded on a bedside chair. Tynan phoned McNulty's number, and the phone vibrated in the jacket hanging on the back of the chair.

There was a bowl of massage oil and a box of tissues on the bedside cabinet, but it wasn't the oil that sent a shiver down Tynan's spine. It was the empty syringe.

Chapter Forty-Three

A mishmash of memories were running through McNulty's head as the world continued to tilt and sway and generally spin out of control. The first was the slap and the cry from Mr Cruckshank's office at Crag View Orphanage. That didn't surprise him, it was always the first thought to go through his head during stressful situations.

The slap sounded like a gunshot in the quiet office. A gunshot followed by a heartbreaking whimper. Young Vincent McNulty dashed into the headmaster's office and saw the half-naked girl on the bench seat in the alcove. Mr Cruckshank ordered McNulty back to his room. McNulty told the headmaster to go to hell. He snatched the heavy Bible from the bookshelf and broke the headmaster's nose. By the time McNulty put the Bible down the girl—who would turn out to be McNulty's sister—had gone.

The second memory was a bit less obvious, although it too involved a young girl in danger, this time from her drug lord father and a California wildfire. Tilly Nutton could almost be a surrogate sibling and a second chance to save his sister.

The eyes that blinked back at him in the dark weren't those of a car thief or a burglar. They belonged to a scared child cowering in the shadows. Amy Moore coaxed the girl out from under the tarpaulin for McNulty with a mug of hot chocolate and a winning smile. The smile had faded when it turned out Tilly's father ran a Mexican drug cartel with a sideline of selling children for sex, his daughter included. The subsequent chase had ended with fire and death at Rancho Verde after McNulty caught up with Tilly and five other runaways at a log cabin next to Lake Piru. The hitman had caught up with them, too. The wildfire caught up with everyone. McNulty had rowed Tilly into the lake, then turned the boat upside down. Flames licked the surface. The scared eyes were more scared this time.

The third memory swirled in a whirlpool of mixed emotions. The eyes that looked back at him were an amalgamation of his sister, Tilly Nutton, and his only real friend. But these eyes were closed.

The hospital in Loveland, Colorado, was busy and noisy. The gurney had rattled as it rushed along the corridor, two gurneys because McNulty was on one of them. The face on the other gurney was charred and blackened and covered in blood. The head had lolled to one side but hadn't looked at McNulty. Jim Grant hadn't looked at anybody. Until later, when he'd said, "You'd think we'd have learned by now, wouldn't you?"

McNulty had been in the next bed. "Learned what?"

"To keep our noses out of other people's business."

"We're cops. That's what we do."

"You're not a cop." Grant, telling it like it is.

A dream within a dream, because Grant hadn't woken up yet after surgery. Something else Grant hadn't said was, "Sometimes I think this is exactly where I belong." McNulty was still dreaming until he wasn't. The beeping of the heart rate monitor had grown louder. Then it had stopped. The green spikes had stopped spiking. Flatline. Grant's eyes hadn't opened again.

* * *

McNulty's eyes flew open, but the light was too bright, so he closed them again. The ceiling tiles were white with wavy patterns. The walls were white too, but he couldn't tell if it was wallpaper or paint. Maybe both. He raised a hand to shield his eyes as he opened them again.

Not everything was white. The walls were tinged with orange, but he didn't think it was part of the colour scheme. He lifted his head and realised he was lying on his back, but he wasn't naked. This wasn't a continuation of the massage by other means. This wasn't a massage at all. He was wearing an orange boiler suit like George Clooney in *Out of Sight*. McNulty thought it was that movie, but his head was still spinning. There was a distant buzzing noise like wood in a sawmill. His stomach lurched, and he closed his eyes again.

The pink light through his eyelids faded to black. The next time he woke up, the buzzing had stopped, but the ceiling was still white. The walls weren't white anymore, though. Not completely. There were splashes of red across the plaster and dollops of thicker stuff on the floor. The world began to spin again. His stomach lurched, and he was sick over the side of the gurney before he passed out.

* * *

"I wondered when you were going to wake up."

The man standing next to the gurney looked as if he hadn't had any sleep, but the lines on his face were more from age than tiredness. The eyes were still bright beneath bushy eyebrows, and the lines creased into a smile. The eyes didn't quite join the smile, but there was no sign of harshness or cruelty. The blood on the walls suggested otherwise.

McNulty asked the obvious question. "Where am I?"

Frank Gardner gave an evasive answer. "In the land of the living. Which is more than I can say for the three men I sent to bring you last time."

The abattoir corridor bounced their words off the tiled walls, but at least it had stopped swaying. McNulty rubbed his eyes and flexed his jaw. His mouth felt like it had been chewing sawdust. He tried to moisten his lips, but he had no spit. Gardner handed him a glass of water. McNulty nodded his thanks. Once his mouth was working, he looked at his captor.

"You should have asked."

Gardner took the empty glass. "I did ask. Just not in the way you'd like."

McNulty waved a hand around the corridor. "Not the place I'd like, either. Reminds me of that scene in *The Long Good Friday* where Bob Hoskins has his rivals brought in on sky hooks like sides of beef."

Gardner pointed at the ceiling tiles. "We don't have sky hooks. But abattoirs have their benefits. If you want to get rid of dead meat."

"Is that how you got rid of the dog? Mum said it was your favourite."

Gardner recoiled as if slapped. "Your mother said a lot of things."

McNulty noticed the reaction. "Yes, she did."

Gardner didn't react this time. He indicated a door being guarded by two men halfway along the corridor. "Why don't we discuss it over breakfast. I'm always hungry after the night shift."

* * *

McNulty felt a strong case of deja vu wash over him. After testing his balance next to the gurney, he followed Gardner through the door and, for the third time, stepped into a mink-lined prison. He wasn't thinking about his mother's luxurious bedroom, though; this time, he was reminded of the exotic reception area in the rundown factory on Southside Industrial Park.

"You can take the X out of Northern, but not the North out of Xtreme."

Gardner gave a little laugh. "Oh, this isn't Xtreme North. We rent apartments for that."

McNulty jerked a thumb back toward the abattoir. "Until you need to get rid of the dead meat."

Gardner indicated a dining table with a nod of the head. "The only meat on offer here is sausage and bacon. Sit."

McNulty scanned the room. Deep-pile carpet and velvet wallpaper muffled the sound of his feet. There was an expensive desk with green leather inlay in the far corner and floor-to-ceiling bookshelves against the wall. Most of the books looked like leather-bound classics and legal books but there was a shelf of paperback originals that included the Pan editions of Gavin Lyall and Ian Fleming and the Midnight Ink editions of Colin Campbell's Resurrection Man thrillers. The books that Jim Grant detested. There was a hardback selection of Lee Child, Ace Atkins, and Nick Petrie alongside the Harper Collins reprints of Elmore Leonard.

McNulty nodded at the books. "The girls like to read before

they get remaindered?"

Gardner glanced at the bookshelf. "Books get remaindered. When they don't sell, and the publisher has them pulped to make paper for books that do. The girls are profitable until they're not."

He indicated the table again. "But let's not spoil our appetites."

McNulty pulled out a chair and sat down. The table was set for two. Knives, forks, and condiments. It was the condiments McNulty was looking at. Brown sauce and ketchup. And a large shaker of table salt.

Chapter Forty-Four

Tynan finished working the crime scene two hours before dawn and sealed the apartment in case he needed to take a second look. The first look was bad enough. It told him all he needed to know. Frank Gardner had stuck his head above the parapet, and Tynan had missed.

SOCO had lifted dozens of usable fingerprints from the bedroom, but the rest of the apartment had been wiped clean. Some of the prints would no doubt be McNulty's, but the worrying thing wasn't the usable prints, it was the unusable ones. The door handles and bedside cabinet had several complete fingers, but none of them had any loops or whorls; they were completely blank. Just finger shapes with no lines for comparison, the prints burned off. That was how serious these people were.

Tynan gathered the evidence bags and put them in a cardboard box, keeping McNulty's personal effects separate from the massage equipment and towels. Jeans, T-shirt, jacket, and shoes were in individual bags. He would label them later if he needed to. The mobile phone was locked using fingerprint ID, so that wouldn't help until the IT Department unlocked it. He doubted it would reveal anything since Tynan had been with McNulty when he'd booked the massage. He slipped the phone in his pocket and locked the apartment. It was time to follow the only other lead, which was currently in a holding cell at Weetwood Police Station.

* * *

"So, Pat. You don't mind me calling you Pat, do you?"

Tubah looked like being called Pat was the least of his worries. His face was a mass of twitches and suspicious glances masquerading as cool after being locked in a holding cell for six hours, then plonked in an interview room with the recorder turned off.

"Why would I mind?" Even that didn't sound convincing.

Tynan didn't sit in the chair opposite Tubah, he leaned against the door, looking down at the table that was fastened to the floor. The chairs, too. The only thing that wasn't nailed down was the steaming takeaway coffee on the table between Tubah's hands.

"Good, because Pat, I've got to tell you, you're fucked six ways from Sunday."

Tubah put a brave face on the situation. "Only way I'm fucked is I need to get home to feed my cat."

Tynan gave a sinister smile. "Yeah, I heard you like pussy. That's why you work for Frank Gardner."

"Who?"

"The fella took over from your old boss."

"I work for Pizza Palazzo. Deliveries."

"I thought they used Deliveroo. You know, pushbikes and mopeds." Tynan paused for effect. "Not stolen Subaru Imprezas."

"I don't have a Subaru Impreza."

"You were sitting in one before you tried to run off through the rose bushes." He put feigned concern in his voice. "How is your hand?"

Tubah covered his right hand with his left. The scratches were still weeping.

Tynan tilted his head. "A rose between two thorns. The thorns being a stolen car and a kidnapped cop."

"He's not a cop." Tubah immediately clamped his mouth shut. He gulped. His expression said, *Oops.*

"And you're not a pizza guy. But I do have a special offer for you."

Tynan pushed off from the door and sat opposite Tubah. He waited until Tubah couldn't help but meet Tynan's gaze. "A one-time offer. A get out of jail free card. Where did they take him?"

Chapter Forty-Five

Where they had taken McNulty wasn't as important as why they had taken him there. The abattoir was part of a meat packing plant, but they weren't cutting him up and turning him into sausages; they were feeding him sausages. And bacon and eggs and black pudding. McNulty left the black pudding. Dried blood wasn't to his taste at the moment. He sprinkled salt on his eggs, then held the shaker out to Gardner.

Gardner shook his head. "Hides the flavour."

McNulty put the salt down. "I heard you liked to drown your food in it."

Gardner paused with a piece of bacon halfway to his mouth. "Who told you that?"

"Same person who said you got angry about losing the dog."

"Ah yes. Doreen. Your mother loved that dog. Named it after your sister."

* * *

McNulty held his breath. That was the first acknowledgement that his mother even had a daughter. His mouth felt dry. He took a drink of tea to cover his discomfort. He watched Gardner with fresh eyes, looking for any family resemblance. The frown lines and creases up the side of his mouth could have been anybody's, but the eyes were brown, not blue. McNulty's were blue, the same as his mother's.

"You knew her well then."

"I knew her well enough to mourn her passing. My condolences."

"You knew her well enough to pay for the best room in the house."

"At Halcyon Court? There is no best room in the house."

McNulty was confused. "You didn't visit?"

For the first time, Gardner looked uncomfortable. "She didn't want me to visit. And by the time I'd plucked up courage, she wouldn't have remembered me anyway."

"She remembered the dog."

Gardner pulled himself together. "But not the person who gave it to her."

McNulty prodded. "The man who liked to drown his food in salt?"

Gardner let out a sigh. "The less you know about him, the better."

The same words his mother had used. McNulty was beginning to think Gardner knew her better than he was saying. The thing was, if she was worried about how angry Frank would get, how much angrier might the man who liked to drown his food in salt get. Both his mother and Gardner seemed to share a healthy interest in keeping that anger under wraps.

"Is that why you sent three men to jump me? So I wouldn't find out?"

"I sent three men to bring you to me." Gardner indicated

the plush decor with a wave of the hand. "I owe all this to you. If you hadn't closed down Telfon Speed and Northern X, it wouldn't have risen from the ashes as Xtreme North, and I wouldn't have taken it to the next level."

"You're bragging about being head of an international torture sex business?"

"International girls. Not international. Just England." He shrugged. "Well, plus Scotland, Wales, and Ireland." A shadow crossed Gardner's face. "International is somebody else."

"They wanted to bring me to you?"

Gardner's voice turned serious. "If you hadn't killed them, you could have asked."

McNulty held up his hands. "I didn't kill them, I caught a bus."

"Really? You expect me to believe that?"

"You caught me with a massage. Did I look like I could shoot three men?"

"You were naked. Makes a man more vulnerable."

McNulty nodded. "Good point. But if I'd shot three men in the alley, would I go into a strange apartment without my gun?"

"You might have had a gun."

"I was naked."

"In your clothes."

"She didn't check?"

"She didn't have time. The police were watching."

"And now they're watching you."

"Nobody is watching me." But Gardner didn't sound convinced. Again, the shadow played across his face. He looked worried. And not about the police.

McNulty misread the signs. "Not right now. But you've

just kidnapped a cop."

"You're not a cop."

That stung, but not too bad. "Once a cop, always a cop. At the very least, you kidnapped an ex-cop. They're going to be watching you until the end of your days."

Gardner spoke softly, almost to himself. "We all reach the end of our days. Some sooner rather than later."

* * *

Gardner tried to put a brave face on it, but being convivial for the benefit of his guest was proving harder than expected. Part of that, he knew, was guilt at having ordered the death of someone he had once felt strongly about. Back in the days of the dog called Susie and the birth of Northern X. The other part depended on whether McNulty was telling the truth or not.

Had he killed the three men in the alley?

And if not, who?

Gardner reckoned he knew who. He consoled himself with the knowledge that Doreen hadn't said anything about her early days with Gardner and, more importantly, her connection to Crag View. Northern X had been a fledgling organisation at the time; an orphanage had seemed like an interesting source of potential sex workers. Getting them in on the ground floor. Catching them young. Gardner felt guilty about that, too.

But McNulty? A trained killer? Gardner didn't think so. Which left the broader question unanswered. Who? He looked at the saltshaker and thought; *We all reach the end of our days. Some sooner rather than later.*

* * *

McNulty watched Gardner's face and thought the boss of Xtreme North was turning a bit introspective. The whisper had almost felt like Gardner was talking to himself. *"We all reach the end of our days. Some sooner rather than later."* McNulty knew something about End Of Days, having survived his own skirmish with it in Loveland, Colorado. Jim Grant had survived, too, by the skin of his teeth, but Grant had flirted with the other side as well, having been dead for five minutes before the ER team brought him back to life.

Gardner had seemed to zone out there for a while, and McNulty didn't think it was because he'd told Gardner the police would be watching him. Gardner forked a slice of bacon and egg into his mouth to buy himself time. McNulty did the same, only with sausage and egg. He was working out how best to push his advantage, because he reckoned he'd got Gardner rattled.

As he considered the situation, he took a small measure of comfort from the fact that at least his sister had the good sense to stay away from this mess. He was thinking about that when he heard footsteps in the corridor and a familiar sound. Two slaps across the face, followed by a scuffle and commotion, then two more slaps.

Chapter Forty-Six

A bacon sandwich from the bakery opposite Weetwood Police Station had joined the takeaway coffee on the interview room table. Tubah was feeling more sanguine about his situation now that he thought he had a bargaining chip. The expiry date on that chip was getting close, though.

"Xtreme North doesn't have a specific location anymore. Gardner learned from Speed's mistake with Northern X. They perform in call services at rented apartments like the one McNulty used."

Tynan had taken his tie off and unfastened the top button of his shirt. It had been a long night. "Not for the extreme stuff. Airbnb don't like cleaning blood off the sheets."

"Single-use girls. Yeah. It's different for them."

* * *

Tynan didn't see it coming. The slap almost knocked Tubah off his seat and crushed the takeaway coffee cup. The lid came off and splashed froth and liquid across the soundproof wall like blood from a gunshot. Tynan looked at the hand that had done the slapping and felt shame mingle with the sudden anger. Single-use girls. He still had dreams about the naked body in the oil drum behind Kwik Save. She had been a single-use girl.

Tubah cowered against the wall, the bargaining chip reduced to a bloodstain that tasted of coffee. He kept his hands up to protect his face. The bacon sandwich didn't smell so appetising anymore.

Tynan's hands were shaking. He sat down and picked up the cardboard cup. He made a big show of reshaping the cup, then used his other hand to squeegee the spilled coffee back into it. Once he'd cleared the biggest puddle, he found the lid and clipped it back on. He made sure the cup would stand up, then carefully positioned it next to the bacon sandwich. He patted it gently as if soothing a cat. After a few moments, he let out a sigh, then gave Tubah a hard stare.

"Your bargaining chip just got fucked six ways from Sunday as well."

He straightened in his seat. "Here's what's going to happen. Either I read you the caution, and you go down for stealing the Subaru, kidnapping, and murder…"

Tubah blurted a defensive riposte. "I didn't kill nobody."

Tynan was calm again. "That's a double negative. You need to be careful about that. Some people would take that as a confession."

"Nobody's dead is what I mean."

"The three fellas in the alley are dead."

"I wasn't there."

Tynan rested both hands on the table. They had stopped shaking. "The Subaru was there. Caught on CCTV. Parked in a side street opposite Hyde Park Picture House. Want to guess who was sitting in the driver's seat?"

That was a bluff, but they both knew who had been driving the stolen car. He pushed the next button, which was less of a bluff. He'd seen the footage. "And do you want to know who got out of the car parked behind you? All three of them."

Tubah whimpered and tried to blend into the wall.

Tynan continued. "That puts you at the scene of a triple murder. Talking to the three men who got killed. In the same car you were in at the scene of a kidnapping. Of an undercover police officer." It was hard to say this next part, but the threat needed to be real. "That's murder number four."

Tubah scrambled himself upright. "McNulty isn't dead."

Tynan felt the anger building again. "Yet."

Tubah could see the anger on Tynan's face. "Not now, not never. Gardner just wants to talk to him."

"What about?"

"The fuck should I know?"

"You know he wants to talk."

"Well, it's more of a guess, really. The three fellas in the alley. They were just supposed to take him to Gardner. Must be why McNulty...you know. Shot 'em."

Tynan bristled. "McNulty didn't shoot nobody."

Tubah held up a calming hand. "Which, according to you, means he did."

Tynan clenched his fists. Tubah prepared to shield his face. Then Tynan's face broke into a slow smile. "Very good. I'm glad you're paying attention."

He unclenched his fists and wiped some of the spilled coffee aside. When he'd finished, he linked his fingers and flexed them until they cracked. Soundproof panels on the wall muted the noise. "Now let's see if you can remember my question."

Tubah cowered in case he got it wrong. "Where did they take him?"

Tynan nodded. "Where?"

Tubah looked down at the table while he marshalled his thoughts. His brow furrowed. His eyes went blank. The concentration showed on his face like a shadow play. The crease between his eyebrows grew deeper then his eyes came back to life and he looked at Tynan.

"I know where he isn't."

"That isn't helpful."

Tubah made circular motions with his hands while he tried to get the words out. "I mean. There's two places. Gardner uses a couple of abattoirs for disposal. But he's not going to have taken McNulty to the nearest one."

"Why not?"

Tubah's face showed how stupid he thought that question was. "Because it's round the back of the police station." He jerked a thumb toward the interview room door. "Over there."

Chapter Forty-Seven

Bodington Abattoir and Meat Processing Plant had been built on the old University of Leeds Playing Fields at Bodington Hall. Some of the playing fields were still there, but they were potholed and overgrown. The surrounding trees had become a wooded glade that hid the factory from Weetwood Police Station. There was easy access from Otley Road to the west and the A6120 Ring Road to the south. There were also narrow service roads that used to give the groundsman access to any part of the sports complex.

The factory was an L-shaped structure with a tall redbrick chimney above the incinerator. The years hadn't been kind to the plant; the entire building looking much older than it was. That was by design, Frank Gardner wanting the factory to look more like a rundown business than a going concern. Hiding in plain sight behind the cop shop.

The car park and loading bays were nestled between the two wings of the factory in the angle of the L. The loading bays were empty, but there were two cars and an ambulance in front of the office block. Two men with serious faces stood guard at the main door. Two more were just visible through the window along the corridor. Four bodyguards, Frank Gardner and Vince McNulty. Not a problem.

* * *

The man with the cold, hard eyes wore a long winter coat, a Peaky Blinders flat cap, and black gloves. The gloves were thin enough to be flexible but thick enough to leave no fingerprints. He crossed the access road out of sight of the car park and carefully walked around the factory, keeping steady eyes on the boarded-up windows and fire exits. The factory looked abandoned. The hitman knew it was a façade.

Once he was satisfied there weren't any other guards round the back, he took the gun out of his coat, checked there was a round in the chamber, and gave the silencer a final turn of the screw. With that done, he kept the gun behind his back and stepped around the corner.

The two bodyguards were busy talking about football. They looked strong and capable, but the thing about bodyguards in England is that they never expect to get caught up in a gunfight. In Yorkshire, guns were even more rare, hard men preferring hard toys, baseball bats, and four by twos. Sometimes knuckledusters and knives. They weren't traditionally tooled up unless they were going to rob a cash delivery. The car park at the abattoir wasn't a cash delivery.

The cold, hard eyes never wavered as the man walked across the tarmac. A slow, steady stride. Not rushing but not taking his time either. The men were discussing a penalty they thought shouldn't have been given and the goal that followed. They caught the movement out of the corner of their eyes, but it was slow and steady. Casual. Non-threatening. The man was almost upon them when he brought the gun from behind his back and shot them both in the chest. They dropped to the floor. The man stood over them and shot them in the head. One shot each. Double tap. He knelt and picked up the shell casings, then went to the front door.

The wired glass in the door was dark and stained, in keeping with the abandoned feel of the factory. He could just about make out the white tiles and the gurney at the far end of the corridor. The other two men were closer, halfway along outside an office door. The man checked the pulse in his left wrist. The pulse had barely risen above normal. He didn't smile, and he didn't nod. That was just the way it was. Normal.

He opened the door and walked calmly along the corridor. Same steady pace. Same non-threatening stride. The footsteps echoed off the tiles but sounded like a friendly stroll. Like a friend coming in out of the cold. Both men were smiling when they got double-tapped.

* * *

McNulty heard the footsteps in the corridor and a familiar sound. Two slaps across the face, followed by a scuffle and commotion, then two more slaps. His eyes registered where he'd heard that sound before, and his nostrils flared. The last time he hadn't realised what the sounds were. This time, he was on his feet before the door opened.

A man with a gun came in. "Sit down, please."

McNulty sat down.

Frank Gardner hadn't stood up. He sat open-mouthed with his eyes staring in panic. McNulty had never seen the boss of Xtreme North looking so gobsmacked. It was amazing how quickly your confidence could evaporate when you had a gun pointed at you. McNulty's confidence was at zero.

The man stepped into the room and closed the door behind him. The gun was trained squarely between McNulty and Gardner. The man took two steps forward, then stopped in the middle of the office. The plush décor felt completely out of place now that death had entered the room. That felt strange since they were sitting in an abattoir. Maybe not so strange since the office, and no doubt the sex rooms, were designed to mitigate the death that was meted out here.

Sirens started in the distance, the sound both frightening and reassuring. Usually, blue lights and sirens were a sign that reinforcements were on their way. The sound told you that the police, the fire brigade, or the ambulance service was on its way. Hold tight, and they'll be here soon. That didn't necessarily apply when there was a gun pointing at you. In a split second, blue lights and sirens don't mean anything at all. You don't need an ambulance when you're dead. This man had killed three men at Hyde Park and four outside. Two more would be no problem at all.

McNulty watched the eyes, not the gun. If there was one thing he'd learned from Jim Grant, it was that the eyes betrayed the intention before the trigger finger squeezed. Looking into these cold, hard eyes, he wasn't so sure. He thought this man could kill without blinking. He doubted his pulse would rise above normal; the man looked that calm.

Gardner wasn't calm. He stood up and held out a hand. "Tell Marat she didn't say anything."

The voice was as cold as the eyes. "He knows."

"And tell him I…"

The man shot Gardner in the chest. Gardner's knees gave way, and he hit the edge of the table on the way down. To add insult to injury, his neck snapped, turning his head backwards.

He crashed to the ground. The blood had already stopped pumping by the time the man shot him in the head.

The sirens grew louder. Coming closer. Then they stopped. The silence was deafening. Then the hitman turned the gun on McNulty.

Chapter Forty-Eight

It shouldn't have surprised Tynan that Bodington Abattoir and Meat Processing Plant was a bloodbath, but it did. He had ordered the response team to turn off their sirens. Silent approach. Standard procedure for any incident where the suspects might still be on the premises. Burglaries, robberies, or rapes. Not so much for violent disorders because then you wanted the thugs to know the police were coming, so they might stop kicking the shit out of each other. With three dead men already at Hyde Park, this was a different scenario.

Silent approach felt like the right way to go.

He didn't think they'd been silent enough.

* * *

Securing the premises had been easy enough; everyone was dead. There was no resistance in the car park and no getaway vehicles. The cars were quiet and stationary. The ambulance was still reversed against the factory doors. Even so, it was standard procedure to send a firearms team in first to make sure there were no surprises. There were plenty of surprises, just not of the gunman variety.

"All clear."

The words were barely out of the team leader's mouth before Tynan pushed his way into the corridor, following the common path marked by the firearms team. There had been two dead men in the car park, and there were two more in the corridor. Tynan kept to the opposite side of the passage and peered through the open door. He could only see one side of the office, but he saw enough to tell it was far more luxurious than a meat processing plant should be. The carpet was deep-pile cream with hints of beige. The desk was carved wood with leather inlay and a pink blotter. The floor-to-ceiling bookcase behind the desk was full of leather-bound books and selected paperbacks. That was all he could see from that angle.

Giving the dead bodies a wide berth, Tynan pushed the door open with the toe of his shoe, then stepped inside. Xtreme North had come to an extreme end. Frank Gardner lay in a crumpled heap on the floor with his head turned backwards. He had a gunshot wound to the chest and a second between the eyes. There were no exit wounds, so it was probably a small-calibre weapon. Hardly any blood, so the first shot had killed him, and the second was insurance. Professional. There were no shell casings, so the gunman had either collected the casings or used a revolver.

Tynan stepped over the saltshaker on the floor and slumped in the chair behind the desk. He let out a long, slow breath. Yes, he reckoned the silent approach hadn't been silent enough.

* * *

The sirens grew louder. Coming closer. Then they stopped. The silence was deafening. Then the hitman turned the gun on McNulty. McNulty kept watching the eyes. No amount of pleading was going to help, so he tried the conversational approach.

"You're the fella from the alley."

The gunman didn't speak.

"Shot three men who were coming after me."

The gunman still said nothing.

"I suppose I should say thank you."

The gunman still said nothing.

"You're the strong silent type, huh?"

The gunman tilted his head and shrugged. The gesture spoke volumes. The eyes softened slightly. Not enough to be called a smile.

McNulty kept his tone light. Jim Grant would have been proud of him. "Back then, in the alley, you shot three men to protect me." He waved a hand toward the gun to get the hitman used to the movement. "I guess your orders have changed."

"They have." The voice had softened, too. Since he'd told Gardner, *"He knows."*

McNulty let out a sigh and drummed his fingers on the table. Next to the saltshaker. Again, to get the gunman used to the movement. He puffed out his cheeks in resignation. The gunman's eyes hadn't flickered. They were still watching McNulty, just not as intensely.

Three cars spat gravel as they sped along the access road. The noise sounded loud in the silence of the office. McNulty recognised the need for a silent approach but reckoned they should have turned the sirens off much earlier. The noise of the squealing tyres was just a sign of urgency as the police skidded to a halt in the car park.

The eyes flickered for the first time. They darted toward the curtained window, then back to McNulty. The flicker was all McNulty needed. He threw the saltshaker at the gunman, then heaved the table up and over. The gunman dodged to one side to avoid being hit in the face, then fired. The small-calibre bullet punched a hole in the heavy wooden dining table but didn't find its target.

The table blocked the view of the bathroom door as McNulty scurried across the floor. One more shot hit the door as it was opened, then there were more urgent things for the gunman to think about. Car doors slammed outside. Shouted voices identified themselves as police officers. The gunman quickly picked up the spent cartridges, then crossed the corridor into the abattoir.

* * *

"You going to stay in there all day?"

"Seems like a good idea."

McNulty poked his head out from behind the bathroom door, then examined the bullet hole in the wood. The bullets hadn't gone all the way through.

"Small calibre. Rattles around the skull but doesn't come out. Good for hitmen. Not good for blasting through doors."

Tynan indicated the dining table. "Or dining tables."

McNulty nodded. The adrenaline dump was beginning to wear off, and the shakes were setting in. He stayed in the bathroom and sat on the toilet seat. Despite the shootout at Loveland, Colorado, he wasn't used to being shot at. Even with small-calibre bullets. He put his head between his knees and took several slow, deep breaths. His hands were shaking. When he finally looked up, Tynan was standing in the doorway.

"Has he gone?"

"He's gone."

Chapter Forty-Nine

Preliminary examination of the scene took until midday. Coroner. Forensics. Photographs. Searching the rest of Bodington Abattoir and Meat Processing Plant took the rest of the day. Documenting it all would take most of the week. What the full search proved was that Pat Tubah had been wrong, Frank Gardner hadn't learned his lesson after Northern X. Because Xtreme North still used service-specific premises for its single-use girls.

Bodington Abattoir was just one of those service-specific premises.

* * *

Since Gardner had taken over and expanded the business model, the only real change had been importing the girls from abroad instead of abducting them from English massage parlours, and spreading his net nationwide instead of just in Yorkshire. Most of the girls still performed massages, but in private accommodations instead of massage parlours. The more exclusive girls used the service-specific premises like Bodington Abattoir.

The initial objective of the police raid had been to find

McNulty and detain his kidnappers. The first part had been achieved when Tynan spoke to McNulty in the office bathroom. The second part wasn't necessary since all the kidnappers had been killed. Apart from the masseuse who hadn't been present at Bodington Abattoir. And the gunman who had done the killing.

Once the site had been declared safe, the deeper search had begun. The office wasn't the only part of the building that was more luxurious than the abattoir. There were three private rooms in the east wing, away from the incinerator. The décor was as plush as the office, with the exception of the floor. Instead of deep pile carpet, the rooms had soft-touch lino that was warm underfoot but easy to clean. The walls, too, were decorated with vinyl wallpaper that could be washed. The bedding on the king-size bed was as disposable as the girls. The torture and bondage equipment indicated how disposable they were. Video equipment suggested the clients liked to relive their visits in glorious colour. Most of that colour was red.

There was a trolley system that was accessed by a discreet door at the back of each room. It linked all three rooms to the abattoir through a long, narrow passage. The plush décor didn't extend to the passage, which was white tile and concrete like the main corridor.

What *was* different from the main corridor was the abattoir.

"Oh my God." Tynan held a handkerchief over his mouth.

He waited until he was sure he wouldn't be sick, then spoke into the radio. "Tell SOCO I need them in the abattoir. And call the Detective Superintendent."

* * *

"How many?"

"Hard to tell. With all the different pieces."

They were back in the office waiting for a fresh ambulance to come and check McNulty out. He had said he was okay, but Tynan insisted. McNulty had been drugged with God knows what; checking him over was not just protocol, it was good sense.

Tynan wiped silver fingerprint powder off his trousers where he'd brushed against the desk. "My guess is you were going to join them."

McNulty shivered. "Sick bastards."

Tynan nodded. "Well, we're closing 'em down now. Tubah ratted 'em all out. Pointed us at the accounts department. Can you believe it? Gardner must have thought he was Richard Branson. Payments. Locations. Everything. The Chief Super is coordinating raids across the country."

McNulty remembered something Gardner had said. *"International is somebody else."* He toyed with the saltshaker. "What about abroad?"

"One step at a time, big boy."

"Some fella called Marat."

"There's a lot of Marats abroad."

"Any of them in Gardner's ledger?"

"No names. Just payments and dates."

McNulty pushed the shaker across the table. He surveyed the carnage that had once been a luxurious backwater in the torture porn trade. Bullet holes in the table and door. Body outline on the floor. Fingerprint powder everywhere. He looked at the spilled salt and let out a sigh. Trying to find out who liked to drown his food in salt had become a distant second in McNulty's priorities. He had a funeral to arrange.

"Any news from Halcyon Court on who was paying for the best room in the house?"

Tynan let out an apologetic cry. "Ah. Sorry. Dropped right off my list of things to do." He indicated the body outline. "He's looking favourite though."

McNulty shook his head. "It wasn't Gardner."

"Because?"

"Because he said so."

"And you believe him?"

"I believe the look on his face. He didn't even know there was a best room in the house."

Tynan waved a hand around the room. "Maybe with all you've been through, you can get Maggie to loosen up a bit. She seemed to like your mum."

McNulty indicated the body outline. "If the accounts department was as efficient as Richard Branson over there."

Tynan pushed off from the desk, smearing silver powder on his trousers again. He didn't bother brushing it off this time. "About your mum. I'm sorry again for your loss."

McNulty gave a sad little smile. "As opposed to giving your condolences."

"Yeah. As opposed to that. I'm sorry."

A shadow passed the office window, and tyres crunched on the gravel outside. There was a single whoop of the siren, then the ambulance parked away from the suspects' vehicles. Tynan looked out of the window. "Your ride's here."

"Ride? Can't they check me out here?"

"I need you out of here. I've got things to do."

"I can help."

Tynan shook his head. "Once a cop, always a cop is a mindset. Not a fact. You need to let the police get on with this."

McNulty tipped the saltshaker over, like knocking over the king in a game of chess. Checkmate. Salt spilled across the table and filled the bullet hole. He nodded at Tynan but didn't speak. He walked out of the office and along the corridor. He'd only been gone a few minutes when the phone in Tynan's pocket began to vibrate. McNulty's phone.

Tynan took it out and looked at the phone. The caller ID showed on the locked screen, with a red and a green telephone symbol.

SUSAN

For a few seconds, Tynan couldn't place who that was, then remembered it was McNulty's sister. He raised the phone to his ear. "Hello?"

III

PART THREE

OPPORTUNITY
Whether or not the defendant had the chance to
commit the crime.
—Blackstone's

Chapter Fifty

Susan McNulty sat in the extra legroom window seat and felt the smooth descent as the passenger jet made its final approach to Manchester Airport. She had never used her maiden name after becoming Susan Carter, but it felt appropriate on her first visit to England since being sold into adoption when she was five. She looked out of the window but could only see brief snatches of ground through breaks in the clouds. The clouds looked dark and angry, but there was only a little wind to try and knock the Boeing 737 off course. Even though Susan was almost back on English soil, the ground seemed to be a long way down. She popped a Werther's Original in her mouth and sucked to ease the pressure in her ears. The plane was buffeted as it hit an air pocket. Her ears refused to pop.

The plane shook again, then levelled out. Susan gripped the armrests, her knuckles showing white in the dull grey light. She couldn't remember Northern England from childhood, but it looked just as her brother had described it, dull, wet, and windy. The whine of the undercarriage being lowered was barely audible above the roar of the engines, the plane slowing some more as the giant wheels caught the air.

Final approach. Five minutes, according to the flight

tracker on the seatback monitor in front of her. Susan looked out of the window. Roads and hedgerows rushed by then there was a long expanse of grass verge, and finally the oil-streaked tarmac of the runway.

She leaned back in her seat and closed her eyes. Despite telling Vince that their mother could rot in hell as far as she was concerned, here she was. She couldn't help but echo her brother's sentiments. What the fuck was she doing coming back to England after all these years?

* * *

The reason she was back in England was simple: her brother needed her. That was the message she'd got via Titanic Productions. Nobody in Yorkshire had her telephone number apart from Vince, and it wasn't her brother who had sent the message, it was some detective. Susan didn't catch the name because it got lost in translation, from Yorkshire to the movie company to home.

The headline was easy to catch, though.

YOUR MOTHER DIED IN HER SLEEP.

The byline was just as compelling.

YOUR BROTHER NEEDS YOU.

The rest of the message made sense if you didn't think about it too long.

Susan was advised to drop everything and come to York-shire because her brother was imploding and needed a shoulder to lean on. A familiar shoulder. A family shoulder. Susan was the only family Vince had left. She had also been told that Vince was putting a brave face on it and was refusing any help from his friends. For some reason, one of the friends was called Donkey, which only threw Susan's mind into more turmoil. The final thread of the message was, don't call Vince because he'll only tell you not to come. Leave it until you arrive, then it will be too late for him to send you back.

Susan left it until she arrived. She collected her luggage from the carousel and wheeled it outside to the ground transport area. There was a general hubbub as passengers queued for a taxi or made their way to the minibuses for off-site parking or hotel transport. There were lots of greetings and lots of laughter. Susan didn't feel like laughing. She found an empty bus stop and took out her phone. It had already pinged several times with welcome messages and telephone instructions. She deleted the messages and dialled her brother's number.

The phone kept ringing. Susan hoped it didn't go to voicemail. This wasn't something she wanted to leave on voicemail. She was about to hang up and try again later when a stranger's voice came down the line. Not her brother.

"Hello?"

* * *

Tynan explained what had been going on without going into too much detail. He didn't mention the kidnapping, or the police raid, or the body parts. He just told the woman that he was sure her brother would appreciate her support.

"How's he coping?"

Tynan shrugged even though she couldn't see him. "You know Vince."

"He's not saying much, I'll bet."

"You'd win that bet."

"But he's taking it hard?"

Tynan let out a sigh. He didn't like getting too personal with people he worked with, but he liked McNulty. He'd liked him all that time ago when McNulty had smiled and said, "I feel like a cop again." He sometimes wondered what *he* would do when he left the job behind. It didn't bear thinking about. He supposed he lived by the same mantra: once a cop, always a cop. Even if cop did sound a bit pretentious in Yorkshire.

"A week ago, he didn't know he had a mother. Then he finds out she's in a dementia care home and meets her for the first time. Then she dies before she can make amends. What do you think?"

There was a pause down the line. "I think making amends was never on the cards. Or she would have made them long ago."

"Maybe. But that doesn't soften the blow."

"No, it doesn't."

There was another pause. Tynan could hear Susan breathing down the line. It sounded as if she was taking it hard as well. Tynan didn't know what else to say. After a few moments, Susan broke the silence.

"Anyway. Thanks for sending the message. Will he have his phone back by the time I get over there?"

Tynan felt on safer ground talking about evidence bags and returning personal property. "I'll get it back to him as soon as I've finished here."

Then he realised what she had said. "Wait. What message?"

"When you called Titanic Productions to let me know about Vince."

"I didn't call Titanic Productions."

Susan sounded confused. "No? So you didn't send the car either?"

Now Tynan was worried. "What car?"

* * *

The car was big and black with tinted windows. It had pulled up at the bus stop when Susan was making the call, and the driver had held a clipboard to the window with her name on it. She had nodded and got in the back while the driver put her suitcase in the boot. The engine was purring while she continued the call.

The driver got in and closed the door.

The conversation took a turn for the worse. "No? So you didn't send the car either."

"What car?"

Susan's door opened, and a man got in beside her. He was big and black without tinted windows. He clenched his fist over the hand holding the phone and squeezed. Susan let out a whimper and released the phone. The big man turned it off and tossed it out of the window. The child locks clicked as the car pulled away from the ground transport area.

Chapter Fifty-One

McNulty didn't wait for Tynan to return his phone; he got replacement clothes from the charity basket and talked the paramedic into dropping him at Halcyon Court. Being the survivor of a police raid had its advantages, but he looked like an inmate freshly released from prison. The sweatpants were too big, and the plimsolls didn't have laces. He felt like the new boy at school whose mother couldn't afford the uniform.

Maggie came down from the office when the receptionist buzzed him in. He wasn't asked to sign the visitors' book. There was nobody for him to visit. Maggie looked him up and down. "You look like you've just got out of prison."

* * *

It was late afternoon, and Halcyon Court looked as bleak as always. The carved stone still looked like Colditz. The naked trees still reminded McNulty of Crag View. That didn't say much. Everything reminded McNulty of Crag View. It was something he would probably never escape. His old adage from *Von Ryan's Express*—"If one gets out it's a victory"—was never going to apply to him.

He stood at the second-floor window and looked out from the office at a particularly nasty looking tree branch. It was almost identical to the one that used to rattle his dormitory window on stormy nights. He let out a sigh and turned to face Maggie, who was busy rummaging through the filing cabinet behind a cheap wooden desk.

He spoke softly. "Thanks for doing this."

Maggie paused in her search and gave McNulty a sad little smile. "Doreen was a lovely woman. You don't deserve to get kidnapped and beaten on top of losing your mother."

McNulty had laid it on thick about being kidnapped. He kept his tone of voice intentionally weak. "I can't pretend we were close."

"You were getting there. She was really looking forward to that coffee."

He couldn't tell if Maggie was lying anymore, so he chose to believe her. "You never know where it might have led."

"Forward. Everything leads forward. But sometimes, jogging their memory helps them look back."

McNulty smiled. "You really are good at this. I can see why she liked you."

Maggie straightened. "Did she?"

McNulty barked a laugh and shrugged. "I don't know. She couldn't remember past the last ten minutes."

"She remembered that your dad used to drown his food in salt."

"But she couldn't remember who my dad was. Kept getting him confused with Frank Gardner."

Maggie shivered. "The man who kidnapped you. What on earth was she doing with him?"

"They had a thing going. I don't know when. I wasn't

around."

Maggie sighed. "Sorry." She knew enough about the orphanage to know it was a touchy subject.

McNulty waved a hand at the filing cabinet. "Anyway, Gardner wasn't paying the bills. So it was somebody else with money."

Maggie took the hint and returned to the filing cabinet. After a few moments, she put an accounts book on the desk and sat down. She leafed through the pages until she came to Doreen Wills. Each resident had a comprehensive history, including relatives, date of arrival, and bank details. Doreen didn't have an open bank account, so all the payments came from a third party.

"Phew. I didn't realise how much her room cost."

McNulty leaned forward. "Christ. You're not kidding."

Maggie ran her finger down the payment history, then skipped to the top of the page to see who was doing the paying. She shook her head. "That's strange."

McNulty couldn't read what she was looking at. "What?"

"Let me check her admission papers."

Maggie went back to the filing cabinet and brought out a creased manila folder. The contents were held in place by a piece of string threaded through the top left corner. The top page gave basic details such as name, age, date of birth, and previous address. There was a brief medical history that recounted when she was diagnosed with dementia, when she was accepted from hospital, how long she had been an in-patient, and who the executor was. There was no executor. There was nobody with power of attorney. There was an addendum halfway down the page with McNulty's name.

"What's that?"

Maggie tapped the entry. "That's when she named you next of kin. Couple of years ago. When she felt her mind slipping."

McNulty looked at the date. He had already been working for Larry Unger in America by then, but he hadn't found his sister yet. Thinking about Susan hardened his resolve. Whoever had been paying the bills must have known there was a son and a daughter, but had never gotten in touch.

"There's no contact number."

Maggie was scrutinising the entry. "No. That shouldn't have been accepted. Just a work contact."

"But somebody found me."

Maggie shrugged. "I don't know. I suppose if it's urgent enough, we can find anybody. Somebody must have thought it was urgent enough."

McNulty remembered the man in black at his motel room. The sombre tone and the funeral director clothes. "The message said she was very sick."

"Yes, that would be urgent enough. End-of-life care always jumps to the head of the queue. I didn't think she was that far gone." Maggie fought back the tears. "Until she was gone."

McNulty rested a hand on her shoulder. "I'm glad I got here when I did. And I'm glad I had fish and chips with her."

"But not coffee."

"Enough is as good as a feast."

"That sounds like something she would have said."

"Really?"

"When she could remember what to say."

McNulty wanted to steer the conversation back to the payments. "At least she had a nice room. Top of the range. Expensive."

Maggie took the hint. "Yes. Bank details." She found

the relevant page in the admissions file, then puffed out her cheeks in disappointment. "No name, just an overseas bank account and a standing order."

McNulty didn't understand banking. "You can do that from abroad?

"You can set up a standing order from anywhere so long as you have our bank details and Doreen's reference number."

"Where was it set up?"

Maggie followed her finger through the fine print, then stopped. "I can't even pronounce that. Sounds Russian."

McNulty felt a shiver run down his spine. Marat sounded Russian too. "If it was Russian, it would say Russia."

"East European then. I don't know. I'm from Leeds."

McNulty leaned forward to scrutinise the entry. "You're not much for taking contact numbers here, are you?"

Maggie tapped the page with one finger. "We could always call the bank. Tell them that Doreen has passed away and ask who set up the standing order."

"Ask an overseas bank to disclose client details?"

"For a good cause."

"International banking. The only good cause is confidentiality."

Maggie leaned back in her chair and let out a sigh of resignation. "Then I'm sorry. We've hit a wall."

McNulty was running all kinds of scenarios through his head, but none of them would help loosen an international bank's lips. No amount of court orders could force them to divulge client information. No amount of threats or bribes could out-threaten or out-bribe whoever it was who could afford the exclusive room at Halcyon Court. He felt so close to the answer and yet so far away.

He replayed Gardner's words. *"Not international. Just England. International is somebody else."* And Gardner's plea to the man who shot him. *"Tell Marat she didn't say anything."* That put Marat at the top of the food chain. If you're at the top of the food chain, you can afford the best room at Halcyon Court. But why would you? Unless you wanted to keep an eye on the woman who might say something you'd rather be kept secret.

Something began to vibrate in McNulty's clothes. He patted himself down and found the burner phone in the pocket of the hoodie. It hadn't been there when he'd put it on. He gave Maggie a hard look, but he didn't think she had slipped it in his pocket. Somebody at the hospital, perhaps? Or the ambulance driver? If you're top of the food chain, you can afford to pay anybody.

He pressed the green button and said, "Yes?"

The voice was hard and guttural with a faint Russian accent. "Now listen to me."

Chapter Fifty-Two

Marat Andrykowski didn't think he still had an accent. He thought his voice was fairly flat and neutral. He put that down to having spent most of the last thirty years in Yorkshire. Whenever he did go back to the homeland on business, his friends teased him about having a Yorkshire accent. When it came to moving away from home, you couldn't win. One way or another, you always sounded like you were from somewhere else.

He ended the call and looked out of the window across the Yorkshire Dales. He loved the sweep of the hills and the lush green fields, even in winter. He loved the slate roofs and the grey stone. When you were an international businessman, you could run your business from anywhere. It was all emails and telephone calls anyway. With a healthy dose of secret codes and hidden messages. That's how you stayed on top. That's how you stayed alive.

It was a pity his brother hadn't been so conscientious. Andrykowski told himself that was a long time ago. It didn't make the decisions he was about to make any easier.

* * *

McNulty had some decisions of his own to make, and using the mantra, once a cop, always a cop didn't help. What he was about to do was very un-cop-like. It was also very un-movie-like. He had grown up watching films at the local cinema or in the TV room at Crag View. In every kidnap ransom film he could remember, there was always a scene where the kidnapper said, "Don't call the police," or, "Come alone." In real life, the sensible thing to do was call the police, and in the movies, they never came alone.

The other thing was, as a cop, you always had backup. McNulty didn't have backup. McNulty didn't have anything. He didn't even have his own phone or laces in his shoes.

Maggie saw the look on his face. "What's wrong?"

McNulty slipped the burner phone in his pocket. "Everything."

Maggie closed the manila file. "We can always send a request through DHSS."

McNulty came out of his reverie. "What?"

"Department of Health and Social Security. The council. It's them that set the resident contribution rate."

"She didn't contribute anything."

Maggie closed the accounts ledger. "The council will subsidise anybody who doesn't have sufficient funds to pay. Your mum didn't have any funds. Once the council assessed her inability to pay, they will have informed the family estate that they'd need to pay the full amount."

McNulty still didn't look fully aware.

Maggie tapped the folder. "They must have had contact with whoever is paying, otherwise they wouldn't know how much to pay."

McNulty nodded, but his eyes were blank.

Maggie pushed the ledger and the folder aside. "That's not what's wrong, is it?"

McNulty took a moment to gather his thoughts, then turned steady eyes on Maggie. "Do you remember when the Big Top burned down on Woodhouse Moor?"

Chapter Fifty-Three

Darkness came early to the house at the end of the cul-de-sac. It came early everywhere. A heavy blanket of cloud hung, low and oppressive, over Mean Wood estate, and the streetlights sensed the gloom and came on. The atmosphere was damp and threatening.

McNulty watched the house from the shadows of a beach hedge that had shed its leaves but was still thick enough to keep him hidden. The downstairs lights were on. The street was still crammed nose to tail with parked cars, at least two of them on stacks of bricks since somebody had stolen their wheels. A Honda 250 motorbike had filled the narrow gap outside Donk's house. There was no PSU van and no patrol cars. The police weren't looking for Donk anymore.

Maggie had dropped McNulty fifty yards from the mouth of the cul-de-sac, and they had said their goodbyes. To Maggie, it had sounded final. McNulty didn't think he would be visiting Halcyon Court again, either, but had asked her to keep looking into the accounts. He didn't think Maggie believed him and took the request with a pinch of salt. He had thanked her again and watched her drive away. Now it was time to re-enlist Donkey Flowers. It was time to send for backup.

McNulty crossed the neat front lawn in the dark and

knocked on the kitchen door. The red and white curtains twitched as Donk made sure it wasn't the police—McNulty still had the copper's knock, so maybe, once a cop always a cop did still apply. The door opened, and Donk stood silhouetted in the rectangle of light. He looked McNulty up and down. "You look like you've just got out of prison."

* * *

The first thing Donk did was get McNulty a change of clothes. The just-out-of-prison look wasn't going to cut it once the night drew in. McNulty stood on the landing while Donk searched the wardrobe and came out with a selection that was about the right size. A bit roomy perhaps, but for what McNulty planned to do, having extra room was a good thing. It was also helpful that Donk didn't seem to like bright colours. Twenty minutes later, McNulty looked like an SAS assault squad in his black cargo pants, dark blue NATO sweater, and dull brown Doc Martin boots. With laces. The green wax jacket made him look like a gamekeeper or a poacher. McNulty was leaning toward poacher.

"Is this your burglar outfit?"

"I was never a burglar. You know that. It was you that kept arresting me to stop me becoming a thief."

"I kept arresting you because your mother told me to."

"Same difference. I didn't become a burglar."

"A poacher then?"

Donk looked offended. "You can always go back to your prison sweats."

"If I get caught out in these, prison is where I'll be going."

Donk got serious. "If you do what I think you're going to

do, the cemetery is where you'll be going."

McNulty got serious, too. "If I don't, the cemetery is where Susan will be going."

That brought them to the second thing. "Is Eric still mad about the car?"

$$* * *$$

Eric Hugunin was still mad about life, but since being mad hadn't changed his life as a dwarf, he had decided to embrace it. *I am what I am, do you have a problem with it,* had been his attitude ever since he'd been old enough to fight. Fighting dirty had been his attitude once he'd realised he kept losing those fights. This McNulty fella seemed to want to fight dirty.

"The human cannonball?"

McNulty nodded. "I heard you could clear three double-decker buses lined up nose to tail."

Hugunin's legs dangled from the chair as he performed a perfect parabola over the kitchen table with one hand. "It wasn't the distance, it was the landing."

"Angle and elevation?"

Hugunin shook his head. "Angle and elevation is the same thing. Elevation and force, that's what hits the target."

"Did you hit the target?"

Hugunin snorted a laugh. "The fella in charge of the cannon? Couldn't find his arse with both hands. His idea was to just use a bigger net for the landing, but the circus owner thought it didn't look dangerous enough."

"Was it dangerous enough?"

Hugunin stopped swinging his legs. "Before they decided on the human cannonball stunt, I used to stick my head in a lion's mouth. The owner reckoned using a regular-sized carny didn't look as ferocious. Using a dwarf emphasised the difference in size. Big mouth, little head. The trainer used to prod the lion so it would roar just before I put my head between its jaws. I could feel the heat. Damn thing used to spit at me. Anyway, this one time, I stuck my head in too soon, and its teeth caught my neck. Blood everywhere. The owner was delighted but confused. How could a dwarf get his head stuck? You see, the difference in height has nothing to do with the difference in size. My head is the same size as yours. It's just the legs and body that make you taller."

McNulty shrugged. "I have no idea what you just said."

Hugunin tapped the side of his nose and winked. "It was dangerous because tall people were making the decisions. Using enough gunpowder to propel a full-size person through the air. A full-size person would have landed in the net. Me, I could have cleared another two buses."

McNulty nodded. "So it wasn't the size of the net but the distance?"

Hugunin shook his head again. "The Big Top is only so big. Distance wasn't the issue; it was the size of the charge. Once I took over the cannon myself, I stopped hitting the side of the tent and found the net."

"Because of the explosives?"

"Big charge big bang."

"Is that why the Big Top burned down?"

Hugunin looked sheepish. "That was something else. My head isn't the only thing that's big. When the circus owner's daughter found out… Well, we should have been more careful."

"And that's why you're not in touch with them anymore."

"I'm in touch with some of them. Just not the owner."

"With the cannonball man?"

"I'm the cannonball man."

"The man in charge of the explosives?"

Chapter Fifty-Four

One thing McNulty had learned from working at Titanic Productions was that the movie life was no different to a travelling circus. Everybody knew everybody else, and they all stuck together. He had even thought about that when he'd applied for the job with Larry Unger. He had felt like a boy running off to join the circus. Now the circus had come back to bite him. In a good way.

The other thing he'd learned was that when it came to weapons and explosives, there was always one man in charge of them all. The armourer. And the armourer had connections that spread way beyond Titanic Productions. The Big Top wasn't the only place a human cannonball could make a bang.

* * *

They hashed out a plan at Donk's kitchen table, using cereal boxes and food containers to form a rough layout of the buildings. McNulty felt like Lee Marvin giving the final briefing to *The Dirty Dozen* just before they were parachuted onto the chateau that was being used by Nazi generals. That would make Donk, Richard Jaeckel's MP sergeant. He wasn't sure who it would make Hugunin; there weren't any dwarves in *The Dirty Dozen*.

McNulty kept interrupting the briefing to apologise for Hugunin's car. He felt he had to promise it wouldn't happen again.

Hugunin indicated the makeshift buildings with a sweep of the hand. "If this goes according to plan." He pointed at the main building. "That Cornflake box is going to end up a lot worse than my Fiat." He twirled his hand around the table. "And the woods are going to need the fire brigade pretty damn quick if you don't want the hill turning into a wildfire."

McNulty held up a placating hand. "It's too wet in Yorkshire for wildfires."

"Not with the stuff my man is providing. It'll suck the wet out of a swimming pool and melt your Speedos."

"As long as you wait until I've got Susan out. After that, you can burn the place to the ground."

Donk's face betrayed his concern. "It's the waiting for you to get her out part that I'm worried about. You sure we'll get the signal?"

McNulty thought about the elevated location and took out the burner phone. "Best signal in North Leeds. I've got you both programmed in. I'll text Go and hit send the minute I've got her clear."

Donk still looked worried. "And you're sure you can get in without them seeing you?"

McNulty thought about the Russian's choice of location. It felt bittersweet that the place he was going to save his sister was the place he'd failed to protect her when he was a boy. "I've been sneaking in and out of Crag View my entire life."

Hugunin concentrated on his side of the operation and left

Donk to bring the reality check. "You were a kid sneaking in and out of an orphanage. This time you're not up against the headmaster, you're up against a Russian oligarch and his pet hitman."

Hugunin couldn't help chipping in. "And however many others he's brought along for security."

McNulty waved their concerns aside. "I only need to swing the Bible at one of them. Break the boss's nose, and the rest will be too busy." He nodded at the makeshift model. "If you can bring the Cornflake box down around their ears."

Hugunin nodded. "Oh, you'll be up to your ears in Cornflakes."

* * *

And that was pretty much it. Hugunin left to liaise with his armourer, and Donk put the Cornflakes away. His mother had always insisted on keeping the kitchen tidy. McNulty composed the text and saved it as a draft message. It didn't take long to compose *Go*. He added two addressees, then came out of the app. All he had to do now was open the messaging app and press Send.

He had controlled his nerves while giving the briefing, but now he felt his hands begin to shake. He had always felt like this before launching an operation, whether it was executing a search warrant or bursting in to arrest a wanted man. The quiet before the storm was always when second thoughts crept in. He was having more than second thoughts this time; he was having second, third, and fourth thoughts. Was he doing the right thing? Could he still remember the secret passages? Did this fly in the face of everything he had sworn an oath for as a police officer? A cop. Once or always.

"Come alone." The standard kidnappers' demand. McNulty was going to be alone when he entered Crag View Orphanage for the last time, but he was just going to have backup nearby.

"Don't call the police." The other standard kidnappers' demand. That one, McNulty was having more trouble with. He couldn't use the, once a cop, always a cop mantra this time. This time, he couldn't claim to be a cop, not even a movie cop. This time, he was going rogue in the truest sense of the word. His anger was about to get righteous and biblical. He might not be swinging the Bible at Mr Cruckshank's nose, but Marat Andrykowski was about to get the full Samuel L Jackson treatment. McNulty was going to strike down upon thee with great vengeance and furious anger. He was going to do more than pop a cap in his ass.

So, *"Don't call the police."* McNulty reckoned he could get away with that one on a technicality. He wasn't going to call the police, he was going to call himself. He took out the burner phone and dialled his own number from memory. The phone rang three times, then Tynan answered.

"You going to do something stupid?"

McNulty still didn't ask for the police. "I'm going to need the fire brigade."

Chapter Fifty-Five

The sharp points of the gable ends stood out like crooked spires above the trees. The chimneystacks looked like broken fingers against the twilight. Brooding clouds hung low in the sky, their underbellies painted orange from the city lights in the distance. Even standing across the road from the woods that surrounded Crag View Orphanage, it felt too close for comfort. Anything to do with the boarded-up children's home was too close for comfort. There was no comfort.

If the carved stone of Halcyon Court looked like Colditz, Crag View was a Hammer House Of Horror. The orphanage could have been any of a dozen haunted houses or vampire castles, but what it reminded McNulty of was "The House of the Rising Sun." The song had always played in his mind when he'd seen the crooked spires standing out atop the wooded hillside. He heard the guitar intro now as he stood in the woods as The Animals sang the opening lines.

The music sent a shiver down his spine. Goosebumps sprang up on the back of his neck. The council should have demolished the abandoned building years ago, the orphanage having been closed in disgrace after the child abuse scandal broke in the news. It had never been sold or redeveloped.

McNulty reckoned there was too much stigma attached to it. Too much pain had bled into the very ground it stood upon. It was never going to be anything other than the place that too many children's lives had been destroyed. McNulty's included. His sister, too.

The heavy gate that blocked the entrance drive still hung from its bottom hinge, the top one rusted away, causing Crag View's main gate to lean like a drunken sailor. Three solid chains had been padlocked around the top, middle and bottom to hold the gates together and a temporary post had been jury-rigged to keep the entire structure upright. The gates didn't need to open. Nobody was going to drive up to the house ever again.

McNulty looked at the main gate for ten whole minutes, then crossed the road fifty yards to the right. He wasn't going through the main gate; he was going to sneak in like he used to when he hadn't been allowed out to the pictures. Even back then, it had been *Von Ryan's Express*, *Where Eagles Dare*, or *The Dirty Dozen*. Some of the spaghetti westerns as well. James Bond had been too sophisticated.

The gap in the hedgerow had filled in over the years, but the dip in the ground where he had burrowed under the fence was still there. He dropped to his knees to dig the hole out again. It was time to parachute onto the chateau.

* * *

Crag View Orphanage had plenty of history, most of it bad in recent years. Before it became an orphanage, it had been government buildings. Before that, in the 1930s, it had been a finishing school for girls. It was the government buildings

287

part that had helped McNulty sneak in and out undetected.

During the Second World War, Crag View had been used as an evacuation centre for government officials and high-ranking military officers. It was far enough out of Leeds to be away from the Luftwaffe's bombing routes—most of their targets being Hull, Coventry and London—but since it housed government officials and high ranking military officers it had to offer protection if the Luftwaffe's strategy changed. The underground passageways and storage facilities were extended and reinforced. Bomb shelters were added in the woods away from the main buildings, the grassy mounds hidden among the trees and connected by utility corridors that channelled power and water from the mains transformer, which was also hidden in the woods.

After the war, the bunkers were decommissioned, and the power turned off, but the corridors hadn't been filled in. The grassy mounds became overgrown hillocks, and two of the passageways had collapsed, forming a sunken channel in the sports field. Over the years, the indentations became less pronounced, but the bunkers were still great places to play. Some of the children had found helmets and webbing belts in the nearest bunker, prompting the orphanage staff to flatten the bunker and punish the children. Punishing children seemed to be their mission in life.

The other two bunkers were left to rot. The tunnels fell into disrepair. There were no more helmets or webbing belts. There was still plenty of punishment, but none of it was prompted by wartime exploits. If you answered back, you got the cane. If you were late for class, you got the cane. If you were a girl, you would get a lot more, some of the boys, too. Fairly soon, the tunnels became a myth that nobody believed.

CHAPTER FIFTY-FIVE

Unless you were a movie fan who was banned from going to the pictures.

Young Vincent McNulty used the tunnel to the furthest bunker, feeling like Charles Bronson in *The Great Escape*—another of his favourite war films. Walking with a stoop to avoid banging his head, he became the Tunnel King during his illicit trips into town. He even nicknamed the tunnels Tom, Dick, and Harry, like in the film. Harry was the tunnel he used, refusing to acknowledge that he would ever take Dick.

He wasn't taking Dick tonight. Creeping through the undergrowth, he moved from tree to tree, always keeping half an eye on the forbidding structure on the other side of the sports field. The windows were sightless eyes, nailed shut and boarded up. Some of the boards were rotten wood, but none of them had fallen off. There were no lights showing through the cracks. The house was in darkness. *Hammer House of Horror* would have been impressed.

He paused on the edge of the woods and slowed his breathing. Eventually, his pulse stopped thumping in his ears, and he could listen to the woodland sounds. Two birds were fighting in the trees. Something was rummaging around in the fallen leaves. An owl hooted, and a dog barked. It seemed that wherever McNulty went, there was always a barking dog. At least there was no noisy TV or husband and wife arguing. There was no traffic noise from the A6120 Ring Road, which was just beyond the hill.

Careful not to snap any twigs, McNulty melted into the shadows and turned away from the house. It felt counter-intuitive to be going in the opposite direction to breach the chateau defences, but he knew the bunker was over there somewhere. The deeper he went into the woods, the better his night vision became. He could see the low branches instead of walking into them. He could sense the dips in the undergrowth before falling into them. He kept low and loose, breathing in through his nose and out through his mouth. The night smelled of pine needles and wet grass. There was a faint smell of rotting flesh, and he knew he'd found the bunker.

The grassy knoll hunched like a sleeping giant in the dark. Wildflowers dotted the crest even at this time of year. Some kind of hardy perennial, or maybe it was just dead leaves standing out in the gloom. McNulty wasn't interested in the flowers; he was looking for the solid square silhouette of the entrance. The undergrowth had flourished since the groundsman had received his final paycheck. It took a few minutes to find the unnatural straight lines that proved the mound was man-made.

He circled left around the end of the mound and pulled at the leaves and bushes that had sprung up over the years. The heavy wooden door smelled rank and sickly. Not rotting flesh, but close enough to make his stomach do a lazy turn. The armour plating had long since rusted and peeled off. He glanced over his shoulder to make sure the lights hadn't come on, then reached in and tore the soft wood apart.

Chapter Fifty-Six

McNulty didn't feel like Charles Bronson tonight. He didn't feel like the Tunnel King; he felt like a sewer rat. Once he was inside the bunker, he took the burner phone out of his pocket and used the light from the screen to get his bearings. The cheap phone didn't have a torch app.

The bunker was smaller than he remembered. He doubted it would have sheltered more than half a dozen people, and even then, not for long. This wasn't one of those survivalist chambers he'd seen in America, where conspiracy theorists built a second home underground, ready for the apocalypse. It didn't have shelves of supplies and bunk beds. It didn't have anything except leaves blown in through the gaps in the door and a pair of fetid carcasses. He couldn't tell if the bones were from a dog, a cat, or a badger, but whatever it was, it hadn't died alone. It hadn't been eaten alone either, the scuff marks in the dust suggesting a whole family of rats.

Yes, not the Tunnel King.

McNulty picked up a thighbone and used it to sweep away the cobwebs that festooned the ceiling and walls. Whatever furniture had been in here during the war had long since been removed. There hadn't even been any when he used to sneak out to the pictures, just random pieces of wood and the occasional seat cushion. All that had been reduced to dust in the years since the orphanage closed down. Now there was just bones, dirt, and dead leaves. And a door that hadn't been opened in over thirty years.

McNulty cleared the last of the cobwebs and tossed the thighbone aside. It clattered on the concrete floor, making him jump. The noise sounded loud in the silent bunker, and he had to remind himself that he was underground and more than a hundred yards from the main building. A brass band could play in here, and nobody would hear it. Even so, McNulty erred on the side of caution. It was amazing how sounds could be transmitted along pipes and conduits. The utilities tunnel had plenty of pipes and conduit.

The door against the back wall was smaller and less rotten than the main door. It didn't have metal cladding because it wasn't designed to protect the bunker from aerial attack. The wood was dry and brittle, though, and the hinges had rusted shut. As McNulty tried to prise it open, the entire door came away in his hands. Ants scurried across the floor. He didn't bother standing on them. A few seconds later, the floor was clear.

The entrance to the tunnel was a gaping black hole. McNulty remembered there was a flight of concrete stairs leading further underground before the tunnel became a straight passage to the house. He was conscious of not wanting to use all the phone's battery, so he used the light to see the stairs, then turned it off.

He went down the stairs one step at a time, testing his footing with the toe of his shoe before moving to the next step. Once he was at the bottom, he used the phone to see where he was going, then closed his eyes before turning it off again. He took a mental picture of the tunnel, then opened his eyes. Night vision didn't kick in. For that to work, there needed to be at least a little light. The underground passage was completely black, so he had to rely on the mental picture. He replayed it now.

The passage was long and straight. It was maybe five feet high by four feet wide, so he had to walk at a crouch. The floor was clear of obstructions, but the ceiling had a collection of pipes and conduits fastened along the full length. The pipes were on the right, reducing the height by another six inches. He knew from the past that the passage didn't curve and there were no bends; it was a straight crawl from beginning to end. When he used to sneak along it as a child, he thought it would be cool to have a little trolley like they had in *The Great Escape,* but now he realised that would make too much noise. Using one hand to test the headroom, he slowly moved along the tunnel, each footstep taking him one step closer to childhood.

* * *

Drip, drip, drip. The leaky pipe and damp smell made young Vincent wish he'd brought a raincoat. The film had been good tonight, even though most of the dozen had died at the end. He preferred *Where Eagles Dare,* a film where the heroes triumphed, and the traitor jumped out of the plane without a parachute. *The Dirty Dozen* didn't upset him as much as *Von Ryan's Express,* though. He'd seen that three times, and it brought a tear to his eye every time Frank Sinatra got shot before he could reach the train.

It was late, and it was dark, but the cover of darkness had

always been his friend when it came to sneaking back in after the pictures. So far, he had never been caught. He didn't think Mr Cruckshank even knew he'd been out, and this was the fifth time Vincent had come back all excited over a film and depressed about returning to his room. There was nothing exciting about living at Crag View Orphanage. There was nothing good about an orphanage, period. Ask anyone who had ever grown up in one. It was a life of shit piled on shit, the shit of becoming institutionalised after the shit of being abandoned. Vincent was beginning to understand what it meant to be institutionalised. Sneaking out to the pictures was his way of fighting against it.

He sparked the lighter he had stolen from the groundskeeper's shed, part of his escape supplies that included a bus pass that he had changed the ID photo on and a pair of leather gloves. He had seen The Great Escape twice and knew the benefits of being prepared. There was no point getting through the escape tunnel if you couldn't catch the bus into town. At least he didn't have to learn German. Look what happened to Gordon Jackson when he had slipped up on the railway station.

The lighter flickered. The tunnel wasn't as solid as it must have been during the war, and there was a draft coming from a breach somewhere along its length. The leaky water pipes added to the general air of dilapidation. That and the rats. It was the rats he wanted to scare away with the lighter.

Drip, drip, drip. The rats were fairly quiet unless he stood on one, then the squeal hurt his teeth. It was like chalk on a blackboard and sent a shiver down his spine. The rats scampered away, leaving his path clear. Keeping his head down to avoid the sagging pipes, he reached the end of the tunnel and began to climb the stairs to the boiler room.

* * *

McNulty paused at the top of the stairs, turned off the phone screen, and listened at the door. Unlike his childhood exploits, there was more at stake than spending a day in the cooler. That's how his mind reshaped the memories, the cooler being Steve McQueen's punishment for insubordination. McNulty's punishment was five swipes of the cane across his bare arse. He hadn't understood why the headmaster needed to drop McNulty's pants until much later, Mr Cruckshank being an equal opportunity abuser. If he got caught tonight, the consequences would be far more serious.

He tested the door. It was old and warped, but not as rotten as the door to the bunker. The leaky pipes and damp had been halfway along the tunnel; now that he was underneath the main house, the passage was dry. The hinges weren't as rusty either. The door swung open with hardly a squeak. He listened some more. When he was satisfied, he stepped into the boiler room. It still smelled of leaked fuel oil and rust. He didn't bother closing the door behind him.

When he clicked on the phone screen again, he realised he'd been right; if he got caught tonight, the consequences would be far more serious. He puffed out his cheeks and got caught tonight.

Chapter Fifty-Seven

"Did you really think you were the only one who knew about the tunnels?"

"I didn't think a Russian oligarch would know much about Crag View."

The best room to hold the conversation was the last room McNulty wanted to visit. Of course it was. The headmaster's office, under the main stairs. Marat Andrykowski's tone hardened. "Tonight is going to be a steep learning curve, then. Because there is a lot you do not know."

* * *

McNulty's heart had sunk when he'd seen the two men waiting for him in the boiler room. One of them he didn't recognise. The other was the hitman with the silenced gun. The gun was held casually, pointing in McNulty's general direction but not aimed at anything specific. The other man turned on a black Maglite torch and took McNulty's phone. Neither of them spoke. McNulty didn't speak either. They were either going to shoot him or invite him for a chat. The gun twitched toward the stairs into the house. So, it was an invite for a chat.

McNulty considered his options. It didn't take long. He didn't have any. If he bolted back down the tunnel, he'd get shot in the back. If he charged the man with the gun, he'd get shot in the front. If he went for the man with the torch, he'd get shot in the side. None of those outcomes would help Susan. None of them explained why the Russian had snatched his sister in the first place, unless it was to draw McNulty in without calling the police. If that was the case, then the Russian wanted to talk, so McNulty took the only option available. He did as he was told.

He climbed the familiar staircase from the boiler room, and his mind drifted back to his childhood. Whenever he got close to Crag View, his childhood was the only place for his mind to go. In his mind, he was sneaking up from the boiler room and waiting until the main hallway was empty. After listening for a few moments, he would cross the hallway to the stairs and creep up to his room. The staff would have all been asleep after McNulty caught the last bus from the pictures. The children's home would have been quiet. He did exactly the same now, but for a different reason. This time, he was listening for more heavies. There weren't any in the entrance hall. There was just the muted sound of voices from across the hall and a sliver of light from a gap in the door.

He half expected to hear a slap that sounded like a gunshot. A gunshot followed by a heartbreaking whimper. It was the right door, and it was the same girl. Except this time, Susan was a grown woman, and the man wasn't Mr Cruckshank.

The two men followed McNulty into the hallway. The gun twitched for him to enter the headmaster's office. The other man confirmed the instruction with a swish of the torch. They still didn't speak. McNulty let out a sigh and stepped through the door into memory lane.

* * *

The slap sounded like a gunshot in the quiet office. A gunshot followed by a heartbreaking whimper. A wounded animal kind of whimper. The man in charge of Crag View Orphanage stood back and leaned against his desk, sunlight from the window glinting off his glasses.

The gunshot echoed in Vincent's ears. Anger filled him like hot oil.

Mr Cruckshank pushed off from the desk, and his bulk hid the bench seat in the alcove. It didn't matter. It was too late. Vincent had already seen the girl, who was too young to defend herself, holding the torn dress across her chest. The girl he would find out much later was the sister he hadn't known he had.

He saw the bright red handprint on her cheek. Picked the biggest book he could find from the bookshelf and hefted it in both hands like a baseball player preparing to swing. The anger boiled over.

The Bible crashed into the headmaster's face and broke his nose.

* * *

McNulty didn't retrace his steps through the upstairs rooms this time. He didn't go up the uncarpeted stairs. His footsteps didn't echo through the dusty corridors, and he couldn't see the peeling wallpaper or the damp patches from the hole in the ceiling, but the place still smelled of damp and rat shit.

Probably not the same rats that had eaten the dog in the bunker. His feet didn't crunch on broken glass, and he didn't trace the initials carved into the banister rail with his fingers. This time it was all about one room. The headmaster's office.

The original desk and chairs had gone, but it was the only room in Crag View that was still carpeted. There were no curtains, but the windows were boarded up. The wallpaper was dry and solid. The bookcase was built into the wall, so that was still there. No books, though. No Bible. And the upholstered bench seat still filled the alcove near the window. There was a fire of splintered wood and old newspapers in the ornate fireplace, and two candles flickered on the wide cupboard at the bottom of the bookcase, moulded in place by dripping wax.

That was where the similarities with his last visit to Crag View—when he'd been on the run from the police for the missing girls from Northern X—ended. He had used Donk's sleeping bag on the upholstered bench seat in the window alcove.

This time, the bench seat was taken. Susan sat with her knees together and her hands in her lap. The man sitting on a foldout camping chair in front of her was preparing a sandwich on a serving tray across his knees. He stopped pouring salt on the sandwich and looked up. McNulty couldn't help noticing the man was drowning his food in salt.

Chapter Fifty-Eight

"Did you really think you were the only one who knew about the tunnels?"

"I didn't think a Russian oligarch would know much about Crag View."

"Tonight is going to be a steep learning curve, then. Because there is a lot you do not know."

There you go, all caught up. The man had finished drowning his sandwich in salt and waved for McNulty to sit in the other foldout camping chair. McNulty ignored him and sat next to Susan. He gave her shoulders a gentle squeeze, then looked at the man who had the same blue eyes and thin nose as the McNulty family line.

"You must be Marat."

Andrykowski nodded while he swallowed, then smiled. "That is the first part of your learning curve. Marat. Yes. Marat Andrykowski."

"Is that like, Bond, James Bond?"

"Clearly not, since I used my first name first, not my surname. But if it makes you happy. I know you like going to the movies. Or is that, going to the pictures, now you're back in Yorkshire?"

"It's the pictures wherever I am."

Andrykowski gave McNulty a wry little smile. "Because you can take the man out of Yorkshire but not Yorkshire out of the man?"

"Something like that."

"They used to say that about Russia. But honestly, the longer I am away, the less Russian I feel."

"You sound Russian to me."

"You don't sound like an orphan to me. And yet here you are. Sneaking back in from the pictures like you were ten years old."

"I was twelve. When I started the pictures thing."

"But not when you broke the headmaster's nose."

McNulty was growing increasingly uneasy about how much the Russian seemed to know about his past. He had only been caught once sneaking back from the pictures, and even then, they hadn't known how he got in and out of the building. The broken nose had been kept quiet too, Mr Cruckshank not wanting to advertise the fact that one of his charges had hit him with the Bible. The punishment had been severe, though. Susan's documents had been destroyed after she was sold into adoption in America, and McNulty hadn't found out she was his sister until he was an adult. McNulty decided to turn the tables and show the Russian he wasn't the only one with insider knowledge.

"You really do like your salt, don't you?"

This time, Andrykowski's smile was sad. "Ah, yes. Your mother. So she did talk to you after all. That's what I was afraid of."

* * *

The candles flickered as the door closed. Susan watched in silence as the Russian waved a hand and the two heavies left without a word. She wondered if now was the time to make a break for it, but since the windows were boarded up and the men were no doubt waiting in the corridor, that didn't seem like an option.

She glanced at her brother. Vince looked pale at the mention of their mother. She wasn't looking very colourful herself. Being kidnapped from the airport and bundled into a derelict orphanage that she hardly remembered could have that effect on a person.

The candles settled down. Susan tried to do the same. She took slow, shallow breaths and decided to follow her brother's lead.

* * *

Her brother's lead was to wait and see. Even though McNulty couldn't send the Go message now, there was still Plan B. Eric Hugunin would have seen McNulty get caught from his vantage point on the landing. After that, it was the fallback position in the annex building. The annex housed the indoor swimming pool and the gym. McNulty didn't know how well that building had stood the test of time, but it had a good view across the grounds to the headmaster's office.

He leaned back against the window and carefully tested the chipboard that had replaced the broken glass. Like any wood that had faced the Yorkshire weather for decades, it was soft around the edges. One good shove could rip it off the wall and give Hugunin a signal. Conversely, Hugunin would have already started the countdown, and if he didn't get a signal from McNulty, would set the explosives off anyway.

That was Plan B. Kind of. For now, he settled in for the steep learning curve.

* * *

Andrykowski looked at the two McNulty's and wondered how much to tell them. Since they were both going to die anyway, there was no reason to hold anything back, but it pained him to admit the truth. He would have been more than happy to let McNulty live out his life in blissful ignorance, probably wondering about the mother who had abandoned him, but not doing anything to find out. That was the thing about America: it gave you distance from the past. McNulty had made a success of himself. His sister, too. Why did he have to spoil it by coming back just because Doreen was dying?

He knew why, of course; because one of the care workers had felt guilty about Doreen dying alone and had taken it upon herself to find the son Doreen had been monitoring from afar. Sending the message via a man in black had been a little extravagant, but Americans loved a bit of overkill. Once McNulty had come back, the main problem was how much did Doreen remember? Now that Frank Gardner had taken it upon himself to have her killed, the only question was, how much had she told McNulty before she passed?

Andrykowski felt a stab of grief. Whatever Doreen had been before age, and dementia robbed her of control, the Russian had still been fond of her. It was that closeness that made it difficult to bury the loose ends. The loose ends were Vince McNulty and his sister, Susan.

Andrykowski let out a sigh. The family resemblance was undeniable, but he hadn't really noticed until he was face-to-face with McNulty. Susan looked more like her mother. McNulty was the double of his father. That made this even more painful. He wondered if it was true what they said: that confession was good for the soul? If so, he decided to get it all off his chest.

"You want to know about the salt? Let me tell you."

Chapter Fifty-Nine

McNulty braced himself for the awkward father-son chat. He knew it would be even more awkward since the son had just found out that his father was the head of an international sex trafficking gang. And a Russian to boot. McNulty was the very antithesis of a Russian. He was about as western as you could get. He loved burgers, movies, and pizza. He hated snow and fur hats. But he did have a habit of putting too much salt on his food. As far as he could see, that was the only thing the father had passed on to the son.

"I know she said my father used to drown his food in salt."

Andrykowski watched McNulty's expression. "Is that all she said?"

McNulty stared back. "She said the less I knew about him, the better. And considering the situation we're in, I'd say she was right."

"Because I drown my food in salt?"

"Because you kidnapped my sister and there's a gunman outside the door."

Andrykowski appeared to consider what to say next. The expression on his face betrayed sadness, warmth, and cold-blooded hardness. "And you think this is where the Russian explains his evil plan before the hero escapes and thwarts the global threat."

"I'm more worried about the local threat."

"Local being Crag View Orphanage with a gunman outside the door?"

"Yes."

Andrykowski took a deep breath. The long, slow exhale was tinged with resignation. His shoulders didn't so much sag as completely disconnect. He flexed his neck, first to one side, then the other. The bones cracked. When he looked at McNulty again, his eyes were steady. "You should not have come back."

Susan shifted on the bench next to McNulty. "That's what I said."

Andrykowski turned his head toward Susan. "Because?"

McNulty recognised the anger building up in his sister. Susan didn't hold back. "Because I told him she could rot in hell as far as I was concerned."

"Why?"

"For dumping me and Vince in a children's home."

"You both survived the children's home."

"Is that supposed to make me feel better?"

"I am stating a fact."

Susan stuck her chin out. "Well, here's a fact for you. That woman was an evil, selfish bitch who dumped her children because she didn't want to provide for us. And the only reason I survived was because my brother broke the headmaster's nose."

McNulty squeezed Susan's knee. "And because Cruckshank had her adopted in America to hide her from me."

Andrykowski waited for the storm to blow itself out, then

let out a sigh. He gave a little nod. "You are both right. And you are both wrong."

McNulty tested the weakened chipboard. "How's that?"

The Russian kept his voice calm and even. "She was an evil woman. But it was not Mr Cruckshank who sent you to America. That was a get out of jail free card that had nothing to do with the paedophile headmaster."

The warmth and sadness crossed his face again. "I only wish I'd had two get-out-of-jail-free cards. But I didn't." He looked at Susan. "So I sent you to America and trusted that you," looking at McNulty, "were strong enough to look after yourself."

McNulty couldn't hide the confusion on his face. "You knew about this place back then?"

This time, the warmth left the Russian's face, leaving only sadness. "I owned the place back then." He shrugged. "Part owned. Along with your mother and my brother." His eyes turned to McNulty. "The man who really did drown his food in salt."

Chapter Sixty

It felt like the air had been sucked out of the room. McNulty slumped against the window so hard that the board almost came off. Susan sat up straight, spreading her fingers as if she'd been electrocuted. The fire crackled in the hearth. The candles flickered despite there being no draft. Nobody moved. Nobody spoke. Everybody listened to the silence and the crackling flames.

Susan spoke first. "You have a brother?"

Quickly followed by McNulty. "You're my uncle?"

Andrykowski answered them both. "My brother was Frank Andrykowski. He loved his dog, which he named after you." Nodding at Susan. "And he loved your mother."

He let out another sigh. "I, however, did not love the dog."

* * *

Love triangles are never a good thing, especially when that triangle involves family. Doing the right thing is never easy, either. To Marat, it felt like there was no right thing; there was just love, the love for his brother and the love for his brother's wife. Of course, Doreen hadn't been Frank's wife when Marat first met her, but she had chosen Frank over

Marat, so the love triangle ended right there. Sibling rivalry was bad enough under normal circumstances, but when the siblings commanded an army of hitmen and knee-breakers, it was sensible to play it straight.

Playing it straight meant watching Doreen from a distance and only interfering when one or the other of them went too far. There were plenty of instances of them going too far but one thing Marat couldn't argue with was the direction of the business that Doreen created, the international sex trafficking business.

"What? My mum was the head of Northern X?"

"Northern X was a local subsidiary, not the umbrella corporation."

"She was the head of the umbrella corporation?"

Andrykowski ignored McNulty's outburst and painted the picture with broad strokes and time-lapse history. Doreen Wills not only created the market for underage girls and boys, she founded Crag View Orphanage as a legitimate cover and plentiful supply. Nobody was interested in unwanted children, so she became an altruistic supporter of unwed mothers and stole their children, all under the guise of an adoption agency that arranged just enough adoptions to make Crag View a legitimate charity.

Then she got pregnant, and life became complicated. Even though she was married to Frank by then, having a child wasn't part of her plan. She gave birth in private and declared the child stillborn before returning to work more motivated than ever. Her son was dumped on the doorstep and became the first of many secret child abandonments that made Crag View famous for helping unwed mothers through their traumatic births. Young Vincent was to be fed and watered until he was old enough to be trafficked, then sold into the business.

"I was a sex slave?"

"You would have been."

"I think I'd have remembered that."

"It didn't happen. Your papers were altered. You became McNulty. And your mother didn't care enough to keep track of you. Once you were in the system, her job was done. In her view."

Marat had been consumed with guilt about his nephew, but consoled himself with the knowledge that he had at least protected Vincent by hiding him in plain sight. An orphan amid a houseful of orphans. Marat also made sure that the boy was never included in the inventory of lost boys for sale and hid his past so deep that even the headmaster didn't know who he was. As far as Mr Cruckshank was concerned, young McNulty was just a thorn in his side.

Life went on. The business thrived. Local subsidiaries were created, and much later, Telfon Speed was put in charge of Northern X. The massage chain thrived in the low-level sex industry before branching out into torture porn itself. Employing disaffected young girls meant there was a secondary supply of girls who would never be reported missing.

In the meantime, Doreen got pregnant again, and Marat had to work his sleight of hand for a second time. Having to protect a young girl was more difficult, so Marat had to be creative. He had given Susan a different surname and put a block on all enquiries when she was old enough to be sold for sex. He had even considered having her adopted by a legitimate family, but wouldn't have been able to hide that from the accountant. Using threats and bribery, Marat had made sure that Susan didn't appear on any lists of eligible girls.

All of that was nearly derailed when trouble reared its ugly head. Twice. Frank Andrykowski was killed in a plane crash on a visit to the homeland.

"My dad's dead?"

Andrykowski held up a hand and continued. The other thing that reared its ugly head was when young Vincent McNulty broke the headmaster's nose with a Bible. Both incidents had turned Marat's world upside down. On the one hand, he had to cope with Doreen's grief and arrange his brother's funeral, and on the other hand, there was the problem of Mr Cruckshank trying to rape Vincent's sister. The paedophile headmaster had overstepped the mark. Marat had considered having him killed, but the Bible incident had already found its way into the public domain. Child abuse and the Catholic Church was already a big news story. Adding an orphanage simply stoked the fire.

"My dad's dead?"

This time, Andrykowski acknowledged the comment. "Yes."

"And my mum knew?"

Andrykowski nodded his understanding. "Because of what she said about losing the dog, you mean?"

McNulty heard his mother's voice. *Frank will be so angry. Best dog we ever had. I don't want to get Frank angry.*

Andrykowski let out a sigh. "The dementia came later. At the time, yes, she knew."

Things began to unravel after the child abuse story hit the news. There were several government enquiries and dozens of local petitions that finally resulted in Crag View

Orphanage being closed down and the children rehoused. The accountant did manage to keep the true nature of the children's home hidden, and the real owners were never revealed. Mr Cruckshank took the blame, under threat of death, and the business moved overseas for a while.

It was McNulty's turn to hold up a hand. "Rewind. You had Susan adopted in America."

"There was a period of uncertainty. I didn't want her real name being revealed. Doreen could be…" Andrykowski struggled to find the right word. "Unpredictable. Volatile. Vindictive. There would have been consequences."

"But she named me as next of kin."

"That came later, too. I don't know why. Maybe knowing she was nearing the end gave her a different perspective. Guilt can manifest itself in many different ways. We weren't talking by then, although I did make sure she was comfortable. It was the least I could do."

"While you were still running the international sex trafficking."

Andrykowski shrugged. "I never said I was perfect."

"You were killing young girls."

"I was running a business."

"A business that killed young girls."

Andrykowski ran out of arguments, his voice flat and unemotional. "Yes."

"And now you decided to tell me all about it."

Andrykowski shrugged again. "As I said, guilt can manifest itself in many different ways."

"You still brought me over from America."

"I told you, that was the care home. I wanted you to stay in America. That would have at least eased my guilt."

"You brought Susan from America."

Andrykowski nodded slowly, his eyes filled with sadness. "Yes, that I did. But only after you talked to your mother. I needed to know how much she told you. What damage had been done? Your sister brought you to me."

"Then you told me everything my mother hadn't."

"Once I knew you hadn't passed anything on to the police, there was no reason for you not to know. So I chose to unload my guilt."

"This being where the Russian explains his evil plan because he thinks the hero can't escape and thwart the global threat."

Andrykowski smiled. "Ah, your escape plan. Because in the movies, the hero always escapes. Let me explain about your escape plan." He clicked his fingers, and the hitman opened the door. Eric Hugunin was pushed into the room with such force that his little legs couldn't keep up with him. The circus dwarf did a comedy pratfall that didn't make anybody laugh.

Chapter Sixty-One

For the second time, it felt like the air had been sucked out of the room. Hugunin lay battered and bleeding on the floor. Susan brought a hand up in shock to cover her mouth, and McNulty dashed across to help the circus dwarf. The hitman handed a mobile phone to Andrykowski, and the Russian held it up for McNulty to see.

"Looking for this?"

McNulty cradled Hugunin in his arms and glared at the hitman. "You like picking on little fellas, don't you?"

The hitman said nothing. Andrykowski waved a hand for him to close the door and stand guard. The hitman stood with his back to the door, leaving the man with the torch in the corridor. Hugunin brought his head up with an effort and, with a voice that was no more than a croak, whispered in McNulty's ear.

* * *

Some plans go off without a hitch, but sometimes you have to resort to Plan B. McNulty didn't have a Plan B; he just had Eric Hugunin. It turned out that the ex-human cannonball had created a Plan B of his own, but McNulty didn't understand what Hugunin meant with the harsh whisper. Andrykowski understood that any whisper was a bad thing and clicked his fingers again.

The hitman stepped away from the door and shot the dwarf twice in the chest and once in the head. Blood and brains splattered McNulty's face. Susan let out a scream that died in her throat. The hitman moved back to his position at the door as if nothing had happened.

McNulty felt paralysed. He wanted to recoil in horror, but his arms and legs wouldn't move, so he was left cradling the dead man like a child in a nativity play. Blood dripped through his fingers. Eventually, his motor functions returned, and he laid Hugunin gently on the floor, then sat next to Susan. McNulty didn't trust himself to speak. The Russian didn't seem any happier.

"I am so very sorry."

McNulty still couldn't speak.

Andrykowski put Hugunin's phone on the other camping chair. "This whole thing has been most regrettable. I thought I had saved you all those years ago. Your sister, too. I thought blood was thicker than water. It turns out it is only blood."

McNulty found his voice. "You should know. Your hands are covered in it."

"Not your blood."

"But it will be. Won't it?"

His uncle's sadness deepened. "I am afraid so. Yes."

"And you thought killing me here would bring things full circle."

Andrykowski appeared to think about that. He glanced around the headmaster's office, sad eyes taking in every detail of the once great institution. Crag View might have started on the whim of McNulty's mother, but his uncle took pride in the fact it had done some good with the legitimate adoptions, even if they were mainly just set dressing for the main purpose. Andrykowski hadn't known that Mr Cruckshank was a paedophile when he'd employed him, and supposed he should have gone deeper with the background checks. Doreen hadn't cared what the headmaster was; he was just set dressing, too.

But bringing things full circle? He hadn't thought about that. Now that McNulty had mentioned it, Andrykowski could see how his nephew might see it that way. Andrykowski shook his head. "That was not my intention. I would have been happy to have never heard from you again. America was a good fit for Susan. It was a good fit for you, too, once you found out that's where she had been adopted."

"You could have made that easier by just telling me."

"I saved you both from the sex trade. That should be enough. Telling you where she was would have also told you who I was. This conversation tonight. It should never have happened."

"You being a sex-trafficking murderer. That conversation?"

"Your mother being a sex-trafficking murderer. That conversation. I didn't want to think about it myself. Sometimes the road we take is preordained. In that way, blood really *is* thicker than water."

"But not tonight?"

The Russian sighed. He puffed out his cheeks with such force that the candles flickered. A knot of wood exploded in the hearth. The fire crackled. The boarded-up window felt soft against McNulty's back. Hugunin's blood soaked into the carpet, proving that blood was always thicker than water.

Andrykowski wasn't looking at the blood on the carpet,

he was looking at his nephew and niece on the bench seat. "Tonight is a special case."

McNulty felt Susan shiver beside him, but didn't want to get blood on her clothes. He let her shiver. This wasn't the time for brotherly love; it was time for affirmative action. He just didn't know what that action would be now that he didn't have his phone.

Andrykowski toyed with the two phones on the camping chair. Eric Hugunin's phone was a shiny, modern full-screen handset. McNulty's was the burner phone that had been slipped into his pocket at the hospital. It was more basic, just a screen and a keypad with no fingerprint scanner or facial recognition. The Russian picked it up and tapped any key. The screen came on.

"The thing that is special about tonight…" Andrykowski held up the phone so McNulty could see the screen. He opened the messaging app. "…is just how many friends you managed to make in such a short time."

He opened the draft messages folder. "The downside of tonight, for you, is that you placed your trust in a circus dwarf and a man called Donkey."

Chapter Sixty-Two

onkey Flowers waited for the call that would never come. He checked his watch for the tenth time in the last five minutes and knew that things had not only gone sideways but had descended into deep shit. He had been living in deep shit all his life. Shit, he could cope with. It was working with the police that left a bad taste in his mouth.

Despite everything McNulty had done to save Donk from a life of crime, and all that his mother had taught him about being honest, kind, and straightforward, life had never been straightforward for the former troublemaker and shoplifter. Take tonight, for instance. This shit was anything but straightforward.

He checked his phone again. No, not straightforward at all. But it was certainly deep shit.

* * *

Andrykowski glanced at the draft message, then looked at McNulty. "You kept it simple, I see."

McNulty knew what the message said. "I didn't want to confuse anybody."

The Russian read the Go message, then checked the addressees. "Not a long mailing list either."

McNulty nodded at the body on the floor. "Even shorter now."

Andrykowski checked the call log. "But you did call yourself."

McNulty was beyond being surprised that the Russian knew McNulty's number. Of course he did. He seemed to know everything about him. "I lost my phone after the massage. I called to see if anybody found it."

"And had they?"

McNulty nodded. "Didn't want to give it back though."

Andrykowski checked the log again. "It took five minutes to tell you that?"

McNulty shrugged. "We got into an argument."

"About keeping your phone?"

"About telling me to fuck off."

"Did you upset him?"

"Who said it was a him?"

It was Andrykowski's turn to shrug. "Figure of speech. So, he told you to fuck off, why?"

"I might have told him to fuck off first. And shove the phone up his arse."

Andrykowski nodded. "That would get his attention." He checked the phone again. "You don't have a lot of friends you could call."

McNulty clenched his jaw. "I don't have a lot of friends. Period."

"Apart from Donkey Flowers."

"I used to arrest him when he was a kid. His mother died."

Andrykowski let out a sigh. "Losing a mother is a terrible thing. Isn't it? Even if you only met her once."

McNulty glanced at Hugunin's shiny new phone on the camping chair, then focussed on the Russian. "According to you, once was enough."

"You were staying with him when you visited her?"

McNulty didn't want Andrykowski checking Hugunin's phone so he kept the Russian talking. "After Gardner's men trashed my hotel room. Yes."

"And you talked to him after your visit."

"I said he was my go-to man."

"Him and the circus dwarf."

"Yes."

"And he was to come running when you sent the Go code."

"It wasn't a code."

Andrykowski smiled. "No, it was very clear. The Donkey and the Dwarf were your escape plan. After you rescued your sister in the same office where you saved her before."

"It didn't work out too well before."

"She went to America. I would say it worked out very well."

McNulty waved a hand around the headmaster's office. The candles flickered. The fire crackled. "Doesn't look that way now, does it?"

Andrykowski held the phone loosely in one hand. "Nevertheless, the Donkey is the last loose end."

"He's not a loose end. He doesn't know anything."

"And I believe that because you told me?"

Still keeping the Russian's attention away from Hugunin's phone. "You believe that because *I* didn't know anything. Isn't that what we've been talking about the last twenty minutes?"

Still focussing on McNulty's burner phone. "He knows enough to come running if you send the Go message."

"So don't send the Go message. Then he won't come

running."

Andrykowski's finger hovered over the send button. "But I want him to come running. That's how we tie up loose ends."

McNulty repeated his defence. "He's not a loose end. He's just a fella I used to arrest when he was a kid."

The button finger trembled. "If he didn't want to get arrested, he should have stayed out of trouble."

McNulty watched the phone in his uncle's hand. "He isn't in trouble."

The finger rested on the send button… "Yes he is." …then pressed it.

Eric Hugunin's phone pinged with the incoming message. It also made another sound that McNulty didn't recognise. For a brief moment he wondered what Hugunin had done then he remembered the whispered warning. "Call forwarding." That also included message forwarding. Not to Donk, because Donk was sent the original text. To the four other phones the human cannonball had got from his armourer. The ping hadn't even died before the first explosion ripped through the east wing.

Chapter Sixty-Three

onk saw the explosion from the main gate and started using the bolt cutters. He cut the padlocks and chains as if synchronising with the other three explosions.

Top padlock. The northeast corner exploded.

Middle padlock. The dining room exploded.

Bottom padlock. The upstairs dormitories exploded.

The night was turned into an orange fireball with flashes of brilliant white light and a shower of pyrotechnic sparks. The same technique as Hollywood explosions, only done on the cheap. Donk forced the gates open as the balls of flame became a raging inferno. The jury-rigged gatepost collapsed. Sirens sounded in the distance.

* * *

"Go, go, go." Tynan thought McNulty had been exaggerating when he said he'd need the fire brigade. The Detective knew there was going to be a signal, but he'd expected a flare or something, not this. Not a derelict building exploding in the night. This was like *Die Hard* comes to Yorkshire.

The PSU van was parked in line of sight of the house on

the hill, but far enough away that the Police Support Unit wouldn't draw attention to itself. The fire engine was a different matter. All the kids on the estate wanted to play on the fire engine. Nobody was interested in the unmarked car with the twin aerials and blue lights in the radiator grill.

Everybody knew what to do when the signal was sent, but nobody expected the signal to be so obvious. Four balls of flame stood out above the trees. Tynan jumped in his car and pressed talk-through on the radio.

"Go, go, go."

The sirens started straight away as the convoy sped through the housing estate like a Chinese dragon trailing blue and red flashing lights.

* * *

The room shuddered from the concussion of the four explosions. Dust and plaster fell from the ceiling, and cement crumbled off the walls. Andrykowski dropped the phone and grabbed the back of the chair for stability. It was only a foldout camping chair. There was no stability. He overbalanced and tripped over Eric Hugunin's body. The hitman brought his arms up to protect his head as three ceiling tiles fell on top of him.

That was all the time McNulty needed. He pushed back hard against the glassless window, and the board splintered. The soft wood swung open, only held in place by three screws in the top right corner. One more push, and it came off entirely. McNulty grabbed his sister and shoved her through the window.

The hitman recovered from the falling tiles and moved

to help his boss. In a situation like this, bodyguard duties took precedence over being a hitman. The sole purpose of a bodyguard is to protect the person you are guarding. The person he was guarding was a tangled mess on the floor. The bodyguard was halfway to picking the Russian up when McNulty hit him with the second camping chair.

* * *

Susan did a backward flip out of the window and landed upside down in the flowerbed. She rolled onto one side and struggled to her feet. The fireball from the kitchen lit up the sports field. Flames reflected off the broken glass of the greenhouse in the vegetable garden. The reflections flickered across the lawn like dancing light off a swimming pool.

She checked herself for injuries, but the landing had been soft. She wasn't smoking, and she wasn't on fire. Looking at the roaring flames, it seemed she was the only thing that wasn't. Crag View Orphanage had been turned into Dante's Inferno, the entire northeast corner having collapsed into a pile of flaming rubble. To the left, the kitchen windows had been blasted open, pockets of fire flickering on the boards scattered across the sports field.

Somewhere on the other side of the main building, an orange glow in the sky showed where the upstairs dormitories had caught fire, the splintered wood and floorboards proving no match for the magnesium, gunpowder, and petrol of Hugunin's human cannonball. As she watched, a section of crumbling masonry tilted then fell over, collapsing into the building and crashing through the floor into the basement.

A man was shouting as he ran across the lawn from the

entrance drive. She couldn't hear what he was saying, and she didn't know who he was. He was waving his hands like a wild man, his screams sounding like a braying donkey. Further along the drive, beyond the collapsed gateposts, blue and red lights flashed in the darkness. Crackling flames drowned the sirens.

Susan ignored the shouting man and the flashing lights. She stood up and looked through the window, then ducked when three ricochets blasted chunks out of the window frame.

Chapter Sixty-Four

"Just like a Yorkshireman. Brings a chair to a gunfight." Sean Connery might not have said that in *The Untouchables,* but he would have if he'd seen McNulty swing the camping chair at the man with the gun. In McNulty's defence, the hitman wasn't holding the gun when the chair smacked him across the head; it was tucked into his belt, but that was small comfort when the gunman drew and fired in one swift movement.

The weight of the silencer affected the speed of the draw, and being hit on the head affected his aim. Noise from the collapsing masonry muffled the already suppressed gunshots, but the muzzle flash told McNulty the hitman had fired three times. The shots were wild, blasting chunks out of the window frame as another section of Crag View smashed through the floor into the basement.

McNulty followed the advice he'd seen in a movie once. If you're facing a knife, keep your distance. If you're facing a gun, close the distance. McNulty closed the distance, grabbing the gun in both hands and clamping the slide so it couldn't fire again, and pushing it upwards. The hammer nipped the fleshy part between McNulty's thumb and forefinger as McNulty brought his knee up into the gunman's chest. He couldn't reach his preferred target of head or balls.

The blow to the chest wasn't enough. The gunman dropped the gun and jabbed his elbow into McNulty's neck. Another miss. Not the gunman's preferred target of face or throat.

The two men wrestled for control, neither of them getting the upper hand. The gunman flexed his knees to form a wide base for balance. McNulty did the same while trying to bring one knee between the gunman's legs. The balls were undefended, but McNulty couldn't maintain his balance and bring the knee up at the same time. He had to sacrifice one or the other. He sacrificed balance, driving his knee into the gunman's crotch but falling over in the process.

The knee in the balls released the gunman's wrestling grip. McNulty fell to his left and became entangled in the folding camping chair, which had complied with its product description and folded. The legs stuck out at awkward angles, the collapsible seat and backrest wrapping around his feet.

He rolled away from the gunman.

The gunman rolled toward the gun.

By the time McNulty had untangled himself and pushed up onto one knee, the silencer was pointing straight at his chest. He knew how this was going to go. He'd seen the results of the hitman's work. "Two in the chest and one in the head, is it?"

* * *

Susan stuck her head up over the windowsill and wished the headmaster's office was still furnished the way it had been on the day Mr Cruckshank tried to rape her. The desk wouldn't have been much help, but at least if her brother had hit the gunman with the heavy wooden chair, it wouldn't have bounced off like the folding camping chair. There was no Bible on the bookshelf either. Her brother was completely defenceless.

She watched the two men fight like boys playing wrestler. She saw her brother grab the gun and force it upwards. There was more wrestling. The gun dropped to the floor, and her brother kneed the gunman in the balls. That should have been game over, but her brother overbalanced and got tangled in the folding chair. He rolled away from the gunman. The gunman rolled toward the gun. Susan didn't wait to see what happened next. She wasn't going to let her brother get shot in the face.

Susan scanned the debris that had come off the roof. There were broken roof tiles and splintered wood. A carved wooden gargoyle was still attached to a short length of guttering. The gargoyle's head was burning. The guttering made the perfect handle.

Her brother's voice came through the glassless window. "Two in the chest and one in the head, is it?"

Susan hefted the makeshift hammer in both hands to gauge its balance, then launched herself through the window.

* * *

McNulty hadn't seen his sister do the backflip into the flowerbed, but he did see her do a forward roll over the bench seat. The cushioned seat softened the blow, and the headmaster's carpet prevented cuts and scrapes. An ugly smiling face with its head on fire came up off the floor, and for a moment it reminded him of Mr Cruckshank moments before McNulty had broken his nose with the Bible.

The hitman couldn't help following McNulty's gaze, and for the second time, the distraction was all the time McNulty needed. He closed the distance again and ducked beneath the outstretched gun. The burning head swung in an arc like a baseball player hitting a home run. Mr Cruckshank's nose was broken again, the man who was threatening a McNulty, defeated by a McNulty sibling. Only this time in reverse.

The gun skittered across the floor. The hitman went down like a sack of potatoes. Susan stood over him and raised the burning gargoyle above her head like an executioner's axe. Her eyes were wild. The rictus grin was terrifying. Bloodlust took over. She was going to bludgeon the man to death for daring to attack her brother.

McNulty stood in front of her and gently took the makeshift hammer. He put his arm around Susan and guided her to the bench seat. The hitman was out for the count. McNulty picked up the gun. The candles had blown out, but the fire still crackled in the hearth. Eric Hugunin's body lay tangled in the folding camping chair. Marat Andrykowski was nowhere to be seen.

Chapter Sixty-Five

All roads lead to Rome. The saying meant that the same outcome could be reached by many different methods. McNulty reckoned what it really meant was that no matter what road you took, you always ended up at the same place. He reckoned for him that place was Crag View Orphanage. Or more specifically, the headmaster's office.

But he was wrong. It wasn't going to end here, it was going to end somewhere else. Maybe the saying should be; all roads lead to hell because that was where McNulty was heading when he came out of Mr Cruckshank's office.

* * *

"I'm staying with you."

Susan was standing beside McNulty when he opened the door and prepared to take on the other bodyguard. He braced himself for an assault by Maglite, but when he threw the door open, the corridor was empty. To the left, the doorway into the dining room was ablaze. To the right, the collapsed ceiling blocked the front door. The main staircase had crashed into the basement when the upstairs dormitories had exploded and toppled the central chimney into the gaping inferno.

The black Maglite torch lay on the floor beside the staircase. The torch and a pair of severed legs that were the only things left of the second bodyguard. The rest of him was somewhere in the basement, along with McNulty's dormitory and the crumbled chimneystack.

He turned to Susan. "I need you to show Donk where I am."

"Donk?"

"Donkey Flowers. He should be here any minute."

She remembered the screaming man who sounded like a braying donkey. The man who had been running across the sports field followed by blue and red flashing lights. The cavalry in the form of a police van and a fire engine.

"Why don't you tell him yourself? Then he'll know where you are."

McNulty shook his head. "Not where I am. Where I went."

Susan looked confused. McNulty indicated the only other door in the corridor. The only place Andrykowski could have gone. The boiler room tunnel. McNulty's *Great Escape* route.

* * *

McNulty opened the door to the boiler room, then stepped to one side. He didn't know if the Russian had a gun of his own, so he followed the rules he had taught Alfonse Bayard. The actor had kept asking why cops always knock and step aside. McNulty had told him the facts of life about being a beat cop; you never know what's on the other side of a door, so you plan for the worst. You don't want to be standing in front of a hidden gunman. Andrykowski was a hidden gunman.

Nobody fired through the open door. Nobody came

dashing into the corridor. McNulty took a quick look through the opening and dodged his head back. Nobody blew his head off. He opened the door wide and looked past the top three steps into the brick and concrete utility room. The rest of the stairs should have been in shadow, that's why the second bodyguard had been carrying a Maglite, but McNulty didn't need a torch this time. The basement was aglow with dancing firelight.

He raised his voice over the flames. "You okay down there?"

There was no reply.

"I'm coming down. Don't go ape shit on me."

He craned his neck around the doorframe and couldn't see anybody at the bottom of the stairs. There were still plenty of shadows, but they were all moving, throwing shifting silhouettes across the walls. Part of the ceiling had collapsed, but the boiler was still intact. The fuel oil drum was rusty and leaking. He was surprised how strong the smell was. The boiler hadn't been working for over twenty years; surely it had been drained of fuel oil.

He went down the first two steps and stopped. "You still there, old fella?"

He wasn't trying to be insulting; he just couldn't bring himself to call the Russian Uncle Marat. He went down two more steps, then scanned the basement. It was separate from the main cellar, but it looked as if the collapsed chimney had crashed through the dividing wall, bringing splintered beams and debris with it. The hole was blocked by masonry and burning wood. There was no escape that way. The only way out was back up the stairs or through the narrow door at the far end of the room.

The door was closed. He wracked his brain to remember if

he'd closed it behind him. He shook his head. No, he hadn't. He'd left it open. Somebody else had closed it.

McNulty took the gun out of his belt. He'd never used a gun with a silencer before and was surprised how heavy the stubby black suppressor was. He considered taking it off, but wasn't sure if it had a screw thread or bayonet fitting. He wasn't sure if there was a safety catch either, so he checked both sides of the grip. There was a small metal lever near the thumb. A little red dot showed when the lever was in the up position. He clicked it downwards. Green dot. Weapons hot.

He brought the gun up in both hands and pointed at the narrow door. He took a hesitant step forward. More masonry tumbled into the basement, jerking his head to make sure it wasn't tumbling on him. A splintered roof beam crashed into the dividing wall. Plaster peeled off the wall. Sparks drifted across the boiler room like fireflies.

The narrow door remained closed. He took two more steps, then stopped again. The boiler was big and rusty, the furnace door hanging open on one hinge. Pipes sprouted from the top and spread across the ceiling. Some of the pipes had cracked and were dangling from the supports. Light from the dancing flames didn't penetrate the shadows between the boiler and the fuel oil drum. McNulty's focus was on the door. If the Russian had escaped, that was where he'd gone. Charles Bronson. The Tunnel King.

McNulty crossed the boiler room and was about to open the door when he saw the blood on the handle. There was a bloody handprint on the door and a few splatters on the floor. The splatters were fat at one end and elongated at the other. Angle and direction. The blood trail wasn't leading to the door; it was leading away from it. He opened the door anyway to make sure it wasn't a double bluff, but there was nobody in the tunnel.

"Are you going to make one last trip to the pictures?"

McNulty spun around. A limping figure emerged from the shadows between the boiler and the oil drum. Andrykowski was cradling one arm across his chest and favouring his right leg. The arm and trouser leg were soaked in blood. He seemed to notice his predicament and let out a bitter laugh.

"I should have had health and safety put a handrail on the stairs."

McNulty looked at the wreck of a man. "Crag View didn't follow health and safety."

"It didn't follow The Bible either, but we had one in the office."

The Russian shuffled to one side and leaned against the oil drum. The seam had split and was leaking fuel in a greasy slick across the floor. McNulty wasn't looking at the flammable liquid; he was looking at the gun in Andrykowski's good hand.

McNulty nodded at the gun. "You going to shoot me now?"

"You don't think I should?"

"I think I should shoot you."

"Are you going to?"

McNulty shook his head. "After all the shit you've pulled? Susan? Me? Shooting is too good for you."

Andrykowski's gun pointed vaguely at McNulty. "I saved your sister."

"She should never have needed saving. You're family. She should have been safe anyway."

"You're family too. Should I not have saved you?"

"I don't need saving."

"Not even back then?"

"Not even back then."

The fuel slick became a trickle as Andrykowski's weight strained the seam. The Russian was leaning even more heavily against the oil drum. The gun was sagging in his hand. He seemed to notice the leak for the first time, then tapped the drum with the gun. The drum sounded hollow. He tapped it lower down. Still hollow. Halfway down. The dull thud showed how much fuel oil was still in the drum. Depending on your point of view, it was either half full or half empty. If the leak caught fire, McNulty was banking on half full.

The burning roof beam leaned some more as part of the dividing wall collapsed into the room. Chunks of stone and plaster tumbled across the floor, and more burning wood filled the gap. The staircase was now engulfed in flames. Raised voices sounded through the door at the top of the stairs, but McNulty couldn't make out who was shouting.

He turned back to face his uncle. "You should have looked after us."

Andrykowski shook his head. "Your mother should have looked after you."

"She's the one that abandoned us."

Andrykowski let out a sigh of resignation. "Yes."

McNulty remembered Larry Unger sending him off to England. *"We might all be family here at Titanic Productions, but you only have one mother."* He'd had more support from that family than he'd ever had from his real one. He felt the anger boil up inside him again. It was never far from the surface. Maybe confronting it now would change that. Slaying the ghosts of the past.

McNulty pointed the silencer at his uncle. "You should have done better."

Andrykowski looked at the gun and gave a sad little smile. "She was family, too. But I never loved the dog."

He tapped the oil drum to find the level, then fired twice. The shots ripped the barrel apart, and the muzzle flash ignited the fumes. Fuel oil gushed across the floor, then caught fire. Andrykowski became a human fireball before McNulty shot him in the head.

The fireball dropped to the floor, but the ball of flame kept expanding. It filled the boiler room and blasted up the stairs. The last word to go through McNulty's mind before the ceiling collapsed was, *family*.

Chapter Sixty-Six

The funeral was a small affair with minimal family. There was hardly any family left. The service of remembrance was brief and lacking detail. With the best will in the world, Susan couldn't think of anything positive to say and had only given the briefest of instructions to the reverend conducting the service. She had considered choosing classic movie themes as the intro and exit music, but didn't think her brother would have approved.

The main problem was that Susan felt no connection to Yorkshire, so organising a funeral at short notice was doubly difficult. The detective, Jimmy Tynan, had made most of the arrangements with a little help from the man who sounded like a braying donkey. Donk had turned out to be her brother's best friend in a world where there was a shortage of friends. Crag View wasn't a breeding ground for friendship. The orphanage wasn't great for family either.

The only people standing with Susan at the graveside were a cop, a thief, and a care home worker. Donk bristled at being called a thief.

"I wasn't a thief."

"He arrested you, didn't he?"

"Because my mum told him to."

Susan let out a sigh. "Yeah. Mothers have a strange way of doing things."

She wasn't sure if that was true because she hadn't known her mother at all. At least her brother had spent a little time with her before the end. She looked up at the grey sky. Northern England was exactly how her brother had described it to her: dull, wet, and windy. The trees surrounding the graveside were naked and windswept. They had a permanent tilt to the right. There were no leaves, just bare branches that were sharp and pointed like witches' fingers. She thought her brother would have appreciated that. Or maybe not. You could never tell with Vince McNulty.

The group stood huddled together for shelter against the wind, but separate in all other respects. Donk looked distracted and kept looking over his shoulder toward the side entrance on New Adel Lane. Maggie, the care home worker, seemed to be the most upset, which surprised Susan since she assumed anyone in that line of work would have thicker skin. Det Sgt Tynan stood with clenched jaw and blank face, a look that was no doubt very effective when conducting prisoner interviews, the face giving nothing away and prompting the interviewee to fill the void.

Susan was simply too numb to show any emotion. She had grown up believing she had no family and then found a brother and a mother in fairly quick succession. Now she felt alone again. She followed Donk's gaze beyond MA Clarke & Son Memorial Masons. The side gate to the cemetery was closed. Mourners and visitors were encouraged to use the main entrance on Otley Road.

Reverend Petrie finished the interment service with the usual, "Ashes to ashes, dust to dust," and carefully tossed a handful of dirt into the grave. He held out a hand to the mourners, but nobody seemed willing to follow suit. Maggie started crying again. Donk checked his watch. Tynan showed a modicum of leadership and picked up a handful of soil from the pile next to the hole. The detective looked embarrassed at the noise when the dirt and stones hit the coffin.

Susan didn't feel like throwing dirt on the memories and held up the bouquet she had bought from Leeds House of Flowers opposite the main entrance instead. She took a deep breath and was about to drop them on the coffin when Donk gave a polite cough and waved a hand toward the side entrance.

A transfer ambulance pulled into the turnaround, and a gravedigger opened the gate. The ambulance reversed along the driveway, then stopped. The driver climbed out, opened the rear doors, and lowered the foldout step. He helped a man on crutches climb down. They exchanged a few words, then the driver closed the doors again. The man on crutches took a deep breath, then turned to look at the group huddled at the graveside. McNulty gave the faintest of nods, then walked between the trees that reminded him of Crag View Orphanage.

* * *

The walking fireball dropped to the floor, but the ball of flame kept expanding. It filled the boiler room and blasted up the stairs. The last word to go through McNulty's mind before the ceiling collapsed was, *family*. He didn't wait to see what that meant. He yanked open the narrow door with the bloody handprint on it and dived through the opening.

After that, it was *Great Escape* time, not the Tunnel King Charles Bronson or the Cooler King Steve McQueen, just a frightened boy escaping Crag View for one last trip to the pictures. The explosion in the boiler room had slammed the door closed behind him, and the mouth of the tunnel had collapsed. The tunnel was plunged into darkness apart from a glimmer of light through the gap around the door. Flames licked at the wood, but the blast snuffed them out.

The long crawl to the end of the tunnel had felt like it took a lifetime, and in some ways, he reckoned that's what it was. The distance between childhood and here. By the time he crawled past the fetid carcasses and climbed out of the bunker, his childhood was ashes and dust. He couldn't stand up, so he sat with his back against the doorframe and watched the burning wreckage of his youth.

It wasn't until the fire was under control that he realised he'd broken one leg and badly cut the other. Donk found him twenty minutes later. Susan hugged him despite the pain in his legs. Tynan brought the meeting to order.

"Next time you want the fire brigade dial nine, nine, nine."

* * *

The fallout from the destruction of Crag View Orphanage was immediate and all-encompassing. Tynan was hauled over the coals for authorising an operation without consulting the Detective Superintendent, and the Fire Chief was criticised for not preventing a fire that everyone knew was coming. Those were the official lines. Unofficially, the police were more than happy, and the fire brigade got to practice putting out a fire without worrying about saving anybody.

Here's what the police were happy about.

Forensics were confident they would be able to match the gun, which McNulty had managed to keep hold of after diving through the door into the tunnel, with the bullets recovered from the eight people who had been shot to death since McNulty arrived from America. The three men in the alley, the four men outside Bodington Abattoir, and Frank Gardner. Nine, because there was also Eric Hugunin. Small calibre was good for preserving bullets inside the body because there was no exit wound; the bullets just rattled around in the soft tissue to cause maximum damage. The gun McNulty had taken from the hitman was small-calibre. What that meant was that eight murders could be recorded as detected, and since the hitman was dead, they wouldn't even have to go to court.

The hitman being dead was another bonus. Plus, the intensity of the fire. Because of the heat and destruction, there wasn't much left of the bodies at Crag View Orphanage. SOCO had managed to find the charred remains of four people, but the forensic teams had found zero identification. Everything had been burned beyond recognition. There was no DNA and no fingerprints. The crushing force of the collapsed building meant there weren't even any teeth to check against dental records. McNulty had identified two of the men who had been in the headmaster's office before the fire as Eric Hugunin and Marat Andrykowski. Hugunin, the police knew about. Andrykowski didn't exist.

"What do you mean he doesn't exist? I talked to him."

Tynan stuck with the facts. "Officially. He's not on any of our databases, and there's no record with immigration. Russia isn't saying anything. He's a non-person and as such is a non-crime."

McNulty clarified. "He shot himself. Suicide isn't a crime."

"I thought you said he shot the fuel drum."

McNulty shrugged. "Same difference. He blew himself up."

So that was one of the bodies accounted for without having to complete a full coroner's report. Hugunin had been shot by the hitman, so that made nine detected murders. The hitman was the only fly in the ointment, him and the legless bodyguard in the basement. There was no record of them as associates of Frank Gardner, and since the hitman had killed Gardner, they were actually working for Andrykowski, the non-person. There were fingerprints on the five small calibre rounds still in the gun's magazine, but so far, no match with known criminals.

The other bonus for the police was Xtreme North. The Northern X replacement organisation had been wrapped up and closed down after the raids sparked by Pat Tubah. Add the fact that the head of Xtreme North—Frank Gardner— was dead, and that was another closed book. Bonus number two was the international sex trafficking ring that was the umbrella company above Xtreme North. The fire at Crag View had cut the head off that snake. Forensic accountants would go through the orphanage's history to find any links from abroad, but so far, all they had come up with was Doreen Wills and Frank Andrykowski, deceased.

McNulty bridled at the mention of his mother. "Marat Andrykowski was Frank Andrykowski's brother."

"Not according to initial findings. There is no brother."

"And what about my mum?"

"Her being suffocated, you mean?"

That part was a bit sensitive, so Tynan had taken his time to explain. Since they hadn't recorded it as a suspicious death at the time, the Detective Superintendent had decided to keep it recorded as natural causes. There was nothing to gain by adding another murder to the case file, especially since they didn't have a suspect.

"The woman. She posed as night staff."

"The same woman who was about to wax your pole, are you thinking?"

McNulty nodded. "The masseuse, yes. Salino."

Tynan sighed. "A complication the Super can well do without. And since your mother was kind of involved with the orphanage and the sex trafficking…" Tynan shrugged. "She was on palliative care anyway. End of life. I'm sorry."

Considering everything his family had put him and Susan through, McNulty had reluctantly agreed. In real life, you never catch everybody. Loose ends are almost never tied up. Somebody always gets away.

Tynan tried to cheer McNulty up. "Look on the bright side. We've shut down two sex trafficking networks and solved nine murders. You're a hero again. Maybe Larry Unger will give you a pay rise."

* * *

The group that was huddled around the open grave parted, and Susan walked over to McNulty. Keeping her face blank, she hugged her brother. McNulty could feel the tension vibrating through the embrace. The blank face was as much a mask as his own. Donk couldn't help but smile at the sight of his friend. He tapped his watch.

"You almost missed it."

McNulty broke away from Susan and shook Donk's hand. "There's nothing to miss. We had fish and chips together. That was enough."

Tynan nodded but stayed on the other side of the grave. Maggie stood beside him. Reverend Petrie had stepped back to give the family some privacy. Wind howled through the branches that looked like witches' fingers, and McNulty touched the tattoo up the side of his neck. He didn't need the reminder anymore.

Susan helped her brother negotiate the mound of earth to reach the side of the grave. His crutches sank into the dirt, and he had to reaffirm his grip. Susan tossed the bouquet of flowers into the hole and stepped aside. McNulty stood alone, looking down at the coffin. It looked so small. He felt emotion well up inside him, but fought back the tears. He knew he would cry, but not here. Not in front of his friends and family.

Family. A group of people related by blood. He felt related to every single one of them, including Maggie, who had cared for his mother in her final years. Whatever Doreen had once been, she was still his mother. He looked at the mound of earth but didn't scoop any up to throw on the coffin. Instead, he took out the saltshaker he had stolen from hospital and unscrewed the top. He filled his hand with the smooth white condiment, took a deep breath to ward off the tears, then drowned his food in salt.

Chapter Sixty-Seven

The woman sitting in the extra legroom window seat felt the turbulence shake the passenger jet as it banked right after taking off from Manchester Airport. She looked out of the window but could only see brief snatches of ground through breaks in the clouds. The clouds looked dark and angry, and a strong gust of wind tried to knock the Boeing 737 off course, but the pilot held firm. Even though she had only just left English soil, the ground seemed to be a long way down. She popped another mint in her mouth and sucked to ease the pressure in her ears. The plane was buffeted again. Her ears refused to pop.

The passenger jet continued to climb. The engines roared, but the crushing pressure in her ears muted the sound. The woman didn't like flying. She reckoned she could count the number of times she had flown on the fingers of one hand, and those had only been short hops to Europe. This was her first long-haul flight.

The Boeing levelled, and her ears finally popped. The engine noise became a dull constant, and she could hear passengers discussing their plans once they arrived in New York. The woman wasn't staying in New York; she was booked on a transfer to Boston. She didn't have anyone to discuss her plans with. Her plans weren't open for discussion anyway. She wasn't quite sure what they were, but she knew they would involve payback and retribution. She gave a sinister smile. Both words meant the same thing.

Then she stopped smiling. McNulty deserved retribution times two. The plane was buffeted one more time, then it settled on its course for America. The woman took her job seriously and, despite not having a boss anymore, felt responsible for letting her last boss down. This job she would do for free.

She tucked her ticket stub in the seatback in front of her and settled in for the long journey. The name on the ticket matched her passport. Salino had chosen the name herself. She thought being called Amy Moore would add a touch of poetic justice. Once the passenger announcements had finished, she closed her eyes and let out a sigh. Payback and retribution. Times two.

Acknowledgments

I am going to go off piste here, and focus on some of the people who were stepping stones to greatness. If greatness has been achieved it is largely down to them. If it has not, the fault is entirely mine.

Firstly I want to thank *Donna Bagdasarian* for being my agent in the early days, and for suggesting that I set my books in America. Good call Donna. Secondly, or maybe he should have come first, there is *Lee Child,* who introduced me to Donna back when I was struggling to get my UK crime books published. He gave me such positive feedback after reading *Through The Ruins Of Midnight,* that his blurb has been front and centre on every new book since. Plus, he allowed me to use his real name for my main character without threatening to sue me. The journey hasn't been smooth. Another helping hand came from *Eric Campbell,* who resurrected Jim Grant for Down & Out Books. The final stepping stone belongs to *Shawn Reilly Simmons* and *Deb Well,* for expanding my reach with Level Best Books.

As always, I've saved the most important for last, you, the reader. This book didn't simply pop into your hands, you made the effort to seek it out. I appreciate your support. Happy reading.

About the Author

Ex Army, retired cop and former Scenes Of Crime Officer. Colin Campbell is the author of British crime novels, *Blue Knight White Cross*, and *Northern Ex*, and US thrillers *Jamaica Plain, Final Cut*, and *Shelter Cove*. His Jim Grant thrillers bring a rogue Yorkshire cop to America, and his Vince McNulty novels bring a Yorkshire *ex*-cop to Hollywood. He has also written several children's books, that his daughter read first, about troubled youths seeking redemption. For more info visit www.campbellfiction.com.

AUTHOR WEBSITE:
   www.campbellfiction.com

SOCIAL MEDIA HANDLES:
   Facebook: https://www.facebook.com/colin.campbell.13 36/

Instagram: https://www.instagram.com/campbell.fiction/

YouTube: Colin Campbell Books, Tennis and Cars: https://www.youtube.com/@colincampbellbookstennisca1275

Also by Colin Campbell

Darkwater Towers

Through The Ruins of Midnight

Ballad of the One Legged Man

Gargoyles: Skylights and Roofscapes

Blue Knight White Cross

<u>Jim Grant Series</u>
Jamaica Plain
Montecito Heights
Adobe Flats
Snake Pass
Beacon Hill
Shelter Cove
Catawba Point
Permission Granted: Grant and McNulty Stories
Chance Harbour
Operation Snow Queen

<u>Vince McNulty Series</u>
Final Cut
Tracking Shot
Northern Ex
Forced Perspective (with Jim Grant)
Swing Gang

Double Exposure (with Jim Grant)

YA Books
Silent Flight Holy Night
The Early Grave Of Sophie Laville

Standalone Books
Devil's Coast